BESTIAL ECOSYSTEMS

CREATED BY MONSTROUS INHABITATION

SPECIAL REFERENCE WORK

A compiled volume of information for players of Classic Fantasy Role-Playing games, including: Speculative origins on monsters, guidelines for creating encounter tables and designing monstrous and magical biomes.

By Courtney C. Campbell

Cover by Karl Stjernberg
Editing by Sándor Gebei
Illustrations by Courtney C. Campbell, Jeshields, Bodie H., Direquest, and Zach Moeller
Extra writing by KingSillyGoose, Lucas Zellers, and Google+

Public Version

INTRODUCTION

I did not write this book alone.

A long time ago there was a place that no longer exists. It was a complete failure in all respects save one. It brought the architects of the old school renaissance together. The name of that place was Google +.

I was looking for a way to create more interesting ecology articles, in the style of old Dragon magazine articles. So I began with Aboleths and began working through an A-Z list of monsters. Posts would go up on Google+, asking for creative ideas about the monsters and people delivered. I wrote about a thousand words of ideas, and collected and presented the other collected ideas for prosperity on my blog where many of them are still there to this day.

I had an inkling I might someday make a work like this, so long before the closing of Google+ I made sure to contact every contributor individually, and ask if they were willing to let me use their work. Some requested money and were paid, a few refused to have their work included (and their entries were removed), but the vast majority were glad to have their work included.

It's here I'd like to thank them for their contributions and work:

Adam Taylor, Andy Barlett, Patrick Stuart, Andrew Shields, Richard Grenville, Nadav Ben Dov, Jacob Hurst, Joshua Blackketter, Harald Wagener, Luka Rejec, Reynaldo Madrinan, Christopher Hatty, James Stuart, Nathaniel Hull, Nobilis Reed, Arnold K., J. Alberto Abreu, Eric Duncan, David Brawley, Evlyn M., Dyson Logos, Justin S. Davis, James Aulds, Noah Stevens, Dave Younce, Dennis Laffey, Jeffrey Turner, John Payne, Jose Carlos Dominguez, Jeff Russell, Jensan Thuresson, Alex Joneth, Michael Fuller, Seth Clayton, Beloch Shrike, Noah Marshall, Chris Tamm, Scott Martin, RJ Grady, Ed Hackett, Louis Swallow, Zach Marx Weber, Peter Kisner, Scrap Princess, Tim Groth, Matthew Bannock

Sadly, since the fall of Google+, many things have changed. Some of the contributors are no longer with us, some are no longer part of the community, and the original posts are lost to time. Several of the names you may recognize, as they are creators in the table top role-playing space. Some contributors commented only once, others had a hand in adding something to every entry. Life has moved on and been kind to some of us and difficult to others. Any of the contributors should feel free to contact me with any thoughts they have!

That said, I am excited to finally have the trilogy of *On Downtime and Demesnes*, *Artifices Deceptions and Dilemmas*, and *Bestial Encounters caused by Monsterous Inhabitation* finished. It is an alternate *Dungeon Master's Guide*, *Player's Handbook*, and *Monster Manual*, suitable for use with any fantasy role-playing adventure game. It explores the things most frequently ignored in those books. Rather than providing procedures for play, they talk about how to construct campaigns in ways that organically drive play forward.

I once had someone ask me "how to use" the information in this book, and that question befuddles me to this day. "Monsters" are animate creatures. If they exist there must not only be reasons and causes, but also myths and legends. It's hard to create all this on your own, so this book is a boon in campaign design by providing a variety of those ideas from many different voices.

There are so many ideas on each page of this book, it's often difficult to read or even look at. So much creativity and strangeness, ready for you to use to make your campaigns a lot more magical while making them more understandable, approchable, and tractable at the same time.

These ideas are the way I run campaigns, and the books were created as a reference for me. The fact that they are useful for other people is just a wonderful bonus. I'm glad to present the final volume, and hope you enjoy using the ideas to create memorable and enjoyable campaigns.

CONTENTS

 BOLETH

"We give a name to a thing, and the name limits it. There are creatures before names. We are foolish to think they are limited."
— Obadiah, Taurian speaker

NOMENCLATURE: Uobilyth, spawn of Piscathces, Agnathans, Pleco

DESCRIPTION: Aquatic respirating, psionic fish-people

THINGS THAT ARE KNOWN:

- They do not display emotion or empathy
- They resemble large (20′ long and 3 tons) rubbery blue-green fish possessing only caudal fins
- Their mucus allows air-breathers to extract oxygen from water. It also prevents them from extricating it from the air
- They have three slit-like eyes, stacked vertically, each a solid color
- They have two pairs of tentacles — two thin ones that are 10′ long and resemble a mustache, and two broader, flatter tentacles that resemble pectoral fins. Outside of water, they use these tentacles to literally drag themselves around.
- They have tube-like orifices along their body that secrete slime
- They have powers of illusion and mind, able to trick and dominate other creatures
- They are assumed to take slaves, though what is done with living captives is unknown
- Their mouth is a giant sucker on the outside
- From corpses it has been discovered that all aboleth are hermaphroditic
- They can breathe both air and water
- Their purposes and reasoning are inscrutable even to the hyper-intelligent

RUMORS AND OTHER WAVES IN THE OCEAN:

- Secrecy is of the utmost importance to the aboleth. It is a biological imperative on the order of reproducing in mammals
- All written language descends from ancient elder Aboleth glyphs. If an aboleth were to become angry and erase the root glyphs to protect them from lesser minds, then language based on those glyphs would correspondingly vanish

- No one has ever killed an aboleth ever. Those who claim to have killed one have fallen victim to an illusion

- The description we have of an aboleth is an illusion. To see their true form would drive the viewer mad

- All knowledge of encountered aboleth comes from the weakest members of the tribe, expelled for being too weak to even survive mental interaction with an average aboleth

- They are long lived, the weak living 1,000 years and the oldest perhaps being immortal

- What they use slaves for is unknown; some possibilities have been raised from reports:

  ° They are used in constructing grand cities

  ° They live on the shore and fight each other endlessly for an unknown purpose

  ° They keep slaves because slaves are for eating. If we weren't meant to be slaves, why would we taste so delicious?

  ° Bonding with slaves improves their own abilities. A strong slave makes them stronger

  ° They need mental fields in addition to physical substance Slaves are subject to deranged biological experimentation

- They pursue the ancient art of super-science, eschewing magic in all its forms

- Aboleth slime is a potent narcotic, and they treat their slaves much better than their previous life. This has proven to be a surprise for more than one 'rescuer'

- They do not track time by days and nights, for the sun does not penetrate so far beneath the ocean. They instead track time by tidal cycles and patterns, a method poorly understood by land-dwellers

- Their mental powers and illusion magics stem from not wanting hordes of crazed, loving, degenerate drug addicts bothering them. It's a defense mechanism developed to protect them

- An aboleth is selected to be a ruler, which is in contact with all other aboleth of the city at once. His mind knows what they know and increases in size to match

- They are said to be magic resistant

- They are worshiped as god-kings by many of the lesser sea creatures like tritons and sahuagin.

- Their eyes are actual physical manifestations of a pineal gland that acts as a light-sensor. This is actually where the strength of their psionic powers comes from
- They do not come from a single world but instead raid many worlds across all dimensions. This means that there is only one aboleth culture
- The aboleth are able to inscribe glyphs that contain eldritch energies.
- The aboleth were the first creatures that existed from all else. They know this because every aboleth remembers it
- They exude toxic slime via both their tentacles and their large abdominal tubes
- They are not actually creatures but simply biological robots doing the bidding of a secret oceanic society
- They aren't simply biological robots but an out of control weapon granted to a foolish race bargaining with the Crossroad God of Unsatisfying Bargains. Once they received their psionic, mind-controlling, amphibious, armored, magical bio-weapon, they couldn't control it, leading to their own demise
- Greed actually is the source of their creation. The desire for wealth, capitalism itself, is not just an idea. Societies that used capitalism discovered it had actual physical form. Once a society accepts capitalism, aboleths became freed from their cage on the Platonic Plane of Ideal Forms
- They are actually just tapeworms feeding on the gut we all inhabit. This theory is in general discredit because it comes from the seers of Kashgar, a kingdom far from the sea
- They were once human who desired to extend their lives. The enlargement of their organs was the only way to accomplish this, and eventually it drove them into the sea. This was long ago and the depths have changed them and made their thoughts and minds grow stranger and stranger; hating the light and land denied them, filling them with the desire to eradicate every hint from their past biology
- They are living fossils
- Their flesh is prized by dragons
- They can easily control anomalocaris and other invertebrates, but the control of vertebrates is more difficult. Chordates have some inborn resistance. They are frustrated at the rise in dominance of vertebrates because it has reduced the pool of available subjects and size of the invertebrate thrall species.
- They are a race of degenerate aesthetes who enslaved people they thought had the ability to make great art
- They are followed by skinless men who babble insane poetry. If they speak to you, it drives you mad and you attempt to unscrew your own head
- They are immune to death and disease because they can psioncially control bacteria, viruses, and even the cells in their own body

- They permanently dominate thralls by absorbing them into their body, completely taking over their circulatory system and birthing them 3 days later with their psyche completely destroyed
- Aboleth possess racial memory, back to the earliest member of their race
- Aboleth are immortal, and the world they were born to inhabit is no longer the world they exist in, leading to the decline of their dominance
- Some aboleth are amphibious or can fly
- They actually evolved from frogs and their jelly has developed from a way to stun prey with goo. Suggesting this to an aboleth would be a unique way to commit suicide!
- Aboleth are actually a small group of leeches that fed from the body of a god. In thanks, they work tirelessly to bring her back to life
- Their psionic powers evolved from their ability to control simple fish to protect their lair
- Some aboleth are said to enter a deadly death frenzy near dissolution
- They are very wary of illithids because they have no memory of their existence. One day they simply were when they were not before. This gives illithids the singular distinction of having the ability to make an aboleth nervous
- Actually, aboleth are a dying race. They have created the illithids with the best hopes they will take their place. They are a new vibrant race created from the aboleth themselves
- Neither of those are true, the aboleth and illithid meet and immediately fight for superiority
- The Illithids are from the end of time, beings created by the aboleth. Upon discovering that the illithids are part themselves, they decided that they refuse to be eclipsed. They seek alliances suddenly with other races for this reason, to assist them in the war against the far future
- Aboleth are related to the illithid (psionic, four tentacles, intelligent, slimy skin, underground, Lawful Evil)
- The aboleth are the progenitor of many monsters: cloakers, mimics and other bizarre creatures under the ground
- Aboleth are said to absorb the memories of everyone they eat. This defines their culture
- They come from Piscathces, the Blood Queen. She no longer cares for her creations. The aboleth possess this knowledge and it liberates them
- They were created by a god to protect his tomb while he rested waiting for the surface to wipe itself out. Being good servants, aboleth have taken steps to make this happen
- The aboleth have been asleep and are really bothered by this terrible monkey infestation that happened while they were asleep

- Aboleth ruled all the world until man created gods. They strive to reconquer the world and will stop at nothing less then the destruction of all gods
- They have no religion and such, but exposure to the elder evils causes them to respect their force in daily life
  - Bolothamogg (Him Who Watches From Beyond the Stars): They leave gaps and space in their architecture to respect him. He is also known as Yog-Sothoth
  - Holashner (Hunger Below): They construct protrusions and use the black bile of the world in their construction. He is also known as Shudde M'ell or Tsatho-ggua
  - Piscaethces (Blood Queen): Red domed windows of red crystal show their respect. She is also known as Cthulhu or Shub-Niggurath
  - Shothotugg (Eater of Worlds): Pools are added, filled with magical, multi-colored liquids heavier than water. Swirls and vortex patterns adorn the floor. He is also known as Azathoth
  - Y'chak (The Violet Flame): Pillars of violet flame that burn underwater are created. These are used to pass information between the members of the city. He is also known as Nyarlathotep or Hastur
- Aboleth are not actually ancient or long lived. They are only recent creations, the function of hyper-evolution. They are literal living cancer
- Icebergs do not drift. They are ice vehicles constructed for the transport of aboleth cities
- Again, they are not immortal. They are in the process of de-evolution and regression. Now they can only walk on the land with difficulty, and each generation is less bright than the one before. They continue to keep slaves because they always have, but no longer grow. It is the last grasp of a society trying to maintain power before they become nothing but simple, albeit delicious, fish
- They are actually the creation of all races. Expelling us onto the surface was for the sole purpose of producing a better slave. We "rule" the surface, in the same way a pig "rules" a pen
- They no longer take all their slaves, leaving some in communities to recruit new slaves

VALUABLE RESOURCES:
- Aboleth Mucus can be kept, stored, and sold as an alchemical grenade

BASILISK

"I can't say if it's a wild sculpter, 'cause if I had seen it I wouldn't be here now, eh?" — Montague Norahiem, ne'er-do-well

NOMENCLATURE: Wild sculptors, "the last eyes", basilískos, little prince, ruler of rocks

DESCRIPTION: Basilisks are eight-legged reptilian monstrosities whose shining gaze turns their prey to stone

THINGS THAT ARE KNOWN

- Basilisks are sometimes confused with the cockatrice
- Basilisks are the ultimate ambush predators, requiring only a single glance to rapidly petrify their prey

RUMORS AND OTHER SCRATCHING IN THE STONE

- Wallows where hunting basilisks lie break up rocky soil and allow plant life to flourish. These wallows are the second thing basilisk hunters learn to look for, the first being exquisitely-rendered statues of amputees
- The petrifying gaze of different basilisks produces slightly different types of porous stone from the flesh of their victims, including sandstone, limestone, shale, granite, and marble. This usually coincides with the basilisk's camouflage for its preferred environment; for example, basilisks in volcanic regions have black-and-red coloration and produce pumice from their victims

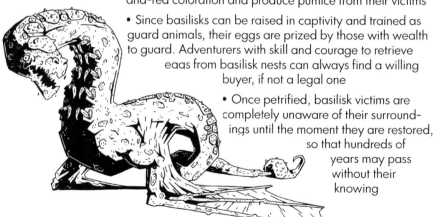

- Since basilisks can be raised in captivity and trained as guard animals, their eggs are prized by those with wealth to guard. Adventurers with skill and courage to retrieve eggs from basilisk nests can always find a willing buyer, if not a legal one
- Once petrified, basilisk victims are completely unaware of their surroundings until the moment they are restored, so that hundreds of years may pass without their knowing

- Even while petrified, basilisk victims are alive and aware of only their own thoughts as time passes without sun, moon, springtime or harvest to mark it. Even a short time in this absolute darkness can drive a victim mad
- The eyes of a victim are never petrified. Victims watch in horror as, piece by piece, their own stone bodies are ground into powder by the basilisk's merciless jaws and eaten
- Rival basilisks fight for dominance by gazing into each other's eyes. Usually only the weaker basilisk is petrified, but in rare cases, both creatures are petrified. The site of such a matched pair of statues is considered blessed or lucky
- A basilisk's victim does not age while it is petrified. Certain religious orders will seek enlightenment in this stone sleep
- In the ancestral keep of a royal family in the east, there is a room full of petrified kings who trusted their descendants to unpetrify them with basilisk oil in a future where their power and wealth have been multiplied by time. They will come again and claim the new world as their own
- The petrified kings will never rise again. Their children have abandoned their trust, and the iron jars of basilisk oil ran dry long ago
- The odor of a weasel or, in a pinch, that of a kobold or gnoll, is the weakness of the basilisk
- Basilisks are, at most 10″ in length, which is why they are so dangerous
- If killed, the miter on the head of a basilisk turns into pure gold
- Basilisks hatch from the egg of a chicken hatched by a toad.
- Basilisks walk upright, heads bobbing as they run
- It is the ruler of all serpents and commands any in its name as serpent king
- The ashes of a burnt basilisk can be used, via a simple process, to turn silver into gold

UGBEAR

NOMENCLATURE: boogerbear, bogeyman, budy, bugge, bogill

DESCRIPTION: Large, stealthy, furred creature

THINGS THAT ARE KNOWN:

- They are squat, man-sized or larger creatures covered in fur
- They have large greenish eyes with no pupils
- They have wedge-shaped ears on their heads
- Their hides range in color from light yellow to yellow-brown, and their fur from brown to brick red.
- Their mouths are filled with needle-sharp teeth
- They have preternatural skills at stealth and observation
- They travel alone or in packs
- They have an exceptional sense of smell

RUMORS AND OTHER WHISPERS IN THE TREES:

- Bugbears will consume food, but they don't need it to live. They actually survive off the emotions of fear or terror
- Bugbears record their history in scars on their body
- The skin and fur of a bugbear can change color to match their surroundings
- Their fur absorbs light like a polar bears and where there is little or no light their coloration becomes pitch black
- Sometimes after stealing a family member, they leave severed fingers or teeth to be found
- Bugbears live in nomadic communities
- They collect mementos of their hunts

- Bugbear is not actually a specific type of creature it's actually an elder hobgoblin. Goblins grow into hobgoblins, and hobgoblins grow into bugbears
- This is especially disturbing, considering bugbears have a ravenous appetite and will eat anything nearby. Including goblins
- They are known to worship various dark gods: Hruggek the Morningstar, of violence and death; Grankhul Two Open Eyes in Darkness, of hunting and surprise; and Skiggaret the Black Claw, god of fear and despair
- Some people say that if you get close enough, bugbear eyes do have tiny pinpoint red pupils
- Some bugbears in winter regions are said to have blue or white fur
- Bugbears have an unnatural ability to use weapons much larger than another creature their size could wield
- They are excellent climbers, with an astounding grip. In fact, it is unknown for anyone to ever be able to remove anything from the hands of a bugbear
- They are actually humanoids who have been corrupted by their bestial nature. Instead of a werewolf, they struggle constantly against the beast in their monstrous form
- This is because they were rejected by god(s) and in revenge they seek to strangle the faithful and civilized
- When they stand still and silent, the faintest breeze can cause their fur to rub together, causing a sound like bugs skittering across a floor, hence their name. This is what you hear before you are surprised by a bugbear
- Their fur is actually bugs. Thousands of bugs
- Bugbears actually use some sort of pheromone or psionic invisibility that allows them to walk around and right in front of other creatures
- It's actually much worse than that. Only clumsy or surprised bugbears are ever seen. The most skilled are so adapt at hiding that they operate freely in human and demi-human society. They adopt a single human to bedevil, continually reminding the human of some petty vexation or minor enemy, until by degrees the human blames that for all their life problems. They then reveal themselves and feed as the human dies from the sight from an apoplectic fit. The bugbear then eats the person and adopts their identity, appearing as a monomaniacal grouchy old man or woman
- Elves are immune to this, being whimsical sociopaths. For this same reason they never mention anything about the bugbear to anyone who can't see them
- They are at home in the wilds, needing no roof or bed for comfort
- They love to construct ambushes, but not from a distance. They want to spring out, choke, and smash
- Wet bugbears look like wet cats. They are only so imposing because their hair is so poofy
- Bugbears are actually a peaceful forest-loving race that once really pissed-off a gnomish PR firm

- Bugbears are the offspring of goblins raped by ogres and giants. They are born clawing their way out of the goblin mother. They are all evil creatures, because it takes a pretty degenerate giant to screw a goblin
- Bugbears are actually ogre corpses animated by the spirits of dead goblins
- They spawn from the friction between the underworld and the overworld. They are tasked with scaring everyone away from the underworld
- They will not do anything in combat to save their allies, even though they attack in a coordinated manner. They believe that the strong will survive and those that survive are strong
- Though strong, they are lazy. Who better to work for them but slaves?
- They are often referred to as having a 'strange gait'. It is true. This is the result of the fact that they have an extra pair of ethereal legs that they use which is the key to their stealth. Watching them move at full speed without making a sound makes them appear to have a very strange gait indeed
- Their feet are nothing so supernatural, just plain padded soft underfeet. When they hunt, they do so on all fours like all silent large predators
- Bugbears are often misrepresented. They are actually half-insect half-bear and they are quiet because their feet are the silent scurrying feet of insects
- Bugbears actually have giant pumpkins for heads (not pumpkin-shaped heads)
- And inside those pumpkin-shaped heads are seeds. . .
- The bugbear is actually an insect torso on a bear's lower body, like some twisted centaur
- They are the creepy uncles of goblin-kind. All of their kin find them disquieting

VARIANTS:

KARDAN: Bugbears with dark-grey fur, that silent as death. They possess the ability to appear as any object: a clock, a tree, a stand, anything.

WIKKAWAK: A local name for the arctic breed of bugbear

MURD: A swamp variety of bugbear. These rural cousins of regular bugbears are fearful of reptiles, and they have the ability to turn into a viscous tar

STALKER: A variety of bugbear that thrives in cities and towns

KOBLAK: A stillborn bugbear that lives. Their eyes are huge even by bugbear standards, and they can see through doors, stone, and earth. They are immortal and undead. They are very resistant to any sort of attack, unless the weapon is coated in fresh grave dirt. Children and men slain by such a beast soon rise again as a malicious spirit

ACELIA

"There's a white worm in the basement of the Collin's estate, and they worship it like a god!" – Magdaline, madwoman

NOMENCLATURE: White worm, worm women, white god

DESCRIPTION: An annelid of the deep earth

THINGS THAT ARE KNOWN:

- They are blind, white annelids that can swallow a man whole

RUMORS AND OTHER VIBRATIONS IN THE SAND:

- Even though cacelia lack eyes, they can sense their surroundings because they have a diamond eye within their brain that lets them see into the astral and ethereal
- Every school child knows cacelia are just immature purple worms
- Vicious rumors have spread that a cacelia can turn itself inside out, revealing a human torso, its rear dissolving into a mass of tentacles. This is clear defamation, and the League of Aligned Taxonomy resents this heresy
- The cacelia attacks by spewing crustrations from its maw. These grapple and attack the prey, dragging it into the worm's great maw
- The moist skin of a cacelia hides hard scales, and its skin secretes a poison that causes rapid bleeding
- These worms emit a soothing psychic emanation, that soon finds them surrounded by cultists
- The bones of the worm are hard to identify, containing traces of human and bovine features
- The skull of the cacelia is thick, blunt, and covered in ridges, which it uses to dig through the earth
- They hunt in areas of loose soil, where they burst from the ground and attack their prey
- They feed extensively on livestock, sometime having whole nests under farmer's fields
- Cacelia are actually the result of sexual obsession. Rapists and other sexual maniacs find their organ grows, until they are nothing but a ravenous white worm

- They have a skull shaped like a salamander, with nine holes on either side
- The oil of the white worm is very valuable, both for its general and alchemical uses
- Upon killing a white worm, they completely dissolve into water
- The white worm is a guardian of gates of death
- The white worm is neither alive nor dead, beyond the effects of life and death
- Some white worms spit acid or discharge electrical bolts

CENTAUR

"It 'twern men on horses. It was men with horses for legs." — Wart, Squire

NOMENCLATURE: Horse folk, keepers of the old ways

DESCRIPTION: Six-limbed creatures with a human torso sprouting from the shoulders of a horse

THINGS THAT ARE KNOWN

- Centaurs live in nomadic tribes that cross the world along ancestral routes that take generations to repeat

RUMORS AND OTHER ROAD STORIES

- The pride of centaurs is as strong as their memory; they repay every slight or honor given them for generations after
- They are so wild as to be near-incomprehensible to the urban or industrial human
- Centaurs have old wisdom about the natural world and can be convinced to give that wisdom in trade
- Centaur lore is passed down through stories in the old Sylvan tongue; these stories are difficult for outsiders to learn, but not impossible
- Centaurs fight to the death in unarmed combat to claim their mates, leaving the losing centaur to rot in the sun
- Asking to ride a centaur is a grave insult. The honor of riding a centaur is given to only one biped in a thousand, and they will never consent to be saddled. If you are given this honor, you must be very careful where you grab hold when they jump
- The waystones along centaur paths are holy ground — no predator will take prey in the shadow of such a stone. Spending three days and three nights at a waystone will give the pilgrim a great revelation, letting them see the world as it truly is
- Some centaur paths cross between the worlds, taking them among the farthest stars or through the deepest fairy forests. Centaurs who walk these strange ways may return changed, with bodies like deer or manes of pure moonlight.

"I once knew a centaur-taur, who had the torso of a human sprouting from the shoulders of a horse, sprouting from the body of an ox where the horse's back legs should be."

"That's nothing. I heard of a centaur-taur-taur, who had the torso of a man, the shoulders of a horse, and the shoulders of ox, all sprouting from the body of a giant elk where the ox's back legs should be."

"I remember when I was like you and knew so little of the world. Then I met a centaur-taur-taur-taur, who had the torso of a man, the shoulders of a horse, the shoulders of an ox, and the shoulders of an elk, all sprouting from the body of a dragon where the elk's back legs should be. It had the dragon's wings, too, so that's 14 limbs in all."

"I give up, friends. It's centaurs all the way down."

-*Conversations Around a Caravan Fire* by Studs T'hulain, adventurer

HIMERA

"A disease of the mind, perhaps a bit of indigestion. A fancy for fools." — Ilx, Naif Merchant

NOMENCLATURE: Triaeon, dewmist,

DESCRIPTION: A rumor of an imaginary beast, one of the mind

THINGS THAT ARE KNOWN:

- It has the head, mane and legs of a lion; the body of a goat; and the tail of a dragon

RUMORS AND OTHER TALES OF THE WYLD:

- A mountain in the ancient land of Lycia had a volcano at the peak which nourished lions, a pasture on its cliffs that is attractive to goats, and the wild grasses and rocks at the bottom were infested with serpents. From this mountain comes all chimeras
- Chimeras are especially vulnerable to arrows, unable to avoid any launched from while in the air
- Sometimes black dark magics merging the flesh of life produce a horrible heresy which manifests as a terrible beast, whose only weakness is time. This is the chimera
- The wise Yang Chu tells us that there are four chimeras that prevent the soul from rest: Age, Rank, Reputation, Riches. Those possessed by these desires are followed by the four chimera. The chimera of life to death brings ghosts, the chimera of power and rank brings killing men, the chimera of integrity bringing light and fire, and the chimera of wealth bringing chains and punishment
- Chimeras are the manifest creations of the astral. They are star-forms sent into the world to penetrate it, and enlighten and align the world to the order dictated by the stars
- Chimeras attack with phantoms and dreams, distorting countenance of creatures, and causing visitation by etheric ghastly visions
- A chimera is a substance that is separate and distinct from reality, eternal, and anathema to gods
- The chimera sits at the end of every universe and is either the first or final cause
- The chimera is actually a three-legged bird-lizard; the goat and serpent heads are simply effective camouflage to scare away predators

- A chimera is a machine woven with silken spider webs by intelligent spiders that they ride within
- Chimeras are a hidden disease. Upon slaying a dragon, the corpse bursts open, and from within a lion attacks. When the lion is killed, his corpse in turn bursts open, and in the interior is the demonic chimera. With its suits of flesh ruined, it attacks with ferocious frenzied fury
- Daydreamers manifest their creations as chimera; lugubrious beasts, they attack the dreamer for daring to make them manifest
- Echidna had nothing left but pieces when she went to forge the chimera
- The chimera is the sister of the hydra; they are two breeds of the same creature
- Chimeras are secretly people who have been infected by other variations of itself, turning into creatures much more terrifying than a lion with a snake and goat head
- Chimera are serpents with two front legs and a whip-like tail
- Chimeras are all immortal and cannot die from natural causes
- The breath of a chimera is so hot that it melts all arrowheads and sets all arrows aflame
- All chimeras are female
- The chimera is just a word unknowing primitive creatures applied to a working forge
- The chimera is representative of seasons of growth, harvest, and death
- Tales of chimera with goat heads and snake heads are just the ramblings of fools, who mistake the chimera's wings for a goat head and its lionized tail for a snake
- Why would one fear a goat? The lion and the dragon are there to protect and shield the goat head from harm
- The chimera is a pale, sickly beast, barely able to breathe and reliant on the kindness of other creatures for survival

VALUABLE RESOURCES:

All parts of the chimera — bone, teeth, claw, and fur — are useful for illusions and dream magics

COCKATRICE

"Those are stone hens up in that den. You'll be a work of art coming out." – Ophid, country rustic

---

NOMENCLATURE: Stone hen, rockbird, cocatris, calcatrix, ichneumon, basilicok, basilikos, cocatriz, velchukruk ("lil peckers" in Stone Giant), skoffin

DESCRIPTION: Advanced reptilian arcane hen

THINGS THAT ARE KNOWN:

- Its gaze or touch can petrify people, even after death
- It can fly short distances
- It is immune to poison
- A cockatrice has the head and body of a rooster, bat wings, and the long tail of a lizard.
- A male has wattles and a comb like a rooster
- The much rarer female appear the same, lacking wattles and a comb only
- It has red or black eyes
- It is about the size of a goose or turkey
- It lays eggs

RUMORS AND OTHER NOISES IN THE WILD:

- A cockatrice is actually a dragon, possibly born from a dragon mating with something other than a pure dragon
- Once the cockatrice has caught the scent of prey, it can unerringly track
- Any toad or snake incubating a cock egg will produce a cockatrice
- The weasel is immune to their petrifaction
- The sound of a rooster's crow will kill a cockatrice.
- A mirror will not stone a cockatrice, but it will violently attack the reflection (or any other live cockatrice) until dead or exhausted
- Its hiss can route all serpents, reptiles, and vipers
- It doesn't actually petrify, but withers plants, scorches grass, and bursts stone from heat and its deadly breath
- Its blood is poison that spreads when struck, up the weapon into the body of the person holding it

- The bite doesn't kill but passes on hydrophobia to the victim
- They are impossible to kill by stabbing. Perhaps this is due to poison, or perhaps their skin is resistance to piercing weapons
- The beak and claws of a cockatrice are made of iron
- A cockatrice has three tails, not a single snake's tail
- It is the mortal enemy of the crocodile
- They are filthy, stupid, and vicious animals
- If in a city, they can kill many with their poison breath. A cockatrice that has done so can only be ousted with the power of the gods
- The cockatrice doesn't actually turn anyone or anything into stone. It has venom that causes calcium to multiply and crystallize, replacing flesh. The stoning that results from this causes a porous appearance versus the statue-like look caused by a medusa or gorgon. It is this calcium that they eat
- The crowing of a cockatrice will curdle the milk inside a cow
- A pregnant sow will birth deaf piglets if exposed to the crow of a cockatrice
- The feathers are quite magical and useful for arrows and quills, but they must be used quickly
- The cockatrice is actually a passive grazing animal and not a predator at all. Their deadly gaze is for insects, not man
- A cockatrice grinds the stone it eats using hard diamonds stored in its stomach
- Sometimes called the "excuse bird" it is often credited with ills it did not cause. They have never been known to eat homework or cause a late snow or poor harvest
- This name offends them and they retreat into their study of geology, hiding in caves
- Cockatrices are actually very wise and know many profound and secret thoughts of the origin of things, learned from the earth itself
- They often correspond with wizards under the guise of being a geothaumatologist or ignohistorian. They pay for their research by providing the locations of gems and raw magic
- These locations are the subject of many treasure maps
- They are not natural creatures; they are created from a rooster of superior chickens and a still living snake plucked from the head of a medusa
- They don't actually consume stone, but eat it in order to help them digest food
- It is actually a being of extra-dimensional origin. It is a normal hunter and scavenger on its home plane, but on ours it is deadly. It has an envenomed beak, and its feathers contain toxic material. It petrifies organic matter, leaving behind crystallized salts

- Cockatrices are quite fecund, but poisoned easily by toxins in this planar environment. Those that survive all learned to bury their crystalline eggs underground
- They have a particular vulnerability to strong acids, sonic vibrations, and metal poisoning
- It has a strong affinity for natural forces
- Cocksatroises was once widely accepted as the plural of cockatrice, now there is debate that it refers to an intelligent breed of cockatrice whose eggs were incubated by tortoises
- Victims do not turn to stone but are nearly instantaneously fossilized. The tap from the beak pulls the victim out of sync with its time frame, stealing all the motion from the target's life. This motion is lost to the universe, funneled into another
- The result of this is every time a victim is refleshed and recovered, that is stealing energy from another dimension. Do that enough and you might be noticed
- They are used to herd stone giant children and keep them safe
- They were designed by the wizard Vora Elgath, a wizard and friend of the stone giants who found them peaceful company
- A cockatrice is not a separate creature but is in actuality an infected chicken This mutated form can only survive on venom, kept on hand by their stone giant keepers
- They are actually the cursed offspring of Ur Kardar, a dragon foolish enough to attack a god. He lost and his eggs were all turned to chicken eggs. A trickster god coaxed the dragonish aspects to the surface by changing how they hatched, the cockatrice becoming his favorite assassins
- That trickster god's clerics can attune to the cockatrice and command its actions; possessing it for a time and petrifying their foes
- The flesh of a cockatrice is quite delicious
- They are vain, bullying creatures and constantly battle for status among themselves
- Females lay 1 to 2 eggs a month at the waxing of the moon. The eggs are brownish-red, flecked with rust-red speckles, and have hard brittle shells. They hatch in 11-19 days
- They love to line their nests with shiny, sparkly items. The more shiny their nest, the higher the status among cockatrices
- Cockatrices have the option of petrifying; They do not automatically petrify by touch
- The feathers of a cockatrice can turn creatures to stone for a long time after their removal or the death of the cockatrice
- The females keep a harem of males and kick their young out at six weeks
- They are the damned combination of a basilisk and its mortal enemy, the rooster

- They grow a crowstone inside their vestigial gizzards ranging in size from a grain of sand to marble size. This cloudy colorless gem is a potent cure for poisons and venom. Swallowing the rank tasting stone is the most effective application. The larger the crowstone, the more effective it will be
- Cockatrice feathers are useful as magical quills because of their durability against caustic substances
- Cockatrices do not always turn you to stone. Some turn you to gold, disintegrate you, liquefy your bones, or turn you into a thrall. Some change your alignment or polymorph you
- The saliva of a cockatrice can turn stone back to flesh

VARIANTS:

- Pyrolisk is a cockatrice that causes opponents to burst into flame
- Cyrolisk is a cockatrice that freezes opponents solid
- Aqualisk is an aquatic cockatrice that eats coral and breathes water
- Perfidalisk is a cockatrice that causes wounds that do not heal
- Regalisk is cockatrice the size of an elephant
- Bicockatrice is a cockatrice with two heads
- Somnolisk causes a deathless sleep
- Miasmalisk breathes a killer venom that spreads out like a fog

CYCLOPS

"It's not an eye it's a time-sphincter."
— Olabuk, mad mage

NOMENCLATURE: One eye, logos-bound, tartaro, siklops, psyclops, kyklopes or kuklopes

DESCRIPTION: Giant men with a singular eye

THINGS THAT ARE KNOWN:

- Giants that have one eye

RUMORS AND OTHER SHADOWS IN THE CORNER OF YOUR EYE:

- Their primary food source is man
- They forge bolts of lightning
- They act as host to annelids, until their lifecycle advances enough to be able to feed from humans. At this point, the cyclops discharges them through their eye into unwilling human hosts
- Cyclopes have vestigial eye sockets with their eye in the center of their head. This is because in order to become a cyclops, one must remove their eyes
- Cyclopes have white marble orbs in place of eyes. These are quite valuable and stealing one from a living cyclops is a feat of great daring
- The eye of the cyclops is unique in that it isn't covered by a lid. It rests as a sphere in the center of the forehead, hence the meaning of the name 'round-eye'
- Cyclopes are excellent engineers, working and constructing factories which produce tekno-steam marvels. They name themselves after elements and machines: bright, thundering, forge, etc.
- They build extremely sturdy walls alternating stacking bricks to produce solid, impenetrable barriers. This brick stacking method is known as cyclopean
- Their creativity spills over into agricultural areas, cyclopes being the first beings to develop agriculture. Legend says that every time they taught it to men, the men slew them
- Cyclopes can control the weather causing winds to bring them ships and dash them against rocks below to feast on the human corpses
- Cyclopes are noted teetotalers, becoming enraged at the thought of drunkards or dipsomaniacs

- Cyclopes cleanse their lands of all other life, having firm and immutable borders that they defend vigorously
- Cyclopes are, at best, as intelligent as a well-behaved dog
- The single eye grants all cyclopes great mental powers, not the least of which is prognostication, allowing them to see and change the future
- The cyclopes are deeply fearful and mistrusting of magic. They are known to skin and mount the corpses of halflings on wooden stakes near their lairs, for they believe the innate qualities of the halflings ward them from arcane energies. The skin is then brine-cured and dried so that it may be crafted into spell-protective clothing
- Cyclopes develop strong sentimental bonds with their livestock and designate individual animals as personal pets that they spare from slaughter. The death of a beloved pet sends a cyclops into a destructive tantrum of blind rage. Cyclopes often injure themselves during these tantrums, as they are prone to kick or punch the stone walls of the caves they inhabit.
- Some cyclopes are jealous of the other races which possess two eyes instead of one. These cyclopes scoop an eye out from a slain victim and then nail the eye to their own skull, fracturing the bone just enough to keep the eye in place while avoiding damage to the brain. The cyclopes will try new eyes or add additional eyes to their skull in a fruitless pursuit of enhanced sight

- The cyclops is no man-like creature, but instead manifests as a stormy sky, and when approached, it reveals a malign milky sphere, a great eye; to witness the destruction it brings
- Cyclopes are bound by sorceries of the Pythagoreans, doomed to live 216 years backwards

# DEVILSWINE

"Ain't every day your food tries to eat you."
— Ropherius, militia butcher

NOMENCLATURE: Pig demons, orcs, beastmen, feral worts

DESCRIPTION: Pigs that walk as men, or perhaps men who are secretly pigs

THINGS THAT ARE KNOWN:

- They are shape-shifters, appearing as either pigs, men, or pig-men
- They cannot change their form under the light of the sun
- They consider human flesh a delicacy
- They are immune to normal weapons
- They have the ability to bewitch, bewilder, and bind humans as servants and slaves

RUMORS AND OTHER NOISES FROM THE PEN:

- All leaders of men, kings of nations, and priests of gods are secretly devil swine
- They lair in forests and marshes because they are grown as fungi on rot-pits built by existing devil swine
- Devil swine aren't devils at all. They are demons that represent human vice run amok. Each one is a personification of a cardinal sin: Greed, Gluttony, Envy, Pride, Sloth, Lust, Wrath. Humans that fall victim to these are transformed into devil swine
- Devil swine never fight fair. They are fond of ambushes
- Their brains reside in their stomach, and they become increasingly agitated as they become more and more hungry
- They have the ability to summon and control peccaries, small omnivorous wiry boars with short straight tusks
- They don't charm humans; they show them their true selves. Their minds are so pure of id that it breaks down any civilization humans have convinced themselves they possess, gaining control of their minds as an extension of the devil swine's own needs
- They have white skin because the outer layer of their skin is a constantly shedding layer of decaying flesh
- Devil swine don't charm men; they are infected with a luminous fungal growth that they spread. This infection is sentient and controls both the devil swine and men
- When you run from suidae, they gain boldness and the character of a man. It is

important to show no fear. The slightest hint will give them the power of men

- Devil swine are invisible to anyone aiming a ranged weapon
- Devil swine are the most filthy of any living creature
- Though they speak and walk on two legs, there is no taming the wild and chaotic nature of the devil swine
- They carry a curse, because they have been the only animal to wound a god
- Devil swine create new children by using their tusks to remove bark from trees; the resultant pulp grows into a devil swine by the next new moon
- Any contact with a devil swine will curse you with a malign disease
- The devil swine is actually the ancestor of man, the legendary pig-monkey
- The body of a devil swine doesn't contain meat, only unwholesome moistures and humors
- It's not moistures and humors that fill the body of the devil swine; once slain their bodies become formless lard
- All devil swine suffer from constant copremesis
- Devil swine do not talk through their snouts, but rather through long slits across their necks, from when they were slain as pigs
- No more than one devil swine is allowed to die on any day, so killing just one will drive them all away

VARIANTS:

Devil swine are shapeshifters, but are not 'true' lycanthropes. But there have been tales of them being able to share or extend their shape-changing magic to dogs, snakes, and rats also, allowing them to take the form of men, so long as they serve the devil swine

COMBAT TRICKS:

FOOD SPRAY: The devil swine sprays out all the food that's in its mouth along with bile, stomach acid, and a bit of wine.

LEG RUN: Instead of taking any other action, a devil swine in combat can drop to all fours and run through the legs of the target

VALUABLE RESOURCES:

A bezor extracted from a devil swine is said to be very powerful, and the rendered fat of their bodies can be a useful base for candles, salves, and waxes.

DISPLACER BEAST

"Are you a good enough warrior to hit where your opponent isn't?"
— Alonvis, Empyrean Knight

NOMENCLATURE: Dirlagraun, phase cat

DESCRIPTION: A feline jungle predator with the wit and will to kill for sport.

THINGS THAT ARE KNOWN

- Displacer beasts project illusion magic from their skin, always appearing 3 feet away from where they actually are. This ability persists even after the beast's death, so that their pelts are prized for cloaks and armor
- Displacer beasts are solitary creatures, living and hunting alone except to mate or raise young

RUMORS AND OTHER VISIONS IN THE UNDERBRUSH

- Wearing the skin of a displacer beast causes the weak-willed to develop a split personality; they come to name and fear their illusory selves. Scholars believe this is because displacer beasts walk on all fours and so occasionally overlap with their illusion, whereas humanoid creatures are upright and narrow enough to remain completely separate from it
- A displacer beast always appears to be 3 feet away from where it is, but it can be in any direction from the illusion, even above it
- Displacer beast hunting grounds are littered with dense undergrowth, sinkholes, and other natural traps, giving the beast the advantage over its prey.
- They hunt anything in their territory they perceive to be a threat to themselves or their food supply. Once that's done, they hunt anything that looks smart enough to be afraid of them
- Those who walk in displacer beast territory should always do so in pairs, and boast loudly to each other of their own prowess in battle. Either the beast will be convinced to seek easier prey or intrigued and keep its distance to hear these stories to their end
- Displacer beasts sometimes fish with their tails, brushing the surface of the water with the black-furred tips like the landing of small insects, then snapping up with their tentacles the fish who come to feed

- Long, spiraling rents in tree bark show the path a displacer beast took to the high branches of trees where they make their lair. Because these rents leave trees open to diseases and invasive insects, dryads and other tree spirits will go to great lengths to keep displacer beasts from hunting within their territory
- Blink dogs, feywild tracking hounds with the ability to teleport over short distances, were bred to serve in ceremonial displacer beast hunts by archfey nobles. This custom has been largely abandoned, but may still appear in more isolated, traditional parts of the feywild
- The memory of a displacer beast is generations old; they keep the lessons of their sires and their sires before them. This is why all displacer beasts have an instinctual enmity with blink dogs and will attack them on sight
- Displacer beasts were bred as soldiers for war, and they got smart enough to wonder why they had to take orders. Even the memory of their creators is now scat on the jungle floor
- Displacer beasts are not native to the planet; they are a transplant from another world nearby
- Displacer beasts aren't natural animals, but a unique type of fae
- This fey ancestry means they were taught warfare by redcaps and are occasionally ridden by them
- This training is what caused them to rebel against the fey and be banished into the prime material
- Displacer beasts love the flesh of goblinoids, far preferring goblins, orcs, and the kind as targets

- Anyone who kills a displacer beast can remove its heart and within lies a pure shard of evil

Valuable Resources:
The pelt and skin of a displacer beast can be turned into a cloak or hide armor. This is very valuable.

DJINN

"That's the thing about wishes. You get what you ask for, not what you want" — Aruzax, Ghazan engineer

NOMENCLATURE: Spirit, sand devil, mazakeen, hidden watchers, genie

DESCRIPTION: Spirits with ties to elemental energy

THINGS THAT ARE KNOWN:

- They are mortal
- They eat, breed, and mate like men do

RUMORS AND OTHER VISIONS IN THE LAMP:

- If struck with misfortune and disease, the cause is likely a djinn

- Djinns cannot enter the prime material of own will. Every djinn in existence was summoned by a wizard

- A djinn is unperceivable to the senses by default. You can only see a djinn if they o you to perceive them

- The djinns bathe themselves in the finest wines. Teams of servants are tasked with keeping a djinn's bathhouse well-supplie with a rotating stock of rare vintages from across the planes. The djinns often drink f the same tubs they bathe in, sending themselves into a euphoric stupor. Djinns do not become intoxicated by alcohol as mortals do; these stupors allow the djinns to experience powerful hallucinations that put them in contact with the divine

- They often take the form of animals in the wastes or areas that are unclean. The presence of one of these possessed animals ensures the area will be foul until it is driven off

34

- Djinns take great interest in carnal experiences with the mortal races, particularly humans. They throw drug-fueled parties that last for days within their palaces, where mortal party-goers often become so intoxicated that they do not sleep for long periods. An offering of bodily or sexual nature goes a long way in negotiating with the djinns. Despite strong interest in casual and fleeting encounters, the djinn love deeply and are known to maintain long-term romantic relationships with the mortal races, sometimes with multiple partners at a time

- It is very difficult for humanoids to spend time around the djinn. Prolonged contact with one of their kind causes whispers in the brain and other madness

- Mold, mildew, and disrepair are all signs of the djinns. They like to lair in dingy, poorly kept, and dark places

- Djinns must eat as humans do, but they prefer rotten flesh and bones

- Djinns fear iron for it renders them powerless

- Djinns live beneath the earth, seething with jealousy at man. They sneak up from their secret cities to poison wells, abduct children, causing illness, and getting revenge against those they believed have wronged them

- Djinns are only invisible because humans lack the sensory organs to detect them

- They will frequently paralyze humans while they sleep in order to wake and communicate with them safely

- Though they may shift their bodies into almost any animal, their preferred animal is a snake. They are unable to take the form of a wolf, due to spiritual law

- They are actually just shadowy forms and cannot exist physically

- Djinns are renowned as soothsayers as their long life spans make them privy to many secrets

- There are seven djinn kings, and each has complete dominion over one day in a week

- They have been known to sneak into houses at night and steal people's sleep

- They have extensive mastery of various craft-skills, and they are rumored to possess the ability to turn barren lands fertile

- Although they appear human, they are actually just forgotten and itinerant human souls bound to elemental energies

- Djinns are agoraphobic. They are so accustomed to their servants and the familiar, often luxurious circumstances of their homes that they develop a deep-rooted fear of the outside world and the unknown. They believe that pain should be avoided at all costs, and unfamiliar environments can quickly become vectors for pain and anxiety. Djinns therefore employ agents to carry out their will beyond their extravagant confines. These agents are often mortals, though spirits are sometimes recruited as well

# DOPPELGANGER

"But you see, I'm not the Duke of southern Ostland at all."
— Last words heard by the knight Fineous, as replayed by the crypt necropticon

NOMENCLATURE: Double goer, doppelgänger, etiäinen, vardøger, ankou, ka, metamorph, skin-walker, mimic, therianthrope

DESCRIPTION: Metamorphs

THINGS THAT ARE KNOWN:

- They are shapeshifters that infiltrate humanoid societies
- They are bipedal, probably
- They can read minds

RUMORS AND OTHER DOUBLES IN THE SHADOWS:

- They derive ecstasy from the emotions of fear and confusion. They thrive on disrupting intimate relationships
- They start their lives by taking over tribes of small dumb humanoids, before moving on to larger, more complicated power structures
- They are humans who receive training from a rare akashic clan. They are trained from birth, given strange potions all in service to their clan. They are the ultimate ninja
- Prestige among their races is dictated by the complexity of their schemes. The most powerful of them simultaneously impersonate dozens of separate individuals
- Master doppelgangers can emulate any forms: fire, fog, any organic or non-organic substance
- There are no doppelgangers. They are actually you, located in another place or time
- They dwell in a place called the black lodge, where they are trapped, until released by a demon or the entrance of a naive humanoid
- They have no shadow or reflection
- They are actually born of rare human children, having no race or culture of their own
- They are actually elven children switched with human children. There is no such thing as an elf, just a face the doppelganger chooses to show us
- In combat, they can change in a dazzling burst, making the opponents uncertain which is the dopple and which is real

- Doppelgangers all suffer from amnesia; they don't know who they are or what they are doing. They are just doing what comes instinctually and seems like a good idea at the time
- They are actually extra-planar and are summoned and bound by wizards
- That isn't true, the wizards create them like homunculi and claim they are from the outer planes
- They bargain with states and other socio-political entities, asking for strange deliveries and indebting themselves to work as spies for short periods
- All rulers of men have been replaced by doppelgangers. They live among us
- They have a compulsion to impersonate and believe they are who they impersonate. They will become hostile and kill anyone who attempts to make them confront their delusion
- No doppelganger ever dies. When killed their consciousness is reborn in a new body
- They can't actually survive in civilization for very long because they are just too alien. They lose their forms both mentally and physically
- They detest others of their own kind
- Doppelgangers are actually very timid creatures having no sense of worth, believing themselves to be a non-entity. They take other forms in a desperate attempt to please others and escape their emotional turmoil
- A long time ago, they made an ancient pact with an otherworldly intelligence. They serve this great outer power in exchange for their abilities
- Doppelgangers may come from any place at any time. They all exist as transient, detached driftwood through the corridors of time
- The outer intelligence that controls them stores all their souls in an ever-changing box
- Doppelgangers are actually magical plants created by wizards. They grow in pods that hang from vines where they ripen like fruit
- They are social parasites, stealing identities to give themselves purpose and meaning
- Doppelgangers gain more pleasure from mental pursuits than physical ones
- Doppelgangers view humanoids with contempt, seeing them as aggressive and egocentric creatures who will never truly know each other
- They are stunted elemental creatures. They steal forms and identities to experience life. In their own form the world is grey and lifeless
- Doppelgangers follow certain people, watching their thoughts like television. They get caught up in their lives and make sure to follow all their favorite characters
- Shape-shifting is their religion, and they will ascend once they have assumed every perfect shape
- Doppelgangers often live in the wilds as animals
- They all live in a great link, a giant pool where they all exist together in liquid form
- They can only hold their shape for 18 hours before they must revert to liquid form

- Doppelgangers are mentally unstable. They quickly adopt any odd habits or beliefs picked up by anyone they contact, which then quickly spread back to their conclave
- In fact, doppelgangers that infiltrate non-doppelganger society for a long time eventually adopt the culture and mannerisms of the locals until they forget they're doppelgangers. They either are the subject of a raid from a doppelganger clan or have an emotional breakdown when they discover they are a monster
- Some of these doppelgangers see the mental instability as a mirror to their physical malleability. They isolate living aesthetic lives trying to quell their inner turmoil by rejecting their ability to shape-shift
- What is beauty to the formless? They only find beauty in their own form when they are isolated from all other races. They wear their disguises with disgust. With no home to go to, they have to wander, disgusted by their forms, terrified by exposure
- When they mate with each other, they produce a doppelganger. When they mate with humans, they produce changelings
- They are thought forms made from concentrated hate and frustrated desires of one or more people and aimed at an individual which is an object of loathing, fear, unrequited lust or one that you wish to subjugate
- It is the double of a person in particular (or more rarely a tribe, corporation, or idea), the master of its face. It is created with the sole purpose of destroying, humiliating, or replacing that master
- But the doppelganger is filled with complexity and incoherence. It creates a double that is self-directed and strongly willed. It borrows features from its hate-donors, shifting faces freely on the way to meeting its master. It pursues its own bizarre agendas as long as they don't conflict with the inevitable showdown
- Once the master is destroyed and its mission complete? The funny thing about hate and lust and loathing is that they don't just disappear. It is now free to explore the meaning of its existence. Very often, it seeks out those who created it, its wrathful parents
- They are actually from elsewhere, visiting humanoids and capturing them for study
- Doppelgangers are like honeybees, led by a queen. The personality of the hive is based on the personalities the queen has copied
- They were originally humans, modified by wizards to be concubines and spies. At some point, the goose got away from the gander
- Doppelgangers are actually an advanced ooze that has recently picked itself up and left the dungeon. They just can't seem to maintain their humanoid form, so they borrow it from others to prevent returning to an ooze like state
- This has caused a rift in doppelganger society: some wish to pursue a hedonistic lifestyle, while others become morose and philosophical, turning violent and loving to inflict pain on those weaker than themselves
- They are secretly a strongly religious culture. They perform rituals in private to help remind themselves of who they truly are
- They are not just men. Werewolves, mimics, trappers, cloakers, all are doppel-gangers in different stages of their life cycle

- They stole the source of true names and fled where only the damned go. They have returned, paying another price — their own visage. They imprinted the book on each of their souls, allowing them to take any form. You may have them do a task for you, but you must give your name to the book, allowing them the right to use your own face
- They are violently territorial sociopaths. They do not experience guilt or remorse. They are driven to succeed and control everything, driven by their utter solitude
- Doppelgangers don't burn
- They pool their memories in clansmen who become memory wells
- These memory wells allow doppelgangers to take on the skills and knowledge of those people's minds contained within
- When unconscious, they revert back to their natural form
- Certain elder doppelgangers can consume the brain of a creature, gaining access to the memories and personality of the victim
- Doppelgangers believe that the world and everything in it is alive and all existence is a competition, a test of physical and mental superiority
- They are failed alchemical creations, the detritus of attempts to create artificial life
- Their origin is human, undeniably. Altered by magic, alchemy, or surgery in some bizarre fashion
- Blood from a doppelganger exhibits life-like traits. It ripples and avoids hazards, oozing away from them
- Doppelgangers eventually replace every building, person, and object in a city with one of their kind
- They do not sweat or produce other skin excretions
- They are the liquid sea-formed soldiers of chaos, walking among the stone of the land to destroy law and all its stable forms. That war never ended
- They often collect rubbish. Small rocks, bits of string, screws, pieces of metal
- Their natural skin appears greasy, but it's actually dry to the touch and feels leathery
- Doppelgangers are able to alter their voice to reproduce any sound
- They are immune to charm, and their ability to detect thoughts operates constantly
- After death, their natural form quickly petrifies
- They evolved in a dungeon environment to take advantage of large groups of unorganized men. A party with more hirelings than it can keep its eye on at once is particularly prone to a doppelganger infestation
- They lust and desire the wealth of humans — wealth they are unable or unwilling to create themselves
- They can only reproduce with the aid of humans and leave their children among human children like the cuckoo

- They do not sleep
- They form their clothing and weapons from their own mass
- They are the stuff of life that first came forth, protean and ever-shifting. Originally it took on the many varied forms, learning to be born, hold a shape, and die. Now it has appeared again, perhaps to herald the end of the race of men
- Doppelganger society is founded on honesty and truth, being unable to lie to each other
- Doppelgangers actually avoid each other because they are the only race they can't read, leading to severe distrust
- When they age, they take the form of large structures, forest glens, or other giant permanent structures and become powerful psionic beacons containing repositories of memories
- This large structure will then birth new doppelgangers
- They respond to their targets, always displaying what each expects to see
- They are each born without a face of their own. They either break off and worship their own lack of identity or, as is more often the case, just steal one
- They are creatures without a conscience. They just kill and replace people on a whim, not from malice but simply from habit and temperament
- Their natural form is non-viable. They must change form to breed
- The doppelganger isn't a separate creature, but your own dark side, released. It kills your mind, in a very real sense taking over your body and becoming the evil that lurks inside you manifest
- Doppelgangers exist only as a curse. They do and accomplish what the original desires, yet cannot itself accomplish
- They are creatures of balance. When a creature, perhaps descended from the divine, drifts from its nature, a doppelganger appears and reasserts the balance by their actions. This always ends in misery, and the balancing creature can only be killed by destroying the original creature
- A religious order is the source of all doppelgangers. Once sought, the god curses the joiner. They must seek out, defeat, and re-assimilate the doppelganger to be inducted. Often they die or fail. Once a great many had, they bound together and brought down the order that created them. They now seek to bring down the god himself
- They are robotic killers from the future to kill those who will disadvantage their creator
- They are servants of the gods who kill those who interfere with worship and their god's divine supremacy
- They are dreams that survive their dreamer's death

"Thus it appeared, I say, but it was not. It was my antagonist—it was Wilson, who then stood before me in the agonies of his dissolution. His mask and cloak lay, where he had thrown them, upon the floor. Not a thread in all his raiment—not a line in all the marked and singular lineaments of his face which was not, even in the most absolute identity, mine own!" - Edgar Allan Poe, *William Wilson*

DRYAD

"Look, it's none of your business what I do with my trees!" — Orane, suspicious homeowner

NOMENCLATURE: Softwood, receptive oak, tree sprite, wood witch, hamadryad

DESCRIPTION: A spirit in the female form, bound to a tree

THINGS THAT ARE KNOWN:
- They are female spirits bound to trees

RUMORS AND OTHER KNOTS IN THE OAK:
- Sometimes, when a man is very, very lonely, he finds a strong tree and carves a gash in it for his relief. It is this seed that the dryad grows from
- The lifespan of a dryad is inexorably bound to the tree's life. As long as the tree lives, the dryad will continue to live
- All dryads have a black heart and only desire the destruction of man
- Dryads lair exclusively within oak trees, Daphnaie within laurel trees, Epimelides in apple and fruit trees, Caryatids in walnut trees, and Meliae in ash trees
- If you impregnate a dryad, the child grows in a seed pod from the tree
- Dryads cannot leave the sight of their tree.
- It isn't true that dryads are tied to the lifespan of their tree; they are tied to its existence. Woe betide anyone who uses the lumber of a dryads tree to build a house or ship, for where the wood goes, so does the dryad
- The dryad exudes spores, so wherever she walks or sits, mushrooms known as dryad saddles spring up
- Dryads play at being rare, but every tree possesses one
- It is impossible to physically love a dryad for the very act itself would burst the heart
- They can send bees to communicate messages in the distance. To refuse the council of a dryad's bee is to incur their fury and wrath

41

- The dryads are born only with one purpose: to attend to the goddess of the hunt as her companions and attendants
- It is always possible to identify a dryad oak, for the tree will be large, and woven laurels will rest in its branches
- Their leaves and features change to match the seasons
- They often take in attractive men who are fond of nature to be their mates and guardians
- They have the ability to bewitch the minds of humanoids, bending them to their will
- Dryads can tree-walk; they can enter any tree and exit any other tree, which means as long as they are within sight of a tree, they are within sight of their tree. This is why they know the forested lands so well
- All children birthed by a dryad are female

# FREETI

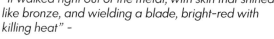

"It walked right out of the metal, with skin that shined like bronze, and wielding a blade, bright-red with killing heat" -

NOMENCLATURE: Fire demon, bronze men, men of bronze

DESCRIPTION: Beings of fire and bronze

THINGS THAT ARE KNOWN:

- They are fire spirits manifest

RUMORS AND OTHER FLAMES IN THE KILN:

- Efreeti are made from a mixture of bronze, basalt, and solidified fire
- They are frequently employed in the creation of magical weapons, not only being excellent steelsmiths but masters of enchantment magic as well
- Just as most life originated in water, efreeti are life that originated from fire
- Efreeti must hold at least 100 ounces of gold on their person at all times; otherwise their strength weakens, and they become easier to imprison by magi or sorcerers. This gold can take any form, though it's most commonly carried as loose coins, jewelry, or carved trinkets
- All efreeti come from a single city, known as the city of brass, which exists simultaneously in every universe
- Efreeti consider themselves too honorable to ever speak a lie. Though they may deceive in other ways or refuse to answer certain lines of questioning, they will never knowingly speak falsehoods
- Efreeti are intolerable narcissists who cannot bear to acknowledge that they may ever fall short. The names and noble titles they grant themselves are exceedingly verbose and change upon a whim. Those who are able to determine and pronounce an efreeti's full name and title when addressing it have a significant advantage in any negotiation with the creatures, for the efreeti become near entranced upon hearing their own name said out loud by another
- Efreeti make their lairs in decorated palaces, villas, or ornate temples of polished stone. They adorn these lairs with countless mirrors so that they may always gaze upon their own fantastical presence. The efreeti commonly enslave goblins or other lesser creatures and foist upon them the single task of keeping the mirrors polished to a dust-free shine

- There is great enmity between fire elementals and efreeti, because the efreeti will not hesitate to enslave and imprison fire elementals for their own ends
- Being made from fire, they can never have qualities granted by water, such as connectedness and empathy; every efreet is a psychopath
- The tongue of an efreet will tie itself in knots if the efreet is ever forced to speak the plain truth
- Efreeti are the spawn of those people who have died in a fire. Their spirit bonds with the fire, and the result is a powerful efreeti
- The fire in their nature represents passions, and they spend every waking moment in a carnival of decadence, ravenously desiring only to fulfill their physical needs, gluttony, mind-altering drugs, lust, and worse
- The efreeti have no power, no magic ,and no strength; they are masters of lies, illusions, deceptions, and the long confidence game, all in order to impoverish nations

# ELEMENTALS

"The earth itself stood against us. Fire walked. What can we do against such enormity?" — Cadrene Sergeant Allanso Illon, shortly before his execution

NOMENCLATURE: Mephits, primordials, weirds, furies, atronachs, daedra, genie, reactionals, eternals

DESCRIPTION: Raw motive elemental energy

THINGS THAT ARE KNOWN:

- They are made entirely of their elemental material
- Except when they are not
- When summoned, they may turn on their creators
- They are immune to their own element and resistant to all but enchanted weapons
- They may be kept at bay using magical circles of protections
- They do not eat, sleep, or breathe; or not at least as we understand it

RUMORS AND OTHER FUNDAMENTAL ELEMENTS IN NATURE:

- There are core planes. They are Wood, Water, Fire, Metal, and Earth. The para-elemental planes are Flowers, Mirrors, Liquor, and Paper
- That isn't true. The core planes are obviously Earth, Water, Air, Fire, with para-elemental planes of Mud, Dust, Smoke, and Magma, and the quasi-elemental planes of Lightning, Steam, Radiance, Mineral, Vacuum, Salts, Ash, and Dust
- The elemental realms are far-off and inhospitable places in the material world
- Elementals come in a wide variety of shapes, sizes, and types, from animal forms to alien dukes, princes, and kings
- Elemental spirits can be summoned to bring the elements in question to motive life. They are bound by ancient pacts they long to be free from
- Elementals can control the substance of their element. Fire can be cool or many different colors, or it can be solid. Earth can be transparent or liquid
- The elements are suits that extra-dimensional spirits wear
- Elements were before us and remember themselves from that time. It is matter that is enlightened and understands itself
- All elementals come from a single contiguous source that touches our plane in different places, but it all comes to our realm from the same place
- Fire and earth are allied. Earth shelters fire, and fire allows earth to move

45

- Water and air are allied, creating weather. They only allied in response to the alliance between fire and earth
- Gnomes are actually the element of earth that has decided to live, walking the earth as wizened, stooped things
- Salamanders are the form fire takes when it wishes to live
- Sylphs are the spirits of wind, and Undines are the spirits of water
- Air and water were stymied, unable to take form due to how fluid they were. Until they stole dust from the earth and heat from fire and together crafted flesh
- Elementals affect your humors, making you sanguine (air or blood), choleric (fire or yellow bile), melancholic (earth, or black bile), or phlegmatic (water or phlegm)
- The four planes are integrated in some Byzantine complex cycle of renewal linking them all together. Although incomprehensible, it does mean that each elemental plane is not purely made up of only its element
- Earthquakes, volcanoes tornadoes, and tsunamis are actually powerful elemental creatures that come to the material plane to retrieve what they need to reproduce
- They are aliens from another planet known as Elementron. They have visited our planet and taken the form of the elements that they found. Now they battle for an esoteric energy source known as elementergon that only they can understand and use. They only desire to collect it, return to Elementron, and continue the only thing they care about their endless war
- Aliens from Elementron are sometimes known as deceptimentals and autorocks
- Planes overlap. Under certain circumstances, you might find yourself shifted between them
- The elements create certain feelings in people. Fire generates all-consuming hunger; water is fatigue, exhaustion, and a wearing away; earth feels like growth, tingling crystalline growth; air feels like a chaotic place of sound and motion
- The elementals personify those characteristics
- They are alien and their motivations are impossible to parse
- Elemental planes don't exist. Magical energy is invisible, and casters clothe them in an elemental to provide functionality. Like a prism splits light, they take the energy of magic and split out an element
- Djinni and efreeti are adventurers from elemental planes exploring ours
- The planes are the divine cosmic energy, split from the world by the gods. They were expelled in all directions. If the world were healed, the prime would again be whole
- The elementals are "hired" out to spellcasters, because each elemental on the prime material plane serves as an anchor. If enough of a certain type of elementals existed on the prime, perhaps a single elemental realm could remerge
- A single elemental realm remerging would be a disaster of incalculable proportions
- Elementals are actually animus spirits that inhabit all objects

- The gods before were slain by trickster demons. The current gods are quite vigilant against their return. To avoid their pogrom, the trickster demons split themselves among many small shards at a time, placing a tiny sliver inside an elemental. Every time an elemental is summoned or used, a small piece is left behind. The tricksters are smuggling their way into the prime, one small shard at a time
- The elementals are physical manifestation of the unraveling in the world
- Elementals are the ghosts of dragons
- Elementals are the pure creative divine energy of a dead god
- Upon death, your soul diffuses into the world. Casters strip out slips of your soul and animate them ahead of schedule
- Proto-creatures unable to wait until the world was finished entered it too early. Spell-casters attempt to snatch them up and re-purpose them until the lazy gods finish the leftovers. This may damage the overall pattern
- Elements vary on local culture, based on what people believe the world consists of. They are made of various conflicting groups:
  - Mutare (Change/Birth/Rebirth)
  - Continuitas (Tradition/Unlife/Death)
  - Mentem (Dark/Mind/Knowledge)
  - Puera (Feminine/Cunning/Beauty)
  - Lumen (Light/Joy/Physicality)
  - Vir (Masculine/Directness/Utility)
- Elementals are the spirits of men who have died from those elements, suffocation, burning, drowning, or being buried
- Real elementals take a shape and stick to it: hellhounds, djinns, mephits. Those elementals that wizards summon are just unformed raw material known as hipster elementals, who were raw material before it was cool
- Mages thin the boundary. Firmament, raw creation, enters our realm and lives. This creates both elementals and undead
- Elementals are from certain types more frequently because pure sources are easier to draw magic from
- Weak mages who thin the boundary indiscriminately create trash, sewer, or blade elementals. Rural sorcerers might conjure ents or shambling mounds
- Necromancers do this intentionally to raise the dead; however few are as skilled as they believe. They downplay the numbers slain by uncontrolled undead
- Strange elementals formed from the space between what is and could be are sometimes formed, being smarter and more unique than their siblings
- Dragons will kill all those who weaken boundaries between worlds
- Elementals are the organs of dead gods. Air comes from lungs, stone comes from bone, water comes from blood, and fire comes from nerves

- Elementals that retain their form eventually grow in sentience
- Elemental planes are actually just demi-planes created by creative pseudo-mortal gods who were masters of wizardry
- What you summon may not be what you expect: a horned snake with bark scales with eyes that beam moonlight or an organic mechanical hybrid that shudders in its movements and bleeds oily black ichor
- They have no souls; its soul and body form one singular unit
- There are also elemental planes of good and evil, meaning that demons and angles are nothing more than elementals of those planes
- This means that there are no fewer than 16 different combinations, good and evil interacting with each plane. Fire, earth, air, and water; cold, mud, magma, and dust; barren, pain, darkness, and endings; light, pleasure, fertility, and beginnings
- Elemental planes are just like material planes but rich in material and magic
- Elementals are the foundations of the universe, the building blocks of reality itself
- Elementals only exist for what states matter can take. Earth is solid, water liquid, air gas, and fire plasma
- Elementals are constraints on infinity itself. Without elementals home planes set in the inner sphere, infinity becomes troublesome, loses definition, and you find yourself simply one among uncountable billions of billions
- Known alignments are not the only kinds. There are elemental alignments, held by animals and raw elementals
  - Air alignments travel, leaving when things no longer suit. Herd animals are examples
  - Earth alignments wait, patiently out-waiting whatever trial assults them. Hibernating animals and animals that trap or ambush their prey are examples
  - Fire alignments consume, devouring and using all they can reach. They are also prone to anger and rage. Lions and wolves are examples
  - Water alignments hoard and steal. Rats, crows, and small monkeys are examples of creatures with a water alignment
- They have a hankering for currency, but not of the material sort. . .
- The plane of air is said to be filled with a Djinn Sultinate, huge airships, and piracy among the floating isles
- The plane of earth is filled with slaves who endlessly toil in mines for their masters. These factions are in constant, endless war. In these lawless lands, coin is to be made among old mining towns, forgotten cathedrals, or lawless freeholds
- An endless desert filled with sultanates of brass, fire, sand, and steel, the plane of fire is a realm filled with obsidian planes, silt seas, and the deadly forces of the sultanate
- The undersea city of glass is a mecca in which all that matters in the plane of water transpires. Guilds, factions, whole cities, and betrayals lie within its walls

There are archomentals, known as the princes of elemental good and evil

- Cryonax, Ice
- Imix, Fire
- Ogrémoch, Earth
- Olhydra, Water
- Yan-C-Bin, Air
- Uzrith, Earth
- Alyolvoy, Water
- Behn-Hadar, Water
- Chan, Air
- Entemoch, Earth
- Sunnis, Earth
- Zaaman Rul, Fire
- Bwimb, Ooze
- Chlimbia, Magma
- Ehkahk, Smoke

- Extremely powerful wizards can summon swarms of elementals
- Some elementals are amalgamates, mixtures of two types, like a burning tornado, or a freezing earthen beast
- In fact, the basic types are only the basic ones in the broadest types. There are actually thousands of different types.
  - Air: blizzard, zephyr, storm, south wind, pestilence, fog, howling, gust
  - Earth: plains, dirt, desert, mud, graveyard, dungeon, sand, mountain, crystal, metal
  - Fire: cinder, lava, forge, pyre, tinder, hearth, flare
  - Water: ice, bog, river, sweetwater, blood, whirlpool, sewer, geyser, bile
  - Wood: thorn, forest, fungal, rose, gallows, moss, vine, rot
- There are four classes of elementals
  - Lesser (summoned by staves)
  - Greater (summoned by devices)
  - True (summoned by spells)
  - Legendary (summoned by ritual)

FLAILSNAILS

"Bwaak!" — A mage who thought it would be a
good idea to polymorph a flailsnail

NOMENCLATURE: Conchlias tribualis, conch hydra, spellshields, spiral defenders

DESCRIPTION: Terrestrial pulmonate gastropod molluscs tri'bula caput

THINGS THAT ARE KNOWN:

- What sorcery is this?!
- They are 8′ tall on average and have a lifespan of about two decades
- Their shells are covered in kaleidoscopic colors
- The shell also reflects magical spells
- They eat lichen and algae using a radula
- They are immune to fire and poison
- In spite of their abilities, they are essentially blind

RUMORS AND OTHER REFLECTIONS OF MAGIC:

- The shell not only reflects magic but can distort it
- The shell can also completely nullify the use of arcane energy
- Whatever the case, it is a very useful property to have in a shield or suit of armor
- They didn't exist until a strange energy surge caused all those doodles in the margins of old manuscripts where knights cowered from snails to come to life. Now they wander seeking truly honorable and chivalrous opponents
- They go through estivation where they seal themselves into their shells, protected by a hardened plug of mucus
- They don't like light
- Salt is as effective as it is against any gastropod. However, at 8 feet high, an attack with 20 lb. of salt is equivalent to an oil flask
- Like all snails, they have 'love darts'. It is as it sounds
- The 'heads' (which are actually just appendages) can smash through wooden shields

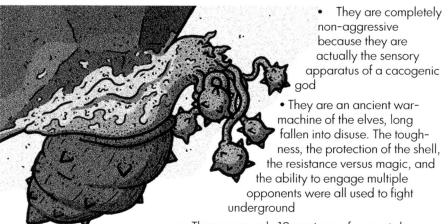

- They are completely non-aggressive because they are actually the sensory apparatus of a cacogenic god

- They are an ancient war-machine of the elves, long fallen into disuse. The toughness, the protection of the shell, the resistance versus magic, and the ability to engage multiple opponents were all used to fight underground

- There were only 12 survivors of a great demon purging of elves, and they were flailsnails — The ancestors of all living flailsnails today

- The snail itself is just a 'ride' extruded from an extra-dimensional portal inside the shell. While the extra-dimensional travelers explore, the flailsnail attacking people is simply an autonomic defense

- Sometimes they are left 'idling', free to roam with no rider

- It is a fleshcrafted masterpiece, representing war. It is big, resists being ended or affected by magic, crushes all in its path, and moves in unexpected ways

- All flailsnails are the result of a wish for a perfect mount by a goblin paladin (or whatever passes for one these days)

- Myconids routinely alter giants snail this way as protection from malicious kobolds

- They are a crossbreed between a giant snail and a very unhappy cleric

- They are the result of magical pollution. This is why we can't have nice things

- There are rumors of a rudimentary civilization of flailsnails underground, aping the culture above in a crude attempt to worship their creators

- This city is said to be ruled by a shelled flumph, worshiped as a flying god

- It is the result of a wish from a greedy fighter. ("I want to have five attacks a round, magic resistance, immortality, the ability to walk on walls or ceilings, an-" "That's quite enough for one wish, mortal")

- Diseased doppelgangers degenerate quickly. The nerve disorder strikes without warning, so they craft a magic shell that prolongs their painful existence

- They are automated organic repair drones. What do they repair? Dimensional rifts. It's not like the gods have time to do so

- Their mucus repairs dimensional rifts and can be useful as a protective ointment in many ways
- They are designed by wizards to be protections for giants. They attach to the giants back and provide protection from magic and attack anything that approaches the flank or rear
- Once worshiped by primitives, the modern design of the mace or morning star is inspired to this day by their appendages
- Their appendages are nature's way of saying "Do not touch." They are clearly labeled and easily avoided
- Wizard pirates entered a contest for "fanciest and most functional ship figure-head". Flailsnail won
- They are pests, optimized to devour whatever is available. Novice adventurers are in great availability
- They were originally an engineered slave species called 'scrubsnails' aboard starships of titanic proportion, working to clean the waste overflow from the engines
  - The engines of these ships were mutagenic reactors running off the raw energies of chaos, because that's the best way to power an intergalactic starship
  - This caused an infestation of mutant microbia, rat- to dog-sized pests. The scrubsnails were modified with weapon appendages to combat this threat
  - This combination of weaponized snails, mutagenic 'God Engine' reactors, and mutant microbes was a perfect storm of safety and performance improvement
  - The resulting damage to the starship caused it to seek planetfall for repair. Many of the weaponized snails went missing at this point. This information was recovered from the records of the Omnipus Unity ST-D :: 13-4321

- The flailsnails are scavengers happily scooshing slowly round dungeons and caves scraping crud and slime from the floor. This includes slimes, oozes, jellies, and puddings. This is the source of the snails' immunity to those creatures and where it gets the weird energy for their shells
- They crawl giddily, seeking desperately to catch a hidden moment or secret glimpse as vengeful peeping toms
- The shells don't reflect magic; they focus it. But the prisms necessary have been long lost. The shells are nearly impossible to be created naturally, so growing them via biological organism is the quickest method
- As an added bonus, wizards who use them to focus magic have found they double as a food processor
- They are actually vat-created sex toys gone rogue and mutated. Six protrusions, slick ooze, shell for kung-fu grip
- They can assign various properties to their mucus and slime at will. It can be sticky or slick, flammable or acidic, or even have more rare properties besides. But never more than one property at a time
- They write great epics in their slime trails
- A great wizard having deciphered the slime trails learned that it is no epics, but simply the names of those people they once knew when they walked the earth as men
- The flails aren't actually bludgeoning weapons. Much like the sundew, they are sticky paralyzing tentacles that begin to digest prey. Once struck, the snail can withdraw into its shell, drawing the victim inside
- They don't actually eat algae. They like to knock their targets prone and then saw them to pieces with their radula

VALUABLE RESOURCES:
The shell can be turned into a shield that reflects all magic

ARGOYLES

"I'm pretty sure that one wasn't there yesterday."
— Egon Burr, Obsward Castle Seneschal

NOMENCLATURE: Stone men, roof demons, stone guardians

DESCRIPTION: Creatures who resemble statuary designed to ward off evil

THINGS THAT ARE KNOWN:

- When still, gargoyles resemble statues
- They are immune to non-magical weapons

RUMORS AND OTHER STONES ON THE PARAPET:

- The stone from which a gargoyle is birthed determines the type of evil it most enjoys. Obsidian gargoyles delight in cooking their victims over open flame. Marble gargoyles prefer to break bones one at a time for as long as possible before a victim is killed. The more fragile slate gargoyles are capable of crude necromantic magic that they use to rot the minds of mortals

- In a nod to their original purpose, all gargoyles can vomit a fountain of rainwater, suitable for drinking and bathing

- Gargoyles turn from flesh to stone, sometimes at will, sometimes tied to the cycle of the heavens

- Damage a gargoyle takes while animate is healed when they turn back to stone, but destroying the statue irrevocably kills the gargoyle

- The claws of a gargoyle can trivially rend stone and steel

- Every gargoyle carries a geas, causing them to compulsively perform some action, or responding with rage when their specific trigger is tripped
- Though gargoyles enjoy working for powerful forces of evil, they will never align with dragons due to their inherent, longstanding hatred for the creatures. The mage that created the first gargoyles was maimed by a dragon, and this infliction has been magically infused into the thin personalities the gargoyles inhabit
- While in their flesh form, they can shift their bodies into different shapes and forms, which become permanent when they return to stone
- The only way to kill a gargoyle is to drown it
- Gargoyles craft musical pipes out of the bones of their victims. When played, these pipes mimic the sounds of pained screaming. Gargoyles use these pipes to lure do-gooders to their lairs for ambush
- Gargoyles are birthed when despicable acts of evil are committed near or within the buildings upon which they were constructed. Sorcerer-kings have successfully created gargoyle armies by building entire districts of stone and then spilling the blood of innocents in the streets
- Gargoyles are actually speakers for the heart of stone, and act as its guardians and hands working within the world
- Gargoyles are created to defend but hated by their creators
- Gargoyles are crafted by kobolds, under direction of dragons to act as spies
- Gargoyles aren't monsters but a broadcast network for wizards. They transmit messages and handle routing local enchantments
- Gargoyles are the final reward for dwarven seneschals. After serving a castle or building for hundreds of years, their final reward is to calcify into an immortal guardian of the place
- Gargoyles are statues animated by gods to protect their temples and riches

GELATINOUS CUBE

"There is a great concordance in the universe, where many places possess the same result but with quite different causes. . ."

— Mordecai, Gahzan royal scribe

NOMENCLATURE: athcoid, kyboid, qulare, geldra

DESCRIPTION: Coagulated viscous transparent hexahedron

THINGS THAT ARE KNOWN:

- Cubes may produce a pseudopod to attack
- The touch of the gel causes paralysis
- They absorb matter. Living matter is digested; non-living matter is eventually excreted
- The do not move very quickly
- They are able to detect and respond to heat and vibration; and they can alter their size to fit through cavities as small as one square foot
- They weigh upwards of 15,000 pounds

RUMORS AND OTHER RIPPLES IN THE JELLY:

- They are not actually cube-shaped; they just expand to fill the available space
- It maintains its shape due to filamentous internal fibers. When killed, these decay and it dissolves into a wet mess
- They asexually reproduce by budding
- In point of fact, they do not bud, but instead leave small gelatinous polyps
- Cubes are highly intelligent creatures
- If you try to trip a gelatinous cube, it is said to tear the fabric of reality
- It's nonsensical to try and trip a gelatinous cube, but if you string razor-wire across a hallway, you can instead fight weakened gelatinous slices
- Trying to slice a gelatinous cube apart won't work, because it will just join and reform again like a jelly
- If you cut a gelatinous cube, the surface begins to bud madly, covered in disgusting polyps, each a baby gelatinous cube
- They were created exclusively to make pit traps more deadly. They are less an independent creature and more a substance created just for pits

- They are simply giant paramecium that have evolved to encompass their local space to compensate for their blindness
- They have a deadly aversion to salt. Its use dries them out
- They are devoid of any thought, simply being a manifestation of earth (making them immune to mind-affecting effects)
- When they meet, they join, doubling in size, but later separate into two normal-sized cubes
- They travel by sliding like a slug
- They travel by rolling from side to side
- Actually, their skin has a variety of properties, and they slide by changing the molecular surface of their surface to increase or decrease resistance, sailing along dungeon corridors
- They don't actually move at all; they are all absolutely stable in relation to the universe and the universe moves around them. The result of all simultaneous cube movement is geography
- The paralysis effect also anesthetizes prey
- The acidic digestive properties are contained within movable elastic cavities inside the cube
- They are said to evolve from grey oozes
- They feed on emotions, which strengthen them
- If you feed the gelatinous cube different types of fungi, it grants the cube different powers, from regeneration to auras to magical effects. People who have experimented with this idea universally end up dead from the plague

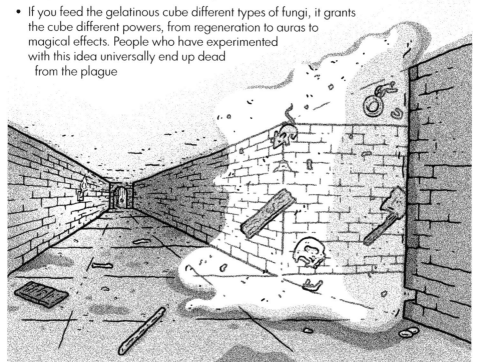

- They can be found underwater but are more visible and have their paralysis abilities diluted
- Gelatinous cubes aren't really an ooze or jelly at all, but a broodmother of goblins. They bud, producing the menace. When goblins age, they crawl into a depression and liquefy. When enough do this, it can create a new cube
- The creature either has a very rapid adaptation process or dungeons have been around for a long, long time, on the order of 100,000 years or more
- It is said that their are races mad enough to become gelatinous cube riders. They wear a ring that surrounds them in a bubble of force and tempt the cube to absorb them. Once within, they direct the cube by slamming the bubble, causing it to move in the desired direction
- They are avatars of Mechanus, a quasi-living engine designed to scour chaotic organic material from the surface of the earth
- Cubes aren't actually living creatures at all, but a square vacuum held between the interfaces of seven dimensional bubbles. Touching the surface of these outer bubbles is what causes the paralysis, as you experience shock. It's not actually digestion, but the exposure to a freezing zero-pressure vacuum which causes it to break apart. This is also why metal and stone are unaffected
- When killed, it maintains its shape and paralytic properties
- They were originally designed as a healing aid and sanitary measure, to prevent disease and rot. They eventually escaped and evolved into their current form
- If you cut off a piece of a cube and cook it with a base such as quicklime, it renders the anesthetic properties inert. This produces a bland, nourishing, protein rich, translucent brown aspic. It is highly valued in subhuman tribes
- Alchemists have a need for gelatinous cubes as an enhancer to extract magical essences
- Gelatinous cubes are actually leftover material from the construction of the sky, making it theologically relevant
- They smell of boiled cabbage
- They are created by gathering minor demons (imps, quasits, etc.) and casting flesh to ooze upon them. The resulting gunk is treated with aboleth slime and purple worm extract before being poured into a mold, most commonly a 10-foot square wooden mold
- They are not silent; when they attack they yell "Cube!"
- Gelatinous cubes can be captured and altered into other forms and creatures
- It's an advanced trap, a container for minds. It intends to lure the party into a trap so that it can exchange minds with one of them
- They communicate with each other by slamming on the ground, sending shock waves back and forth
- The cubes aren't the size of the corridor because they expand to fill the space. The cubes adolescent stage is a rarely encountered volcanic cube that hollows out new dungeon corridors, perfectly fit for gelatinous cubes deep within the earth.

- On death they ossify and turn into giant cubes and shapes of bone. Sometimes their sides harden and pit, and giants collect them for use in divination and games
- They have a membrane (skin) that holds their insides in. When killed, everything inside leaks out

VARIANTS:

UMBER (OR DUNG) CUBE: It is said that using these to dispose of waste in an earth closet causes this mutation. This is identical to the normal cube, except the stench within 10′ is nauseating. They also carry many diseases

VOLCANIC (OR FIRE) CUBE: This is a larval form of the cube. Being more dense, it has between 4-6 hit dice. It does not paralyze but is resistant to physical damage, taking half damage from melee attacks. It is also immune to fire and has a fire aura. These are never found except in the deepest corridors far away from wandering characters. It breaks down the nuclear bonds between the material, fueling its terrible growth

GREY (OR PSIONIC) CUBE: Certain otherworldly experiments on crossbreeding cubes have given them psionic powers. In addition to their normal features, they have psionic abilities

EBONY (OR BLACK) CUBE: Crossed with black puddings, these cubes are no longer transparent, but much more acidic. Their strikes also do an additional die of acid damage and have a chance of degrading armor and weapons

ELECTRIC (OR YELLOW) CUBE: Can discharge an electric aura every 1-4 rounds doing damage and causing targets to be stunned.

FROST (OR DIRTY WHITE) CUBE: A hybrid of brown mold, these cubes grow when exposed to heat and have an aura of cold doing subdual damage to anyone within 10′

SPELL (OR PINK) CUBE: This brain cube is brilliant and can cast spells

STUNJELLY (OR DUNGEON) CUBE: This is a cube that adapts by not being transparent, but by taking on the appearance of nearby walls. It smells of vinegar

# IANTS

"Yes, I would say we have a big problem" — Todis Aldan, neo-empyrean archaeologist

NOMENCLATURE: Titans, big folk, goliaths

DESCRIPTION: Large humanoids

THINGS THAT ARE KNOWN:

- They are large creatures that resemble men
- They vary in height from 8′ to the size of small mountains
- They are fond of throwing things

RUMORS AND OTHER RUMBLES OF DISTANT FOOTSTEPS:

- Many people differentiate giants by the terrain in which they live. That really has little affect on the nature of the giant
- They are hated by certain breeds of gem dragons
- The terrain actually differentiates the race of giant. Cloud giants are elves, fire giants are dwarves, etc.
- Fire giants are actually ancient dwarven gods. They fled their home plane where they were the smallest creatures and came here. To their surprise they were much larger than even the largest creatures here
- Giants traditionally live in sky castles. There, they mine the clouds for silver
- Giants are all living on a clock. As they age they gradually turn to stone
- Stone giants are giants that have found a way to overcome this curse
- They are a proto-stage of titans or gods
- Gigantic ruins suggest they may have at one time ruled the world
- Certain giants, like fire giants, are the result of ancient arcane experiments that ruined their civilization
- The giants are nature's only response to the giant dire cow
- Giants are bestial creatures, collections of the worst emotions of man, too large to be contained in his small form. They enjoy eating the flesh of creatures that beg not to be eaten. Instead of cooking their food, they torture it for flavor
- Giants consume as humanity does, just proportional to their size. This is beyond any sustainable rate, leading to fighting with other races

- That consumption is intentional, the giants being the harbingers of the apocalypse, bringing famine and leaving destruction in their wake
- The giants are a rare species whose size determine their intelligence. Once they were wise titans whose heads touched the clouds
- Giants are good eating
- Their toe jam is surprisingly sweet and delicious. Served with giant toes, it is a royal delicacy
- They were cursed by the Mother Maggot and have been shrunken and debased. Hill giants, ogres, and other brutes are all that is left of their once majestic race
- Giants retain magic enough to extract the energy they need for food. Some giants of course have simply adapted to eating anything, usually stone. This works out fine until the weather patterns start to change as the mountains are ground down to nothing. Eventually they move below ground and begin to consume the earth
- They are the result of gods mating with mortals. They carry traits of their divine fathers, often seeing themselves fit to rule. However, this is a terrible idea, as they are a nexus for forces both mortal and divine that prevent them from being balanced or reliable

- All giants are slaves to their addictions, either alcoholism or worse
- Giants are a first draft of creation, messy and still mixed with the primal elements. They envy and hate the pure humans who are free from elemental bondage
- Giants are simply men of fame and power. As you accomplish more and more deeds, you absorb the energy of shrines and artifacts of the ancients, and your stature grows. Eventually, this could lead to divinity
- Giants are animist avatars that become associated with an area. They manifest around large natural structures, mountains, volcanoes, storms, hills. . .
- Some manifest around temporary things e.g. Fog giants in the morning mist that fade away as the sun rises

- Like most fantasy taxonomy, the sages have only covered the most common breeds. There are cactus giants who stand still in the desert, coral giants who lie in wait in oceans, giants of waves of grain. . .
- They survive by drinking the blood of men. The magical force inside the blood provides hundreds of thousands of calories. It is also why giants have developed such a keen sense of smell
- Everything large fades. The largest fade the quickest. Giants were the first to leave the mortal realms, followed by ogres. Now humans and demi-humans are fading, and the time of goblins is coming. Following them, even smaller creatures will dominate. Giants are only the echo of the past and regret; tales of a world more filled with magic and truth than the one that exists now
- Giants are fed not by food but by their elements. They are guardians of the natural world, a literal physical defense mechanism
- They kill humans, of course, because humans are locusts, all-consuming creatures outside of the natural order
- The giants are hired by the gods. They are masters of reality building and dimensional manipulation. They come from a realm beyond that knowable by humanity. After a lifetime of service, they retire, content to be revered as creatures of ancient wisdom in the shadow realms they once helped construct
- Giants are a form of lycanthropy
- A little known subset of arcane lore stipulates that any elemental subject to summoning by the wizard is allowed to return and engage in some form of obscene congress to obtain key genetic materials. Once completed, the elemental returns and gestates a humanoid. The resulting humanoid is a giant, a creature that one day the elementals hope will replace all life with their own chosen race
- Giants are actually domestic spirits. Ettins come to vent wrath upon those who anger you, ogres of rebellion, and true giants of emotions more powerful. Fire giants are a miasma of rage, mountain giants depression. They are emotions made manifest
  ° This is also the reason giants are so human-looking, they are simply manifestations of what lies within all men
- Because giants are simply psychic projections, you don't fight them by dodging them physically. You manifest a psychic projection of a giant version of yourself to fight them. These projections may or may not look like giant bad-ass robots
- This is why dwarves and halflings get their bonuses versus giants: because they are so full of themselves and overconfident
- When the wickedness of humanity becomes too great, it bleeds over into the fey kingdoms. They, being wise and long lived, collect and concentrate this evil until it reaches an intolerable level. They birth this destruction into a giant form which then haunts the kingdom that created it. Giants are the conscience of man
- They are prideful and arrogant creatures
- Tiny dimensional beings wanted to visit, so they took a friendly meat form of the enormous humans they saw. They overdid the size a little. Oops

- They began by trying to pretend they were normal sized, but that didn't work very well. Now they are stuck and regret their initial miscalculation. They keep trying ways both physical (hunching over) and magical to become smaller. Many have just become bitter, frustrated, and angry and lash out
- Wizards who lost control of incantations like 'enlarge' and 'flaming sphere' often found themselves stuck in strange magical forms. Those that were stuck this way were hunted and eagerly vivisected by their peers
  - This led to the current situation today, those crusty nutjob social pariahs who couldn't even master magic and then were hunted by their peers were off to a misanthropic start. Things did not get better as time marched on
- Giants come from a fallen other world. In this far realm, everything was much larger, and giants were unaware of their size
- A great disaster came as gravity became heavier, and all the giants' plants died. The few giants that remain are brutes, who stoop while they scavenge what is left. Only the smallest and least capable were able to survive by hibernating, only waking to consume and destroy huge amounts of food and human lands before sleeping again
- They are recruited as siege weapons and can catch rocks. This is often a surprise to the catapult team that targeted them with the rock
- Giants do not actually have a stable size. When you face a giant in the distance, they appear to be huge monstrosities But if you face one bravely in combat, you discover it is not so large. The giant shrinks even further when struck, until finally it shrinks down upon death to a mere eight or nine feet tall
- Giants keep giant animals as pets. Giant goats, beavers, and hamsters mainly
- Giants are said to have magical powers to control the weather, levitate, hide themselves in fog, or more
- There are six true giants; all the rest are reflections
  - Cloud, fire, frost, hill, stone, storm

COMBAT TRICKS:

THE SWEEP ATTACK: Hit multiple man-sized targets and knock them back or prone

THE THROW: Pick up a single man-sized target and hurl them

THE BITE: Pick up a single man-sized target and bite off their head

THE ROCK HURL: A ranged attack

THE EARTH STOMP: Stomp the ground causing everyone within a radius to make a saving throw or fall over

THE SHOUT: A scream that stuns all targets in a cone

THE HOT AIR: A blast of wind that knocks targets over, extinguishes flame, and prevents ranged attacks. For giants over a certain threshold of hit dice (or cold-natured) can also be a freezing attack

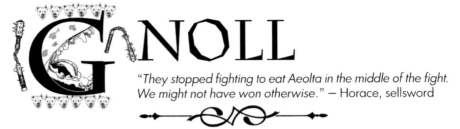

GNOLL

"They stopped fighting to eat Aeolta in the middle of the fight. We might not have won otherwise." — Horace, sellsword

NOMENCLATURE: Hyenamen, fleshgnawers, yeenoghumen, flindservants, hunger-men, laughing death, tantekurash, fangs of Yeenoghu

DESCRIPTION: Upright, humanoid hyena-men

THINGS THAT ARE KNOWN:

- They live in nomadic pack societies in plains or foothills, surviving as hunter-gatherers and scavengers

RUMORS AND OTHER SHRIEKING HYSTERICS:

- No two gnolls have the same pattern of spots or stripes. These patterns are as unique as a fingerprint
- Gnolls cannot see creatures clearly, only their shadows. They use these shadows to determine the power and strength of their opponents
- Gnolls gather and hoard such shiny objects as they can carry with them like seashells, broken glass, and precious stones. They guard these small hoards jealously. Gnolls treat the priceless and the worthless with equal devotion and would kill as swiftly for a bit of broken glass as they would for a fist-sized ruby
- Female gnolls can consume the still living, and then mate fervently with a summoned demon. After this mating, they immediately give birth to a litter of demon-gnolls, who mature within the day. This ritual can be performed continuously as long as their are living victims available to feed the matron
- If a demon infested gnoll kills a creature, immature gnolls who feed on that corpse become adult gnolls at the setting of the sun
- A gnoll never keeps his word. In fact, the surest way to survive an encounter with a gnoll is to make it promise to kill you
- Gnolls often exhume fresh graves to eat the heart of the deceased and gain its power
- Meeting a gnoll's gaze allows wild magic to crawl through your eyes and steal your soul. Their laughing barks in the night are captured souls trying to escape from the gnoll's clutches
- Not all gnolls are touched by evil; some are avatars of nature and serve the interests of fey and the natural world
- A gnoll's laughing howl is the fragment of an ancient spell. If all the fragments could be heard and understood, the spell within could grant any wish

- The brutality of gnoll torture is ecstasy, causing some slaves to turn and follow their masters into battle
- A child who wanders into a gnoll camp is lost for certain, for if it is not killed and eaten, it will be claimed by a gnoll mother and raised as her own. No one can say which of the two will happen, or which of the two is worse
- Gnoll packs constantly battle. If a pack lord is defeated, he is dragged onto a cairn of stones and his still-beating heart is eaten from his chest in front of all his followers
- Those who accept wildness for its balance among all things may pass through magic and become centaurs. Those who thirst for violence and chaos may be cursed to become gnolls
- Gnoll psyche requires a pack, and they will adapt to a 'found' pack and its morality if separated from their own kind
- The title for gnoll leaders is "Hogger"
- Gnolls are both anthropophagous and necrophagous
- Gnolls are actually a very chill and relaxed people, but demand a fight before they can relax and be more civil
- Gnolls consider pickled chicken eggs a delicacy of sublime euphoria. They will go to any length to acquire them. Sadly vinegar is toxic to gnolls and their presence causes chickens to go insane. This puts making the eggs themselves out of reach
- Gnolls love gold, as the touch of it to their skin causes them to experience a mild buzz, but despise the actual labor of mining gold. This leads gnolls to enslave others to create working mines, or raid areas known to possess large amounts of gold
- Gnolls hate manual labor and are fanatic stans of torture. Not only do they use torture to force other creatures to serve their will, every gnoll has extensive knowledge of torture techniques and lots of opinions about the effectiveness and quality of different types. It is these differences of opinion that cause gnoll clans to war with each other
- Gnolls were once the wisest creatures to walk in the darkness when the world was new. Then they looked and had compassion on the lower creatures who could not smell the worm in its tunnel or hear the fish in its pond. So the gnolls used their great wisdom to speak to the sun and convinced him to come nearer and brighten the earth. But the blinding light of the sun's gaze and the shattering scream of his voice drove them mad. Now gnolls wander the low places of the earth as wretches and vagabonds, for no good deed goes unpunished

GOBLINS

"Can't get rid of 'em 'less we get rid of nasty thoughts."
— Unknown

NOMENCLATURE: gobblin, gobeline, gobling, goblyn, gobino, and gobbelin

DESCRIPTION: A monstrous creature, small and grotesque, malicious, and full of greed

THINGS THAT ARE KNOWN:

- They are never more than half the height than the most intelligent creature they know of.

RUMORS AND OTHER ECHOES OF GIBBERISH:

- Some say goblins can fly, using wings. Sages have never found wings, but some skin that stretches between their arms and body allow them to fly. Still others claim these are nothing more than matted cloaks, not part of the goblin body
- Goblins are creatures that haunt a specific place or country
- Goblins are born every time an evil thought or idea occurs. Once the mind is done with it, the thought seeks out a pile of filth and animates it, becoming a goblin
- They are a fungus that grows on the unburied dead
- Goblins are a myth; the name is simply a slur for a tight-knit guild of craftsmen who make and sell tumblers, beakers, and cups — they are Gobloters
- They rest in hollows made in rocks and earth, making it dangerous to have unpacked and wild earth
- The belief that they rest in hollows is wrong; those are actually access points to the world where goblins live. It's how they enter the prime material plane
- Because goblins primarily take items from all humanoids, locating a goblin market will give access to many unique, rare, and hard-to-acquire items
- The problem with goblin-grown fruit is the uncertainty of what soil they fed, hungry thirsty roots?
- The only thing more delicious to a goblin than horseflesh is man-flesh
- Goblins are both mechanically and magically inclined, but their thoughts run counter to all right-thinking people
- Goblins are manifestations of chaos, limbo made manifest, and they are driven mad by the structure around them

- Goblin isn't a name for a race; certain creatures are just born too ugly. This physical grossness corrupts their spirits, turning them into the spiteful creatures we all know
- Goblins are invisible to everyone; only their target of mischief can see them
- Goblins have terribly sensitive feet; this is why smart goblins wear stone shoes
- Goblins are actually sentient toads. They have grown larger and more disgusting. This is why they all wobble when walking
  - This is actually why their voice sounds so cracked and broken; they are just croaking words
- Goblins are clearly tiny narrow creatures whose limbs look just like sticks, and whose heads look like piles of refuse
- Goblins, like moles and other burrowing animals, can burrow through earth and stone; this is why all gnomes know the goblin speech
- Goblins are disturbed by cleanliness. Where humans have a disgust threshold, goblins have the opposite. Goblins are repulsed by areas that are well-kept and are free of germs, dust, bacteria, fungi, mold, rot, filth, refuse, and insects
- Goblins are so hard to catch and kill because they move through the most difficult lands as if blessed by the god of swiftness. Briars, bushes, trees, boxes, limbs, rubble — none provide any impediment to their speed.
- Pious men and women are blind to the presence of goblins
- They will flee from the crowing of a cock because they fear the coming of the day
- Fully half of all grown-ups and one-sixth of all children can never see goblins, even when capering in front of their noses
- Goblins have no language, communicating in grunts and shrieks like monkeys
- Goblins are a special promotion mission for demonic larvae. It's a test to see how much chaos they can cause, to see if it's worth promoting the demon
- Goblins speak a tonal language with dense, layered meaning; it is nearly impossible for non-native speakers to achieve fluency
- Goblins will beg, cower, and plead at the slightest hint of aggression; they don't even have a word for "courage" in their language
- Goblins have a face-saving culture based on honor and shame. They live in a complex class system with a thousand and one courtesies and privileges due the ranks above them
- Goblins are the most persistent threat to an organized society. An adventurer can have no higher calling than to slay goblins and only goblins
- Goblins build clumsy, ramshackle shelters because that is the limit of their ability
- Goblin numbers are far higher than anyone can believe. There are millions of goblins for every humanoid. If they ever were to swarm, it would be the death of the world

- Goblins can make more from twigs, string, and other refuse than a skilled architect can do with quarried stone and mortar. Their ingenuity is limited only by their resources
- Goblins are agile and quick because their marrow is like rubber—their bones bounce
- Every time your focus drifts, it gives birth to a goblin
- Goblins aren't evil, just filled with energy; they are unable to feel fear or pain, and have no impulse control
- Goblins range from slight and nimble to broad and ponderous; the only way to know whether you're dealing with a very large goblin or a very small dwarf is to pull on its beard
- Goblins are masters of poisons because each goblins blood is a unique type of poison. The most deadly become "poison mothers" for the tribe, as they are tied up and fed as their blood is drained to become poison for other members of the tribe

VARIANTS:

REDCAPS: Some goblins stain their bodies and clothing with human blood; they are aggressive and violent

HOBS: These are masters of deceptions, pranks, and tricks, following a target and helping luck turn against them

ERLKING: A forest goblin that stalks children for not giving them respect when they enter their land

TRASGU: This is a nervous goblin with holes in his palms who move things around at night while making spoooooooky noises

COMBAT TRICKS:

SLIPPERY: When an attack misses against a goblin, they have scrambled out of the way and may move anywhere nearby: behind a table, on top of a helmet, hanging on to the wizards backpack. . .

GOBLIN SHAMAN: Goblin shamans can summon swarms of stinging insects, entangle players in writhing vines, and curse enemies with misfortune. When they do any of these things, goblins heal and gain morale

LEADER STRIKE: When a goblin leader strikes an enemy, it provides all of the goblins surrounding that person the opportunity to strike

POISON BLADES: Goblins coat their weapons in mild poison. Goblins with goblin poison cause people to become sick when struck, causing nausea

RIDERS: Goblins tame and ride wolves and horses

VALUABLE RESOURCES

Goblin bezoars are said to be of great use for enchanting potions, able to reduce the cost of crafting and increase the power of the tonic by intensifying ingredients. Like all things goblin, this is not without side effects

GRIFFON

*"They say the griffon can't live without her man, but I seen
more than one man broke by the loss"* — Edgar, houndsman

NOMENCLATURE: Bird-horses, grifforse, gracks, fonhorse, griffin, gryphon, shirdal

DESCRIPTION: A creature that is a mixture of eagle and horse

THINGS THAT ARE KNOWN:

- They can fly
- They can be ridden by men

RUMORS AND OTHER CURRENTS IN THE SKY:

- Griffons are bred and raised exclusively by cyclopes who live near gold mines
- Griffons will only lay their eggs in a nest filled with gold nuggets
- There are different breeds of griffon, depending on the bird or horse used: corvid-griffons, hawk-griffons, and more
- Corruption will cause a dragon to be born with a lizard-like head. These are exceptionally dangerous and must be killed, as they corrupt the land and animals around it
- Griffons are amazing mounts
- In order for a paladin to bond with a griffon, he must trade hearts with the griffon, tying their lives together
- Griffons have the ability to summon storms and winds with their wings
- Griffons pair for life. If their mate dies, they will go for the rest of their life without taking another mate. If they bond with a rider, they will never mate
- The claws and feathers of a griffon possess healing qualities, said to heal mortal wounds and allow the blind to see

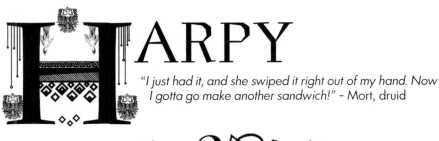ARPY

"I just had it, and she swiped it right out of my hand. Now I gotta go make another sandwich!" - Mort, druid

NOMENCLATURE: Karens, harpyiai, harpyia, hounds of Zeus, air hags, xanthippe, termagant, scolds, fishwives, sea eagles

DESCRIPTION: a creature that is a mixture of woman and bird

THINGS THAT ARE KNOWN:
- They can fly

RUMORS AND OTHER CONVERSATIONS WITH THE MANAGER:
- Sometimes, women who used their beauty to manipulate men, when their physical beauty fades, become bitter and resentful and transform into a harpy
- Birds who are fed human milk mature into harpies
- Harpies are what naughty boys and girls who talk back to their parents will turn into
- Harpies use the disemboweled corpses of their prey as natural incubators for their eggs. When harpies mate, their murderous bloodshed only increases as they seek to gather enough fresh corpses within which all of their eggs may hatch. When the babies are born, the parent harpies nourish them from the same corpse, feeding them the flesh, sinew, and bone marrow that has not yet decayed
- Their faces are always ragged with hunger, and they only desire to fill their gullets and abate the constant pain
- Harpies decorate their lairs and mark their territories with the bones and desiccated entrails of their victims. They construct foul gore amalgams called "flesh scarecrows" using the body parts of various corpses. When working in the service of hags, as they often do, the flesh scarecrows are animated by the hag's magic to serve as mindless servants or protectors
- They are spirits of the wind and lurk nearby humanoids to steal food or other items at hand
- Harpies don't actually lack for male affection it's just that the men are usually married or want to keep the relationship on the down-low, leading to the traditional harpy mood

70

- There is no force on the earth below or the sky above that rivals a harpy's wrath

- Harpies hold grim, primitive torture festivals during the waxing moon. Multiple victims are saved for a single night of sadistic debauchery, wherein each participating harpy is assigned a single victim. The harpy that causes their victim to scream the loudest and longest until death is determined the winner and granted the reward of first rites to eat the still-warm hearts of every victim before the remaining meat is divided amongst the rest of the tribe

- They live in an environment of filth and stench, and they contaminate anything they come near

- Harpies are an essential part of the ecosystem, for it is their wings that stir the winds to blow

- Harpies are very nimble, and their feathers are said to deflect the blows of weapons

- It is uncertain if harpies pick twisted black knotted trees as nests, or whether the harpy nest causes trees to become twisted, black, and knotted

- Harpies are born when women ensorcell men in falling into love with them, by skinning a freshly buried corpse and wearing it as a belt while entreating the devil for aid. After one day and night, she ties it around the man whose love she desires, and when he wakes, he willingly marries the now cruel and evil harpy

- Although beautiful, all harpy songs are death to those whose souls are soothed by the music

- People do not regret their debauchery among the harpies, but their friends and family that they leave behind mourn the person who once was

- Harpies are like vultures, but instead of seeking meat, they seek to snatch the soul at the moment of death

- Harpies are the children of gods and responsible for bringing and removing the nighttime

- Harpies love to torment the blind, moving things around them, and snatching things from their hands, and when the blind seek help, people tell them it's just the swift storm winds

ELLHOUNDS

"No, Prince Erik, the hellhounds Neves released cannot be ignored for your spring retreat." — Lambert, exhausted seneschal

NOMENCLATURE: Nessian warhounds, demon dogs, garmr, death hounds

DESCRIPTION: A hound of fire and flesh

THINGS THAT ARE KNOWN:

- They are intelligent hounds
- They have the ability to breathe fire

RUMORS AND OTHER FLICKERS IN THE FIRE:

- Hellhounds are the guard dogs of hell
- They have pitch black fur, are larger and stronger than normal dogs, and have red eyes
- A true hellhound is bound with a collar and chain of hell-steel that trails along the ground
- They have the ability to step through shadows
- Hellhound pelts are permanently stained with the blood of their kills
- The "fire" that hellhound breathes is actually a form of acidic bile
- Hellhounds are what happens when a fire gets bored and decides to go exploring
- Warlocks who have sold their souls to devils can only take one form, that of the hellhound
- Hellhounds are spawned in pairs, as servants to devils, and when the keymaster reaches the gatekeeper, the devil is summoned
- Hellhounds can only sleep in graveyards
- Although cruel and vicious, they are exceedingly loyal and protective
- Everyone sees a hellhound once in their life, soon before their death

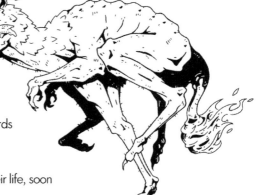

- They smell of brimstone and burn areas through which they pass
- Hellhounds are just rumors spread by ignorant peasants who didn't know how else to describe a mechanical dog
- They hunger for the flesh of human children
- You can breed a hellhound by feeding the burnt flesh of a unicorn to a trained hound. Soon a hellhound will grow inside its guts, until it bursts free, killing the host and eating its flesh for sustenance
- Hell hounds are the only way to banish demons without magic. They can consume the demon, banishing it from the prime material
- Hellhounds are what happen to wolves that feast on goblin and greenskin flesh

HYDRA

"At first I thought it was a snake, den two snakes. 'da third head gave it away."
— Holfandun, Othlandic cook

NOMENCLATURE: Reptilia hydroza, many-headed reptile, chthonic water beast, hydroraptor, water serpent

DESCRIPTION: A water reptile with multiple heads

THINGS THAT ARE KNOWN:

- They are reptiles
- They often live in swamps or near water
- They have multiple heads

RUMORS AND OTHER SERPENTS IN THE SWAMP:

- Hydra isn't a separate creature. They are actually reptile elementals
- Each hydra starts off as a genius. However, when they are forced to regenerate or grow a new head, their intelligence is forced to be split between each surviving head
- Something about the regenerative powers is easily influenced by the elemental planes. When fire influences a hydra, you get a pyrohydra, and when ice does, you get a cyrohydra
- Hydra does not refer to a specific creature but rather a mutation or disease that grants extra heads
- There are rarer elements that affect hydras, from chronohydras to mirror hydras, radioactive to vacuum hydras
- There is always one head that plots against the others. It strives to secretly acquire aid, which is difficult being that it is attached to the other heads
- Hydras are not quadrapeds. They are actually bipedal
- Several varieties of hydras exist: winged dragon types, slow moving swamp types, serpent types, and even types that walk like a man
- There is a dimension of snakes, and hydras are just ancient reptiles who contain a genetic code that grows a mobile portal to that realm
- Killing the snakes just allows more to work their way through the portal, but whatever you do, make sure to close that gate. If a hydra body ends up wedging it open, a whole circus of snakes can pour out

- Hydras only have a single head, but it is displaced throughout time. That is how so many heads appear from a single neck

- A hydra's heads are not actually heads. They are just tooth and spiked tentacles that appear to be heads. Its actual head is in its tail

- That is a particularly nasty rumor that has no truth to it. Its brain and organs are all safe inside the armored body, and its real mouth is a sucking orifice in its belly

- Hydras don't really 'grow new heads'; they are just actually better regenerators than trolls

- That said, each part of a hydra cut off will grow a new hydra. Once there was just one, chopped into a million pieces by brave heroes

- The hydra isn't a predator at all. It's a freshwater filter feeder, needing many heads to siphon plankton, small fish, and algee from the water. They are the most peaceful of swamp creatures

- Hydra isn't a creature, but the titanic form that the apocalypse comes in, each head devouring a part of the world

- It isn't just the heads but all limbs that grow back, hence the origin of the hydra-centipede

- Not only is their breath poisonous, but also their blood and even the tracks they leave on the ground

- Hydra is simply a word to describe the endless hordes of reptile peoples in the swamp. They are the hydra, stealing and raiding from the edge of civilization

- The hydra is a boneless creature, supported by hydrostatic pressurized vesicles

- Hydras don't eat meat; they actually drain all liquid from their prey. They are hydroraptors (water-thieves)

- Hydra heads once cut off leave stumps that regrow new (or multiple) heads. This can be cauterized by fire

- They can also be effectively cauterized by electricity or acids, which can work much faster than fire and reduce the risk of blood poisoning

- Hydras are actually squid

- A hydra's tongues can predict the weather by changing colors

- If cauterized, the heads never grow back

- Hydras are docile herd animals, raised for food. They have multiple heads due to breeding practices to increase the yield of the head which is used to make delicious soups and jellies

- They hydra will continue to grow heads as needed, but when it reaches the high teens, its blood pressure goes too low to maintain consciousness. Slowly, as it rests, many of the heads are reabsorbed after a number of hours

- The above is a lie, because as magical beasts, the hydra has nothing so prosaic as blood. The growth is caused by the salty tears of innocent slaughtered animals, slain without propitiating the spirits of the forest.

- Hydra eggs are quite valuable
- The hydra is no reptile, but a mobile aggressive plant
- Hydras, experiencing aggressive unpopularity due to their "All mobile things are food" international relations policy, have a strong preference to lair in dismal out of the way places
- The hydra has only a single brain, meaning psionic attacks, charms, and other features do indeed only need to be applied once against the hydra, not against each head
- The former piece of information is an ancient propaganda piece by the hydra ministry of public relations. Don't be caught off guard!
- Hydras love riddles; in fact, it has one for each head. If you can solve all the riddles, it will allow you to have its hoard. Answer incorrectly, and the hydra will attempt to make you into dinner
- Yuan-ti are servants of the hydra, each desperately hoping to be blessed with the honor of becoming a hydra itself
- Hydras are the weaponized result of possibility harvesting. The hydra is just a single large snake, but each head is simply the altered positions all manifesting at the same time. This means on any give round a hydra has 3-18 heads
- A multi-headed hydra only has one head, inside the mouth of which is another head, like a matryoshka doll. It's heads all the way down
- Hydras are living beings with fractal DNA
- Someone once made a wish to never be lonely. Every hydra ever is the result
- The hydra has a regenerative organ deep within its body. It is coconut-sized and gristly and is called a terratocopia, shaped like a strange, juicy sea-shell.
- Many people, especially elves, believe that powered terratocopia is the cure to any ills. Especially erectile dysfunction
- Each hydra is not a separate beast but an individual sensory organ of a much larger creature. They are extensions into this dimensional realm and learn about it much like babies, by taking the things within it and consuming it
- A hydra is like a rat king but for dragons
- Hydras are an endangered species. This is purely coincidental and has nothing to do with the terratocopia or any culture's specific believes about said organ
- A maiden per head surrounding the hydra works as an effective method of neutralizing the beast. Spread in a circle equidistant from the hydra results in confusion
- The hydra is a natural apex of Lamarckian evolution. The regeneration abilities of the lizard are taken to extremes and produce a succession of multi-headed beasts, not immediately or obviously related to the hydra
- All hydras are related to the ur-hydra and as such are psionically linked

- Hydras gain immunity to an attack that removes a head, making the single or double-headed hydras the most dangerous
- Hydras aren't monsters! It's the name of a refreshing summer pastry with ice-cream filling and seven raisins served at the forty-four courts of the vile queen Ayuwainya
- Each head believes itself to be the main head and is conflicted between protecting the body and eliminating its competition
- There are no hydras, but there are anti-hydras, with one head and multiple bodies
- Hydras are kept as pets by ettins who give them each one name per head
- Hydra, reproduce asexually by budding
- Hydras have horns that are not used in combat. The females' horns are shorter than the males'
- They can see in the dark with no problem
- The hydra isn't a reptile but is actually a type of land jellyfish, distantly related to coral
- Hydras are magic creatures that require no food. They kill out of inborn aggression and pleasure. Soon even this grows dim, and they become insanely aggressive
- Hydras are actually a larval form of medusae
- It's actually the other way around: a medusa that lives long enough becomes a hydra
- Hydras are former pets flushed by elven owners once too big for their aquariums
- They hydra is actually a normal river serpent, affected by a terratic virus. It reproduces by shedding the virus in waters where it prefers to live. Eventually, it becomes ill and overwhelmed, resulting in a frenzied, demented final stage characterized by staggering regenerative powers. If it survives long enough, its whole body sloughs away and collapses in a mass of aggressive tumors
- Fish & Game designed and introduced the hydra as a simple fish control measure. The fact that they aggressively eat every native species, including humans, was an unfortunate side effect
- Hydras are actually mutated fish or possibly plesiosaurs
- Hydras fling themselves at knights and other monsters, because when they have too many heads, they can't move to feed themselves and starve

"The hero Arthix promised the Lord of Thambar that he would nullify a particularly troublesome seven-headed hydra that dwelt in the bottom of a well and guarded a gem called 'the Heartstone' that the Lord coveted. Arthix asked for the loan of seven of the Lord's tenderest and most desirable concubines. These he chained in a circle around the well, each one the exact same distance from the well and an equal distance from each other — like numbers on a dial. The hydra crawled up from the well with each head looking in a different direction as was its custom. Each head saw a writhing, shrieking, delicious concubine and each head strained to pull the beast towards that desired morsel, but each head was equally strong so the beast remained stationary. Arthix snuck in, stole the Heartstone and buggered off. One of the concubines managed to wriggle free of her chains, and, likewise, buggered off. The head that had been eyeing her turned its attention to the next concubine in the circle. . . suddenly that concubine had two heads looking at her, and the hydra pulled itself in her direction, devoured her and then devoured the other five concubines in turn. The Lord of Thambar was furious. The escaped concubine followed Arthix back to his boat and professed her undying love for him. After they escaped the island together, she chopped off his head with his sword while he slept, threw his body overboard, sailed for the mainland and used the proceeds from the Heartstone to live life on her own terms rather than having to be a concubine for the Lord of Thambar. The Lord of Thambar was furious, but wasted his time looking for Arthix (who was fish food)."
- Stephen Poag

IXITXACHITL

*"There's no debate about how to say the name!
Don't be absurd."* — Nenemith, sage

NOMENCLATURE: Intelligent rays, demon rays, devil fish

Ixitxachitl is pronounced:

- ish-it-SHACH-itl
- iks-it-ZATCH-i-til
- ik-zit-zah-chih-tull
- iks-it-ZAK-itl
- iks-it-SHAK-it-ul
- ih-SHIK-sha-chi-tul
- iks-iks-a-CHIH-tul
- ick-ZIT-sah-chittle

DESCRIPTION: Evil intelligent clerical manta rays

THINGS THAT ARE KNOWN:

- They are highly intelligent and wield malicious divine powers
- They live underwater
- They are shaped similar to manta rays
- Their lairs are often hidden quite well
- Members appear to be vampiric in nature

RUMORS AND OTHER STORMS IN THE DEEP:

- They have their magical powers because they sacrifice to the old and forgotten gods
- They sacrifice not just the flesh of men and treasure, but also sculpture and metal-works. In times of scarcity, they must occasionally sacrifice one of their own number
- They are particularly deadly to rangers. Crikey!
- They dislike having their name mispronounced
- They kill and sacrifice opponents because they desire to turn their life energy into magic items

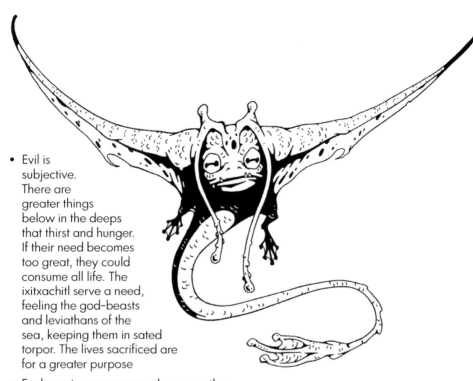

- Evil is subjective. There are greater things below in the deeps that thirst and hunger. If their need becomes too great, they could consume all life. The ixitxachitl serve a need, feeling the god-beasts and leviathans of the sea, keeping them in sated torpor. The lives sacrificed are for a greater purpose

- Each carries an energy; when more than 20 gather the barriers between the prime material and the realms of the old gods weaken, and they feed their gods directly by draining the life from those they face

- They are mercenary, hiring out their services to any deity meeting their horrific demands

- Vampiric ixitxachitl are conduits for the Great Administrator, She Who Waits Beneath The Sands. They gather blood and funnel it to her vats, to be turned into pucks, shaped like pontefract cakes

- Any who consume these pucks is turned into a wooper (an infant ixitxachitl)

- The ixitxachitl are actually just sentient coral. They aren't evil but seeking revenge for the destruction of coral by surface dwellers. They are focused on finding a way to flood the world

- Ixitxachitl like poetry, haunting organ music, and whale song

- Ixitxachitl can be tanned into scrolls. These scrolls allow the spell on them to be reused up to 1d12 times, but there remains a small (~5%) chance that the spell will be changed from whatever it is to summoning vampiric ixitxachitl

- Ixitxachitl have one six-fingered hand on the end of their long, prehensile tail

- The vampiric ixitxachitl vary in size. The smaller they are, the more of a knack they have for traps and mimicry. They will often disguise themselves as treasure in order to access secret places. They favor disguising themselves as one of the following: Bag of holding that can hold up to 2000 coins. After that, it explosively vomits them out. Tricorn hat, Book dust jacket, Girdle of uncomfortable looks

- Ixitxachitl believe sea cows are sacred manifestations of their deities and must never be harmed

- Vorpal ixitxachitl have poisonous spines on their tails. On a natural 20, the spine pierces the heart of their enemy, causing instant death

- They create forbidden alien intelligences as recreation

- They are arrogant and self-important to a fault. Anything that does not concern their world is of no importance at all to them

- In the deep heavy ocean trenches, portals are refined by the crushing pressures of the deep. The dark intelligences of that place send their scouting spells through to see what the thin space is like, alien astronomers exploring our airy realm. Their magic is more durable than our weak magic. If the portal closes before the spell returns, it cures taking on intelligence and independent life. It maintains a thread of connection and can draw energy from its ancient source. The ixitxachitl have not forgotten their original purpose and they secretly labor to build chambers for when their masters arrive to claim this realm

- They worship dark gods like Demogorgon

- Ixitxachitl worship the death cult of Skulli, the six-flippered manta of destruction

- Ixitxachitl explosively expel their guts to entangle foes. This is why ixitxachitl become vampiric: they need living blood to regrow their intestines

- Ixitxachitl implant their eggs in the posteriors of their victims. There the eggs hatch into little mantas that eventually emerge from the victim's mouth

- Ixitxachitl aren't aquatic. They are amphibious. Out of water they are called cloakers

- Stupid wizards. Valek the sea wizard wanted a magical cloak. He wanted it to see and warn him of incoming attacks. He wanted it to channel divine magic to heal him and refill spells. He wanted it to help him swim like a creature of the sea. Imagine his surprise when it grew weary of his endless pedantic speechifying, stabbed him, and swam off. It dug into the glimmering cosmic connection infused by Valek, found a patron and had but one wish: a mate

- Male ixitxachitl paint their flippers with gaudy patterns of green, red, and mauve to woo females. They also enjoy wearing kilts

- They are not cruel. They just don't understand that other creatures besides ixitxachitl are sentient. They treat the whole world as if it exists for their use and pleasure

- Despite looking like manta rays, ixitxachitl actually taste like beef

- Lochsbaed, a cruel sea goddess, subjects all sahuagin clerics to judgement when they begin to attract attention with their spell demands. The failures become ixitxachitl, scales cast from her divine body
  - This is true, and the ixitxachitl are literal scales, seeking to construct her body on earth. When a critical mass of failure is reached, she will be drawn to the frame of her scales and her avatar will cleanse the earth, boiling them with blood and death
- When the moon is full the ixitxachitl can fly through the air in bubbles of suspended water. This makes them more difficult to hit
- They originally are space creatures and came here clinging on the hulls of spelljammers
- They dissolve into hundreds of pearls when slain
- They are parasites of the cosmic life force, sucking divine energy. The most refined become vampiric. Every god wants them killed, but a cult is studying them to learn how they steal energy from the gods without worship
- The vampiric ixitxachitl are actually ancestors, the source of their clerical spells, and summonable through pheromonal and ink gestures from the Great Swimming Grounds beyond to act as champions and protectors
- A defected drow faction moved to the deep sea, worshiping an ancient monstrosity they crafted with atrocity and deep magic. They worship it, granting it power, and it flakes off ixitxachitl like dead skin. Now, however, it favors the ixitxachitl more than the drow
- A city of bloodthirsty killer cultists worshiping evil was flooded by a group of powerful adventurers. However, some were saved with new bodies granted by underwater darkness spirits
- The ixitxachitl do not serve gods. They take divine power from lost underwater temples. The vampiric ones serve as hosts for stolen divine sparks
- There is a caste of four-armed engineers and builders among the mantis folk called the fixitxachitl
- They are symbiotic with evil halflings that live on tropical islands. They surf the large ones and use the small ones as frisbees for sports. The dead ixitxachitl are made into hide shields and armor. Their spines are wonderful spear tips and daggers. What's the exchange? The halflings make sacrifices at a dark altar. All ixitxachitl magic is fueled by that altar
- The ixitxachitl are pure vegetarian nature-lovers. Their clerics are really druids and the vampiric ixitxachitl use mouth daggers to perform sacrifices to balance the ocean
- Ixitxachitl are hunted by the penguin folk to be made into cloaks and jackets of warmth and spell resistance

- An aboleth from the elemental plane of water (or more likely, mucus) crafted a magic item that devours its victims. When successful, they are transformed and excreted onto the prime material as ixitxachitl. The aboleth does this without concern but the thought of destroying the item might appeal to mortals
- They are obsessed with acquiring slaves that can function underwater
  - Although they can raise dead, they are unable to control them, due to the enmity of the gods of death (e.g. Orcus)
- Ixitxachitl are the larval stage of the space manta, sailing through the folded planes of the multiverse, spreading their dark blood cult to primitive worlds
- The vampiric liches of Sonburnne wanted to invade their elven rivals across the sea. However, the sea was too dangerous to sail so the elven navy prepared with magic and arms for every incursion. They experimented with various options, transforming soldiers into rays, event transforming some of their own vampiric number. They eventually abandoned the plan and the tests, discarding them into the ocean. Some lived. They blame the elves
- Riverine ixitxachitl enslave elementals to carve maze-like branching canyons and canals in which they raise their young
- For the mermaid festival the princess trained her ray friends to form a bubble and force out water to reduce the pressure. She would show off a hot air balloon underwater and use it to sing her solo. But an evil sea witch had cursed her rays. As they approached the crowd, they turned black and scattered, stabbing and casting and sucking. The problem was solved, but the sea witch achieved great fame as a result. All the other witches wanted to know the curse, and the witch was able to sell it and retire in style. Enough castings have assured the remains drift around the sea, forming a people of her own. A few have begun to question where the witch got her curse
- The ixitxachitl are not sea creatures at all. They live in a city on the dark side of the moon, traveling to the sea on moonbeams for their coming of age rituals
- The truth of their origin is that they are simple shed skin from greater evil gods, who would sooner invent a creature to eat them than listen to their endless pleas
- Dried ixitxachitl brains are used to make the traditional elven soup of wisdom which grants a bonus to intelligence and wisdom. With each serving you risk addiction
- The females breed annually and are seeking to improve the race by engaging in a selective breeding program
- The Zzar wizard house was trying to build a godzilla-class undead monster. However, the tank began to bloat and rot. They repurposed local rays to eat flesh once it was ripe, but the profound necromantic energies had unpredictable effects. Not only did some of them become vampiric, but they began to grow a vague malign intelligence. One of the Zzar necromancers staged a coup using these as foot soldiers, then using the brainjuicer increased the intelligence of his minion. It worked too well. They ate him and escaped. It has been speculated that they continue to have the goal of building a leviathan of the deep to rampage across the surface

- They come from one of the seas of the moon or from within the great reservoir inside it
- Certain varieties have adapted to thrive in sewers
- Ixitxachitl are forbidden from dealing the killing blow to a creature. This is why they swarm, because there is some question as to who the killer is. A lone ixitxachitl will prefer to injure and leave a target bleeding. Vampiric ixitxachitl are created when they knowingly take the life of a victim
- Vampiric ixitxachitl are treated with suspicion by other ixitxachitl and are worshiped by kuo-toa
- Aberrant mermen or triton mages have grafted ixitxachitl to their backs, learning to adopt either form and increase the arcane powers they wield
- Powerful ixitxachitl know the spells *Desalination*, *Wall of Coral*, and *Squirming Doom*
- The name ixitxachitl is a cruel joke played on outsiders, seeking to twist their tongue into perfidious knots. The malicious creatures have a different name for themselves
- The ixitxachitl grow an extra eye for every sentient creature they kill
- The ixitxachitl are not vampiric. This is poppycock based on magical thinking. Much like the mosquito, ixitxachitl females need mammalian blood to produce eggs
- The ixitxachitl believe that negative emotions are destroying the balance of nature. They seek to provoke other creatures to draw them out. This is why some ixitxachitl are vampiric. Others feel 'drained' after being drawn out. The ixitxachitl are only acting as supernatural psychotherapists. "Survivors" of ixitxachitl "attacks" report that they feel more positive and motivated about themselves, and they feel less depressed or angry
- Ixitxachitl may only be turned if their name is pronounced correctly
- They will burrow underneath the sand to hide or surprise opponents
- They can swarm creatures, losing their individual attacks but doing automatic damage

 # ERMLAINE

"Arrrgh! Untie me!" - Slive

NOMENCLATURE: Little men, gremlins, bane-midges, jinxkins, smurfs, atomites, minimi (sing. minimus), troublemaker, twik-men, dinkos, globbos, scrabblers, rat-brothers, flappies, flabbies, squeakies, squnities, verminites, trapsters, point-heads, mouselings, minimen, tiny terrors, minscules, manikins, rodent riders, peewees, diminumen, jermies

DESCRIPTION: Small troublesome fae who associate with rodents and other small creatures

THINGS THAT ARE KNOWN:

- They are fey creatures
- They associate with rats
- They dwell in warrens beneath the ground
- They shave captives

RUMORS AND OTHER NOISES IN THE WALLS:

- They are actually gremlins called by an incorrect name. Being given a separate name, they desperately sought to differentiate themselves from gremlins to maintain their existence and avoid being absorbed into other beings
- Their natural language sounds like a high pitched squealing or keening
- Rats gnawed loose the bonds of a bound fey prince once. The prince bestowed upon the simple creatures a boon; when they were killed in great numbers, from a mass grave would rise a jinxkin, which would avenge the fallen by undoing the strength of all would-be oppressors. With multiple mass graves, multiple jinxkin arose, and they bred true.
- During the Great Winter, when the rats and their hunger outnumbered the people a hundred to one, the whole city had to be abandoned when the jinxkin rose up in numbers and force.
- Every time a person says or does a mean thing a jermlaine is created from that thing. This is why they are so terrible
- Jermlains shave their victims because hairlessness is a sign of weakness. Elder jermlains are honored for their braided back and armpit hair. Shears are considered cursed, and all shaving of victims is done with a dull knife

- They do not do much damage when they strike, which is good. The poison and other alchemical substances used have their full potency however.
- Once an elven army rose up in hubris to take the City of Brass. The rulers of that city twisted reality itself to turn the invading elves into vermin. The jinxkin resulted, their minds enfeebled towards history and sense of self, but still expressing all the malice that the City of Brass felt from the invading fey.
- The excrement of jermlains is a peculiar pink paste. It can be used to treat skin complains, cuts, bruises, and protect from insect bites and allergies. It restore an additional hit point per day
- The fae have many defended gates from the Ardenwald to Prime. One of their favorite auto-immune systems to put in place is the jinxkin infestation. It is enough to keep normal people away; it commandeers local rodents (and there are ALWAYS local rodents); and it is only mildly murderous. The jinxkin pay for their fey powers by making gifts of hair to their eldritch masters, to show that they are performing as intended (and should stay in the energy budget). This hair gives the fae a sense of who is lurking around their portals.
- They seek a new king with a birthmark that, according to prophecy, is hidden by hair
- They often dwell in cities and aristocrats and criminals are very interested in buying the secrets they gather, especially their own
- Fey nobles usually have a pouch or two of banemidge eggs. When they are treated poorly in an area, they toss a handful of eggs into the local water supply. Like mosquitoes, the banemidges rise and cause mischief. They need hair to reproduce; some populations shave so the pests will die off. The banemidges usually survive because humans are so reluctant to shave everywhere . . .
- They must eat hair in order to reproduce. It is unpleasant, but allows the males to perform. Females make elaborate macrame items or knit clothing from hair to attract mates
- They scavenge for treasures off dead bodies. If you are looking for someone that has disappeared, they are the people to talk to
- They are highly allergic to dander; shearing their captives makes them less likely to irritate their skin
- They burn the hair after soaking it in rancid-smelling oils to serve as an aphrodisiac
- They are prodigious collectors. That slightly chipped silver button on your trousers is worth a small fortune to the right jermlaine
- They will ally with humans, especially if bribed. They have a strong tendency to betray those they help
- Jermlaines love wild hair, and they don't excrete feces but instead multi-colored rays of light
- Children love the taste of jermlaines
- Jermlaines lay eggs

- The reason jermlaines have saggy skin is that they are actually a breed of gnomes that was struck by a magical illness that shrank their bones but not their skin. Gnomes become quite hostile if asked about this

- Jermlaines reproduce by constructing hair effigies and breathing life into them

- Jermlaines are born from the filth and detritus left behind by adventurers. They are iron ration scraps, bits of 10' poles, torn scrolls, warrior blood, and rogue sputum imbued with crafty hatred by spirits of the underground who loath, and resent intrusion

- When a fairy fountain is corrupted, the energy does not stop gushing out. If the conduit is broken, the energy saturates the "groundwater" energy of the area, corrupting things that are not meant to sit in the wash of alien energy. Things are changed. The banemidge vermin are the least of the worries from such a site. The main way to end the problem is to either cap the energy source, or rebuild its proper flow path

- Jermlaines quadruple in hit dice (but not size) if they eat human food after midnight

- If jermlaines get wet, they begin to duplicate

- The skin color of jermlaines reflects their temperament

- The idea of smurfs is fae propaganda to portray them in a positive light

- Rats carry fleas that carry plague. Rats also carry mites that become banemidges. When anything with hair travels through the Ardenwald and gets back to Prime, they have traces of the parasites of that alien place on them. Without natural predators, the banemidges emerge and latch on to a hot-blooded and plentiful population of rats, then proceed to become a real problem. The banemidges are the primary reason travel to the Ardenwald was forbidden, even to elves. After a century of determined efforts to rid a kingdom of the banemidges, the prospect of tracking more in became a capital offense.

- They are actually sentient fay fruit. Archfay sometimes use jermlaine in their potions. They taste bitter

- The juice of jermlaines is delicious, and the high lords of the elves pay ridiculous amounts of money for it

- Some jermlaine, domesticate species other than rats, like frogs, bats, and lampreys

- Princess Kavastra was too kind, and she hated seeing rats poisoned and trapped. She approached the fey in the nearby woods and asked if the population could be managed in a kinder way. The fey provided rat herds to balance the needs of the Jermlaine with those of the men, and all was well. A century later a descendant of Kavastra demanded the rat herds be repurposed for spying, assassination, and war. The hard-eyed fey replied, "Do as you will. Teach them what you want them to know." It didn't end well.

- Some ride small animals into combat like foxes, chihuahuas, or rats

- Leprechauns actually breed jermlaine as pot-of-fool's-gold guardians

- They have wellness anxiety and despise germs, which they are small enough to see. This is why they shave all their captives before dragging them into their lair
- They use the hair gathered from captives to build nests. They need it to retain heat to hatch their bejeweled eggs
- Jermlaines are elementals from the Plane of Frustration they waylay, trick, embarrass, drain, and eventually kill. Their offerings are collected by the leaders, feeding back to a sphere in their lair that becomes a gate back to their plane when they've harvested enough suffering
- Rats worship them instinctively, and in return they get protection and food
- They actually are just obsessive wig artists and like throwing wig parties. The best wig at the party wins the Fuzzy Sceptre of Jermlainishness for a month
- They are obsessed with numerology and particularly the number 23
- They are passionate about interpretive dance their firelight dance parties are profound
- Jermlaines are actually the most beautiful of the fay but project a glamour of ugliness to keep away humans. The hair is used to produce glamour powder which causes people to wince at their ugliness
- A mirror of burnished silver will reveal the true form of a jermlaine, or capturing one and putting it inside an iron cage for three and thirty days
  - The pygmies of the Nil-shuth Valley know this and capture them for the pre-marriage arrangement. The arrangement is a formal and ritualized limited term where the men lose innocence and become men. The jermlaines are not amused by this
- The wizard tower Alcanth had a testing-ground below, where young wizards had to succeed against trials of their hearts, minds, muscles, and magic. Each wizard crafted a homunculus to add to the stable of threatening creatures used to train and test apprentices. In a weird turn of events, when the Alcanth wizards were at war with the eladrian, some of the fae made friends with the homunculi, who turned traitor and gave the wizards up to the elven knights before eloping with the fae. However, the story did not end happily. When the fey knights discovered what their underlings planned to do, they were uncomfortable. So, they banished all their fey helpers back to the Ardenwald and abandoned the homunculi (and the weird hybrids from their loving unions) in the ruin of the wizard tower. A few hundred years later, embittered magic fey construct colonies were heading out with legions of rats, finding the only way to blunt their misery was to spread it
- They can use specific frequencies of light to transport themselves instantly. Rainbows are sure signs of jermlaines
- Gnomes are steeped in fey energies. They know the languages of burrowing creatures. They are widely disliked. They tend to spend a lot of time in their secluded homes, amusing themselves with magic and illusions, and getting cozy with rodents about their size. They won't talk about jinxkins. Not even with other gnomes.

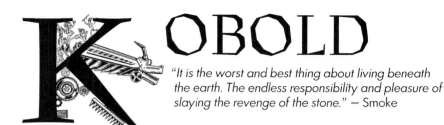

KOBOLD

"It is the worst and best thing about living beneath the earth. The endless responsibility and pleasure of slaying the revenge of the stone." — Smoke

NOMENCLATURE: Cobalts, koboldi, knockers, the bold

DESCRIPTION: Underground demons spawned from earth

THINGS THAT ARE KNOWN:

- They are small
- They hate gnomes
- They have an aversion to melee combat
- They are sensitive to light
- They have facility with traps and mechanical objects
- They can see in the dark

RUMORS AND OTHER KNOCKS IN THE MINES:

- They are actually halflings. When a dragon swallows a halfling whole, the resulting egg hatchlings are kobolds
- Kobolds are related to kabouter, common garden gnomes
- When moving alone through tunnels, kobolds are capable of dilating time, allowing them to reset traps faster than humanly possible
- Kobolds have a secret penchant for tipping cows. On adventurers
- A secret breed of kobolds in the eastern mountains, called Perkmandelz, can turn invisible and run around with a lantern, imitating a subterranean will 'o wisp
- Kobolds are not scaled. Those are actually dermoliths: little stones that grow in kobold skin, letting them blend in with their rocky habitat
- They are immune to petrification because they are already petrified creatures
- Kobolds collect coins quite quickly and quietly congregate in clammy caves to count and cackle
- Kobolds feel compelled to count a loose pile of coins lying around. Then they store it in a small sack with the value written on the outside. The reason for this compulsion is unknown. It does irritate dragons who just want to sleep on coins, not little sacks filled with sacks of 100 coins each

- A kobold can count 50 coins in a combat round
- Kobolds are the animate leavings of slain dragons
- They lust and revenge themselves against man-races, trying to reclaim the glory of their dragon creators
- Kobolds and dwarves are related, which is why they are often found as dungeon maintainers
- Kobold horns are noted aphrodisiacs among orcs. Kobolds themselves cannot breed until their horns grow back
- A kobold's horn is regenerative, and a whole new kobold can grow from one horn. This explains the difficulty at eliminating the infestation. A single kobold can break apart its horn and grow a whole new batch of fresh kobolds
- Kobold horns grow all over their body
- Kobolds wouldn't be the problem they are today if it wasn't for the early kobold genocide attempts. The bodies were hacked to pieces and the horns often became shattered. Each kobold then became hundreds
- Trapmaking is the highest art among the 'bolds
- Kobolds have serrated beaks, not teeth
- "This is absolute nonsense. The Kobolds of Underpnod have mobile, wrinkled faces, like disgusting little monkeys or withered, wizened halflings." — Vaziry of Pnod
- Kobolds are untamed feral dwarves, murdering and eating trespassers and hoarding ancient treasures
- Kobolds work for death and keep the damned as slaves to toil in the mines
- A dwarf is a civilized kobold that lives among humans and speaks a human language
- Civilized kobolds ("dwarves") no longer burn in the sun, but they cannot see in darkness. Kobolds and "dwarves" are both misshapen little old men with flinty, inhuman eyes, knobby joints, and at least one exaggerated facial feature. Beards are optional
- Kobolds turn to stone in the sun and are often collected as garden ornaments
- Kobolds are to goblins as gnomes are to dwarves
- This being the case, they are smaller, lighter, and unlike gnomes being focused on trickery, they are more direct than goblins. They use magic that causes explosions of spellfire, telekinetically hurled objects, and tunnel collapses. Even with their magic potential, the kobolds themselves are small scrawny things that rarely go into combat
- Kobolds are very good with animals and often train small and medium creatures like boars, spiders, and giant weasels as mounts
- They create their homes using telekinetic magic used while in a meditative trance. This allows them to function as if they were humanoid sized
- Kobolds have remarkable singing voices; however, they are unlikely to share this

with outsiders due to their terrible stage fright

- Kobolds are to gnomes as drow are to elves
- The viciousness and cruelty of kobolds has absolutely nothing to do with height envy
- Kobolds are castaways from another dimension, pulled into ours by the smelting of ore. They emerge under darkness from the slag heaps
- They breathe stone, swim through air, and walk on water, They need air to drink, but wind is a very dangerous current. Near slag heaps you will occasionally find drowned kobolds. Cave systems and mining tunnels are more like gentle rivers and much safer
- They collect metals that they can find, hoping their shamans can use them to find a way home
- Kobolds have multiple rows of teeth which grow and grow until they die. Perhaps they are the humanoid descendants of sharks?
- Kobolds like the color blue
- Kobolds sometimes live in the forest and have adapted to survive. They defend and mark their territory well, with guerilla patrols, snares, traps, deadfalls, and other deadly protections
- One reason for the effectiveness of kobolds is their shamans focus on divination magic, and their easy access to communication methods (familiars, magic) and crystal balls (dug from the earth).
- In southern lands, they are seen as less evil (koboldi) and can be entertaining, due to the fact that they are always aroused and can drink to bacchanalian excess
- They fill mines with foul air, poison gas, toxic minerals, or worst of all, koboldium, the burning metal
- The kobold god has a harem of chosen kobold maidens. Many semi-divine kobold warriors are born, whose skin blunts weapons and when slain, curse the killer
- Kobolds are not only mechanically inclined but also alchemically skilled with black powder, incendiaries, mines, and poison gas
- The entrance to a kobold lair is always disguised
- One fated night, long ago, a very drunk, lusty, and desperate gnome had relations with a giant salamander he 'surprised' and took advantage of. The resulting spawn from this rape was several hundred kobolds
- They speak the language of insects and all crawling creatures. This is why the most poisonous and deadly don't mind being dropped by them through muder-holes on passing adventurers
- Kobolds speak no languages. They capture poisonous insects and torture them till they are only filled with rage and evil, then they release them through murder-holes on passing adventurers

- Kobolds have no noses. That is why they smell terrible
- Kobold tails are a delicacy. Even kobolds themselves think so
- Kobolds feast on dragon corpses. This is the reason for their magical nature
- Kobolds have very specific dietary needs. This is why they are never found away from underground complexes and tombs
- Kobold shamans smear gold, silver, and copper coins on their skin, forming a heavy, glittering, armored layer as a ritual to fuel their spells and magical abilities
- A kobold that has lived an extended life and died of natural causes is reborn as what the kobolds call an Earthen One, who can pass through any type of earth. This includes metals
- Kobolds specialize on setting traps because eating tendons from the flesh of a living creature while they scream is the greatest delicacy.
- The first kobolds emerged from the torn tooth sockets of the titans that tried to destroy the world. The pain and death of those great forms was too great to be contained, and the kobolds were forced from their gory, cracked jaws. Their word for themselves is "homeless," and their mission is to harvest parts to build a new titan home. The trouble is, they don't know how, and all they remember is pain. So they collect that in jars. But they can't actually collect it. So they hurt people and wave glass at them. It's their religion.
- Kobolds have a flying relative – the Urd. Urd are tougher, more intelligent, and nastier. Their existence has nothing to do with the depredations of the kenku
- Kobolds will hate gnomes until Garl Glittergold ceases his never-ending teasing and trickery of Kurtulmak
- Kobolds are bastard children from wild bacchanalian parties among the wood-lands keepers, being a cursed combination of druids, rangers, animal companions, fey liquor, and practical jokes
- Kobolds are the immune system of an animistic living earth. The scar tissue from gouges and wounds on the surface takes the form of kobolds defending their mother
- Kobold eyes, when plucked and dried in the light of a full winter moon, will become semi-precious stones. If dice are made from these stones, they are magically loaded that shift +1 in the direction you prefer when you roll them.
- Kobolds who do enter melee often have tail attachments that they use to wound opponents. These have been know to throw black power, alchemist's fire, or substances even worse
- They hate gnomes because gnomes are cheaters; dirty, nasty, lying, cheaters. Illusions aren't fair; traps are. Using illusions to win prank contests isn't fair. You can't win if you're dead
- Stupid wizards. The combination of a ring of wishes, a German shepherd familiar, and some inadvisable things said about the usefulness of said familiar led to the kobold removing the ring from the wizard's fresh corpse. The last charge is the

cause of the piles of kobolds everywhere

- Kobold lariats are woven from the skin of sentient creatures. They are fascinated by hides
- If a kobold is skinned, the hide dissolves into sand in 1-4 days, no matter how it is preserved
- Kobolds were originally swarming, agile, flexible, and mechanical boarding constructs for spelljammer ships. A bribe of being both made of flesh and fertile to breed was made. Their original creators, furious, rounded up all they could find and marooned them on a quarantined planet. Releasing them is a capital offense
- Kobolds are fleas that have fed on the blood of dragons
- In ancient times, when all races were reptilian, kobolds ran the oppressive empire. All other races did their bidding. To this day they seek to manipulate and control the other races
- In the far future, humanity seeks to save themselves from a seared sky and fouled earth. They built a time gate and sent a group to save humanity from itself. Upon arrival they became sick and only their young survived. In three generations, all was forgotten, leaving a primitive culture seething with hatred for humans
- Kobolds are the progenitors of the elves, banished from the surface and forgotten by their children
- Kobolds wear lederhosen and make beer from rock
- If a kobold becomes wet, he flies into a rage. A great artform is creating intricate dust and soot patterns on their skin to mimic scales
- A kobold can transform into mist on nights with a full moon. This is how they migrate from cave to cave. The mists are cursed and many believe can cause migraines, ague, and loose bowels

COMBAT TRICKS:

AGILE: Kobolds are small and flexible They can move in, around, and under other creatures bypassing them easily and immune to any bonus attacks gained via opportunity or due to fleeing

MOB ATTACK: Kobolds receive bonuses to hit equal to the number of kobolds in melee with a target.

BOMBS: Kobolds can throw bombs with various alchemical effects (alchemist's fire, smokesticks, tanglefoot bags, etc.)

TRAPPERS LUCK: Kobolds can attack a player and do no damage but move them into a nearby trap

MAGICAL BLAST: Kobolds can generate and throw energy orbs that focus their magical force. The type of energy is dependent on the strain of kobold

EARTH STEP: Kobolds can meld with the earth, allowing them to disappear into the ground. They move incredibly quickly this way, reappearing anywhere within 100′

PAINFUL STABS: Kobold attacks do little damage but really hurt. When striking, after rolling damage, they can choose to do only 1 point of damage but apply a circumstance penalty to that target's combat rolls (attack and damage) until healing is recieved

SLUGGISH STEP: Kobolds can cover the floor with bags of their sticky poop. These cause people moving in those squares to move at half speed. Kobolds themselves are unaffected, of course.

VALUABLE RESOURCES

"The element Cobalt is actually named after Kobald, an earth spirit. The miners who dug out and smelted ores to find useful metals, which included the cobalt ore, which was poisonous with arsenic and ruined other metals, blamed Kobald when things went wrong because the spirit didn't want them down there.

When Georg Brandt found out what was actually poisoning the miners and ruining their ore, a new element, he named it after the spirit in tribute to the men who dug it out." - Patrick Stuart

LAMMASU

"The offer she makes you seems like a good idea, but so does the worm on the hook to a fish."
- Aldervile, neo-emperian speaker

NOMENCLATURE: Lamia, manticores, nagas, sphinx, shedu, lilith, empusa

DESCRIPTION: Creatures that have the head of a human and the body of a lion, goat, deer, or snake, said to eat children

THINGS THAT ARE KNOWN:

- Humans are their prey
- They are intelligent and have powers of illusion
- They like to live in arid desolate places
- They have the heads and/or torsos of humans, with animal lower bodies
- They can see in darkness
- They bait and trap men, using them for sex, sport, and supper

RUMORS AND OTHER SECRETS WHISPERED IN THE WILD:

- They aren't evil monsters, just superior beings who view our children as a delicious source of tender veal
- Their morality is complex, beyond human understanding. Amashotep's seminal works, Beyond Good and Evil, Also Sprach Lammathustra, Ecce Lammia, and Antilamia address the vast subject
- It is a well kept secret that there is no separate species as lamia; it is the curse of all human females one night a month to become one
- They are fond of associating with various other half-breeds, such as harpies and centaurs. Whether this is due to distant relations or some other reason is unknown
- They aren't any special — lions are just super horny and have no problem mating with human females. Lucky to survive, this rape is rarely mentioned. Lots of half-lion monsters though
- The gods dream secrets, and these secrets slip into the world. They find a feline form, because those receive and transmit secrets. The forcefulness and power of the secret can sometimes mutate and warp the feline
- Were a mortal to unravel the secrets of the leonine dreams, then immortality, even godhood, may be within reach. Two gods in the pantheon ascended in this way, and a secret order pursues this murderous quest

- They are actually Zensunni post-buddhists, explaining their preference for arid, dune-filled environments
- They are likely jerks
- They keep dustworms as pets, from which they harvest mysture, a substance used to make lions and snakes grow human-like faces and intellects.
- All lions are inherently evil. They lust after human flesh, and when they consume enough, they become a monster. Manticores come from the flesh of old men; young women produce lamias, and kings produce sphinxes
- They are a species that breeds true, and they suffer no defects from incest. The meaning of this is uncertain
- Demons don't just tempt men: sometimes noble lions fall prey, and the demonic corruption causes this horrific change
- The lamia-kind are neither good, nor evil, being beyond such matters. Some follow chaos and others law. Mortals try to ascribe morality to their actions, but they are simply angelic messengers of the balance, disinterested in the fate of men
- A lamassotto is an underdark version of a lammassu
- That Which Prowls stalks the trade routes and celebrates melding the creatures of the wasteland and the humans who trespass into it. Some of the survivors swear loyalty to That Which Prowls and assist in playing out the long, incomprehensible, sadistic game of cat and mouse with humanity that may end in the elevation or destruction of the world.

- They are truly vegetarians and child-like, playful beasts. Guarding wastelands and other desolate places, however, poses them as a threat to the Lords of Law. The end result is that they are portrayed as a vicious, blood-thirsty, childnibbling beast
- A male lamia is called a lamio. Rare creatures with silvery hides and prodigious. . . manes. The lammassu is a protector of lamia
- They are not half-lion; all of these creatures are simply torsos on swarms of countless insects, each representing the soul of a living creature
- Simply another form of an aberration of chaos, like satyrs, centaurs, minotaurs, and platypi

- The Goddess of Trees was struck ill and barely managed to escape the battle of the gods, stumbling into civilization. There she was cared for by the awed and ignorant human savages. She saw their lives up close; the way they turned to meat and away from the energy of the sun and the plants. She saw how they kept cats to eat meat that threatened what they wanted to protect. And, as we all know, the war of the gods caught up to the village, and the terrified villagers betrayed the Goddess of Trees to the Master of Forges. Her dying curse was that humanity would become the mice, and their hunters would bear the cruelty of their faces

- The spectacular orgies of the Arch Magus Wyvaria tended to focus on reptiles. Lilariasha tended to use shape-changing (mercifully) or just gear (best not to think about it) for coupling with spiders. But Vashtoor. . . he had a thing for lions. There's a reason we've killed all the wizards we could catch.

- The Kingdom of Farragut does a spectacular trade in lamia-sized slippers. They are fascinated by wearing soft, woolen booties while at home

- Their internal organs are suffused with magic—their guts can be used to make magical bowstrings +2 of distance and deceit

- They are not actually lion-headed creatures. They are penanggalan, which many people believe are vampires but are actually a type of sky demon. If they feast on the flesh of men, a body eventually grows to support them. This body is feline. If they feast on other creatures, they become other creatures. Horses and steeds make them into centaurs, felines and cats into manticores, etc.

- Lamias have no digestive systems; in fact their bodies are purely mechanical support systems for their heads. Their heads are the last remnants of an ancient empire that depended on machinery for survival. They were cursed by the gods for the misuse of their physical bodies and now suffer, eternally

- Lamias and lammasu can remove their own eyes. When they do so, they loudly utter prophecies. No one knows the accuracy of these prophecies; it's hard to listen after you've just seen something rip out its own eyes

- They are difficult to perceive, and viewing such creatures is difficult on the mind, draining sanity or wisdom

- No matter their form, they detest combat. Much better through spell, word, or deed to have lower forms do their fighting for them

- Each is violent and aggressive because when they tear themselves into existence a dark shadow is created at the same time. This shadow form hunts them to destruction

- Each is a different manifestation of a pure emotion or ideal, lammasu's are intelligence, lamia's jealousy, manticores are anger, etc.

- All of these are in fact guardians of thresholds, doorways, and portals. It is impossible to cross one without being within their vision. This is the root of their knowledge and power

- They are all just different lineages of rakasta bloodlines

- It is the name for a female vampire. Their powers of mentalism are so strong, that the only memories are those of a beautiful woman crossed with a deadly predator
- They are actually enlightened ascetic beings who have chosen to remain behind in earthly form
- House cats were ordered to play nice with humans so that they could serve as a spy network and witness of human deeds to the dark judges that await them. When enough intelligence about humans reaches them, these strange leonines transform in a more human direction, shaped by the nature of the insights the cats send them about what humans really are
- The leonines are assigned by the cosmos to shepherd the human race, but they chose servants of the wrong temperament. They were unable to agree on how best to handle humanity. Those that insisted on control, pushing and goading humanity to achieve its destiny, became male. Those who preferred seduction, trickery, and thinning the herd became female. Their task is a failure and the disappointment of the cosmos is palpable
- Leonines once ruled the world. Humans could only ascend by wielding chaos magic and crushing human frailties into the animal perfection of the world's rulers. By forcing human flaw and personality in to permanently shatter the balance of these once-regal beasts, they destroyed their ability to work together
- At the end, the heroes faced Gozer, who insisted they choose the form of their destruction. All Rae could think about was Mr. Mittens, his innocent and wise house cat. Since then, the leonine form of the destroyer has gained in power and aggression in the corners of the world, as a millennial-long agenda of destruction unfolds
- The foundation of the world is not stone, but secrets. The leonine guardians of the world are tasked with protecting it. However, their society is matriarchal. The men dislike their servitude and the discrimination against them. Some slipped out of their enclaves (a man's place is at the hearth) and try to support and encourage the seekers of secrets, the faster to erode the world's underpinnings so they can transcend to the next world. Meanwhile, the ladies seek out the races that are addicted to riddles and puzzles, and finish them off as cruelly as they can — still, they cannot quench the thirst for mystery that humans stole from the cats long, long ago
- The priests of the Rakasta are gifted by their feline goddess with more and more leonine features as they are infused with more and more cosmic and divine energy, eventually becoming immortal. Therefore, when slain, they must contextualize and motivate their existence as they re-exist. They go insane a little, but the better they manage their obsessions, the more lucid they remain

LIZARD MAN

"Shame that they just happened to be on our land before we got here." — Melbert, gambler

NOMENCLATURE: Lizard men, swamp folk, scale men

DESCRIPTION: Reptillian humanoid

THINGS THAT ARE KNOWN:

- They are reptiles that walk upright

RUMORS AND OTHER SOUNDS IN THE SWAMP:

- Lizard men are cold-blooded. They have discovered that the warmer their eggs are when being hatched, the more intelligent the lizard-men are

- Lizard men are amphibious and can breathe both above and below water

- Lizard men are undecided if orcs or humans taste better

- Lizard men, due to their lizard brains, don't experience emotions urgently. Fear, hunger, sorrow, all are treated with quiet detachment

- All lizardfolk can regrow their limbs

- Lizardfolk are the ultimate paranoid survivalists, convinced the entire world is about to collapse, and treating any event as if the end times have arrived, which is why they react so violently to unexpected events

- After several interviews with lizard men who join adventuring parties, it generally seems that they display no long term fondness for their friends or their well-being. In several cases, they had consumed the body of a fellow adventurer because it would go to waste otherwise. Their motivations seem exclusively mercantile

- Some lizardfolk communicate their emotions and feelings via scent glands and pheromones

- Lizardfolk were the original people, and they carry on the old traditions, not ignorant of more modern techniques, but in rejection of them

- They serve their old masters, creatures of creation, and base chaos beyond the understanding of the lesser races

- Like all lizards, they have two

LYCANTHROPY

"Yeah, I'm fine. It didn't bite me." — Kald, were-toad

NOMENCLATURE: Werebeast, versipellis, loup-garou, werwulf, lukanthropos, weriuuolf, gerulphus, garwalf, wariwulf, varulfur, warwoolfes

DESCRIPTION: A shape-shifting transmissible condition

THINGS THAT ARE KNOWN:

- They can change form between an animal and human in a cycle governed most frequently by the moon
- They have a vulnerability to silver

RUMORS AND OTHER HOWLS IN THE NIGHT:

- You turn into a were beast when you consume human flesh, becoming a wolf or other predator
- If you're a wolf-friend, wolf-trainer, wolf-speaker, or other person who consorts with wild animals, it's the same as having lycanthropy. It's an illness that gets into your brain and makes you become and like wild things
- The real lycanthropy is alcoholism. Man by day, monster by night
- Lycanthropy is a symptom of war, for they are men when they are home, but monsters when they are warriors
- The devil possesses people and curses them with lycanthropy
- Certain hidden tribes have a moon week, where they spend an entire week each year transformed into animals
- To become a true person, you must enter a marsh, shed your clothes, and live with the wolves for nine years. If during this time you abstain from tasting human flesh, you may return from the marsh and become human again
- Lycanthropy isn't a disease or anything of the sort. Just a few natural herbs and medicinal plants, and you can take the form of a wolf, or something even stranger
- The act of changing form damns your soul
- You don't need any fancy herbs to turn into a wolf. Just pile your clothes on the side of the road and piss in a circle around them. You'll turn into a wolf, lickety' split
- You need a skin of the animal you wish to change into
- A werewolf is what happens to a divorced man

- The dreaded beerwolf is a tyrant who must be resisted
- Lycanthropy is no physical illness, but a disease of the mind, where one believes one can turn into an animal and back, but sadly it is simply a delusion they hold that they cannot be shaken from
- The real thing that transforms you into a werewolf is serial murder
- The werewolf is a double who leaves the body of man unchanged and seeks out into the night to express forbidden desires
- The physical body doesn't change; instead victims of lycanthropy have their minds and senses transferred into the body of a wild wolf nearby
- You can always tell a werewolf because their eyebrows meet and they have curved fingernails, low-set ears, and a loping stride
- If you cut a lycanthrope in human form, the wound will be filled with fur
- In wolf form, werewolves have no tail, so they run with a strange three-legged lope and trail their fourth leg behind them
- Lycanthropes are frequently blamed for the exhumation and devouring of recently buried corpses, but the culprits are much more frequently graverobbers and ghouls
- To change form, you must collect rainwater out of the footprint of the animal, enough to drink a whole glass
- If on certain Wednesdays or Fridays you were to sleep and let the light of a full moon bathe your face on a summer night, you can gain the powers of a werebeast

- Addressing a lycanthrope three times by their birth name will cure it of the disease

- A werebeast isn't an animal at all. It's a disease where a recently deceased corpse rises in the form of a predator and searches battlefields to drink the blood of dying soldiers

- When werebeasts turn into human form, they hang their skins nearby. Burning this skin is the only way to kill the beast

101

MEDUSA

"What are the snakes for?"
— Peterson, area simpleton

NOMECLATURE: Gorgon, snake-lady, maedar

DESCRIPTION: A humanoid monstrosity with a head covered in snakes, whose gaze turns all who see it to stone

THINGS THAT ARE KNOWN:

- They are humanoids whose gaze turns people into stone

RUMORS AND OTHER FADED ETCHINGS:

- Medusae weep tears that turn to diamonds in their eyes. A medusa's heartbreak is a king's ransom
- All medusae suffer from a curse, to have everything they see petrify. It afflicts young women who bargain with devils and demons out of fear of losing their beauty
- Medusae and maedar are actually just a type of humanoid. They don't literally turn things to stone, but instead have a superior culture and judge those from other cultures very harshly, leading to the legend of a 'petrifying' gaze
- Medusae have been known to lead soldiers into battle. With their face always to the enemy, they can never mistakenly curse those who follow or protect them
- Neither medusae nor basilisks are immune to the petrifying gaze of the other; capturing a basilisk first is one way to hunt a medusa
- A medusa's severed head is still capable of petrifying those who look on it. One such head was used by a great warrior to petrify a kraken. You can still make out the shape of the kraken in the great stone spire it left in the bay
- A warrior sect from the desert lands swears its acolytes to an oath of invisibility to better hunt medusa. These warriors cover themselves head to toe in cloth and armor and veils, and will let no outsider see their face once they have taken the oath. They are known far and wide for their prowess in battle
- "Medusa" is the name of an individual, not a species; she is the most famous example of a creature called a gorgon. Anyone who says otherwise is ignorant and uneducated
- Gorgons are a distinct creature, a metallic bull-like construct unrelated to medusae. Anyone who says otherwise is elitist and boring at dinner parties
- Medusae are made when people are cursed for their vanity. Since no creature may see them without being turned to stone, not even themselves, their beauty goes unseen forever

- Medusae are made when jealous or vengeful gods punish beautiful women for arousing their passions or stealing the attention of others
- With the snakes on their heads hidden by a veil or a hood, a medusa may hide her true nature so long as she never looks another creature in the eye. Many have entertained medusae unaware
- Medusae are a variant of lizard men; no petrification but scaly skin, and an eruption of serpent cysts covering its body
- If a medusa lives long enough, her entire lower body becomes that of a serpent. She grows to tremendous size dozens of meters in length
- The 'petrifying' gaze of a medusa is just shock and wears off shortly
- The deadliest poisons in existence come from medusae
- The medusa's gaze is petrifying because it's a side effect of her having vision into the astral and ethereal simultaneously. When you meet her eyes, those forces align, leaving only a stone shell where you were
- Medusae curate their own legends, spreading rumors of their unparalleled beauty and vast hoards of treasure to lure in foolish adventurers and trap them in the horrifying statue gardens they make with their petrifying gaze
- Because they are cursed with such a terrifying visage, medusae despise beauty above all else. They petrify beautiful creatures and hoard the statues so that their beauty can never again be fully enjoyed by anyone save themselves
- Because they are cursed with such a terrifying visage, medusa love beauty above all else. They petrify beautiful creatures and hoard the statues so that their beauty will never be lost
- Medusae are uniquely skilled at intrigue and power. They frequently like to rule from afar, as a distant noble or hidden spymaster
- Medusae can unpetrify their victims using their blood or saliva. A skilled healer may also be able to do the same if a medusa's blood or saliva is available
- Medusae are particularly sensitive to sound, finding loud or disruptive noises damaging
- Anyone can become a medusa; pride and hubris cause the snakes to grow
- The actual true form of the medusa is a writhing mass of tentacles on a lumpy meatball-like body, covered in eyestalks and mouths filled with jagged sharp teeth; they are spawns of the deep elemental earth
- Some medusae are said to be able to pass through stone as easily as they walk
- Medusae mate and lay eggs in clutches, after hatching they are fully grown and mature at the age of five
- Medusae are brilliant archers, crafting wonderful bows and knowing ancient techniques
- The medusae love beautiful objects and collect paintings and objects of art rarity and exquisiteness

MINOTAUR

"What lairs in a maze is good hunting." — General Zaroff

NOMENCLATURE: Tarus, taurian, bull-man, brutal beast

DESCRIPTION: Taurine humanoid with the head of a bull

THINGS THAT ARE KNOWN:

- They are fond of mazes
- They are terrifically strong

RUMORS AND OTHER TWINE IN THE MAZE:

- It is very important that the labyrinth the minotaurs inhabit contain no furniture. They must be bare of decoration
- They are actually terrible at mazes. If they were any good, they'd all be living in sunny little villages, eh? No minotaur has ever escaped from a maze, and they are all a bit sore about it
- They fight and slay all intruders because they are endlessly seeking someone worthy to end their eternal vigil over the infinite labyrinth
- Any mortal that isolates themselves over a long enough period will slowly change and shift into the form of a minotaur. Dwarves who do so turn into particularly powerful minotaurs, larger and more powerful than the default beast
- It isn't only isolation that causes the change in form. It's also stubbornness. This is the origin of the phrase "bull-headed"
- Minotaurs are all autistic, hence the predilection for mazes
- Sometimes this happens quite quickly. The most infamous incident was Tartocrate the philosopher who transformed in the middle of a debate. His bewildering and confusing argumentation made of layers of unassailable facts manifested as a maze around him
- Minotaur shamans wear human masks for their ceremonies
- All minotaurs are hermaphrodites that can reproduce by parthenogenesis
- Though known for the axe, this is actually confusion of the word labrys, considered to be more than just a word describing the narrow mazes they inhabit. They actually prefer daggers and poignards, weapons much more suitable for tight quarters
- The labyrinth is the eternal equilibration matrix of the universe, and minotaurs are its defense vectors, much like white blood cells

- They are actually mechanical and scientific geniuses, and the labyrinth is a training ground for their young. They are so aggressive because they are arrogant teens, who know their species is vastly more intelligent than other humanoids. And what they do in the labyrinth is never spoken of once they escape
- It is said were-minotaurs lair in the tangled groves of Kalabrinthia
- The construction of labyrinths is an insane compulsion that overcomes them, until such structures reach a certain size. After these unknown criteria are met, they abandon their maze
- There's just one minotaur and just one labyrinth, but the labyrinth is very, very large, and the minotaur is very, very good at playing dead
- The labyrinth is a physical representation of their crazed mind and changes and shifts with their schizophrenic thoughts. An entrance or exit only appears during the rare dawns of lucidity and it never lasts long. Once slain, the labyrinth is disconnected from reality, and as a chaotic thought it is transported to the plane of Limbo, where it will slowly degrade over time. . .
- Minotaurs aren't evil, just virile and well hung, causing writers and chroniclers (mostly male) to depict them as monsters, helping to exterminate them across Priapia
- The first minotaur was an unsanctioned and terrible union between a god and a woman. It was not a god of men, but one of beasts and the wilds that took her. This abomination at birth bred true with both beast and man. The labyrinths are their temples to their father, their savage rites honor their animal nature, their war, weapon, and brew craft, homages to the race of their mother. They are the true hybrid, both man and beast, mortal and divine
- The labyrinths of particularly devout minotaurs can serve as gateways to other realms
- Minotaurs are builders cursed into terrible shapes and obsessed with labyrinth building as punishment for cutting corners when building the temples of Zoes the Munificent and Magnificent in Phthyria Minor
- Minotaur horns are indestructible. It is not possible to take one as a trophy. Other parts, however. . .
- A minotaur feels compelled to peel the skin and pull the nerves and muscle fibers apart in their prey. They do this because they know the soul is aware of the body for days after death, and it clouds its travel into the far planes, leaving it adrift. Such suffering feeds the taurian's dark heart.
- Having the head of a bull, they also have the teeth. In order to swallow flesh, it must be in large chunks, hence the popularity of axes among their kind. They also have trouble digesting it, giving them foul breath and a terrible temper
- The (sunny?) disposition of the minotaur gives it an aura of inspiration, improving the morale of all bovine attacks and defenses within 35 feet
- They are usually quite pleasant and docile, but at some point they all turned anthropophagous. This is attributed to the spread of mad minotaur disease

- The minotaur is a weak subspecies of a beast called a majotaur which is 13 feet tall and breathes smoke and brimstone from its nostrils
- The devil-man city of Trumachi is the source of all minotaurs. The future king would not pay homage to their throne, instead wanting to cast down the battlements and shatter the dark tower. The king's sappers who wore hides of the bull were fused to their trappings. They entered the devil maze beneath the tower and found that the tower went into them. Curses shot, crackling and ricocheting through their ranks. Both the high king and the city are hollow ruins, and the wash of monsters fills the ancient guts of the broken, unassailable fortress
- All minotaurs are actually vegan
- Minotaurs have no sense of smell
- The Hurrian sages disagree, claiming it is by smell and hearing alone that the beady-eyed beasts navigate their mazes
- The Samnitians go one further, claiming minotaurs have the ears of bats and use echolocation
- They await the end-times, heralded by the coming of the great two-headed bull-man
- The bull god Dongbah insisted that all bulls be given free range. When economy-minded humans (who cared about not having their children trampled and so on) began to pen them up, Dongbah punished them by creating prisons to herd humans, to see how THEY liked it. Now Dongbah is quite unintentionally the Gaol God, and the wardens are vestigial symbols from his pastoral history
- They all actually have the scrotum of a snake, but few know this
- Perhaps somewhat surprisingly, minotaurs never eat beef
- The archmage Alsaziar was an arms dealer, specializing in organic siege engines. The minotaur was his greatest success, the ultimate berserker warrior that breeds true. The only way he found to control them was to lock them in mazes. Inevitably, Alsaziar was slain, and his island was left alone for many many years. A thousand years later, the minotaurs emerged, eyes brimming with magic and insanity of dark mazes, wielding massive shackles as weapons. Their mazes had grown dull, and they now sought new entertainments
- The Daedelmar fleshcrafters blended men with horses to guard the plains and blended men with bulls to guard the mountains. They explained that all that was required was a burning heart of anger and a gut that trembles with lust for man-flesh. In the aeons since this event, minotaurs worked their way in and along the roots of the mountains and they are nothing but one large connected maze, bound by magic where it is not bound by stone
- They are considered a delicacy by the Paztecas, eaten with pasta al dente
- The bellow of a minotaur can attract cows from up to 3 miles away
- Minotaur milk is said to be liquid gold, prized in the markets the world over
- Their tails are components of magical whips
- They don't construct mazes but actually live in labyrinth-like towers

106

- There is a rare subspecies of minotaur, the 'dwarf' or 'pygmy' minotaur; whose body is that of a halfling and head is that of a calf

- Emperor Flanyeer enjoyed board games, so he created the grandest game as creatures and men were coerced into costume to play at a life-size board. Mages would gain favor for creating the most spectacular pieces. Magus Dulwither created the minotaur which was considered a superb creation till it ran amok, killing and eating several other pieces. Dulwither made several other minataurs to protect him, and that was the downfall of the empire. They smashed and destroyed that city, and now they still play the grand game, making up their own rules.

- They all have a third eye hidden under the skin on their foreheads, which allows them to see the true path through any maze or labyrinth

- Savage tribes wear masks to take on aspects of the spirits. When a tribe nears its end, those who go into the last battle or journey take the form permanently, and some always survive the death of their people

- When ranchers moved in, spoiling the land of the peaceful halflings of Vestilech, they protested. The protests were of course ignored. The halflings captured the horsemen and painfully mated them with large stud bulls, using powerful curses learned from the spider folk. The monsters that were made fear halflings as elephants fear mice, but hate humans with a burning passion. It was not long till the minotaurs managed the herds, treating the halflings with respect. The halflings are now long dead, but the minotaurs still tend the herds

- There is no such thing as a minotaur. It is just tribal shamans wearing masks

- Boiled minotaur tongue is an aphrodisiac, sold in the markets of Farkathae, hence the rarity of said beasts today

- The first of them were spelunkers. Shamans would mark the known routes on a bull hide magically melded with the explorer. They would become bigger, stronger, and have their explorations marked on the hide. Some few got trapped, the hide unremoveable, and with time became terrible beasts under the earth

- They are a nasty joke perpetrated by the god of fertility while drinking in a bar where strippers rode a mechanical bull

- Some star-crossed lovers were involved in a theater production practicing out in the woods with fae watching. One of the fae enchanted the dour pimp of the group, giving him a bull head. He was not a good sport, and he ended up slaying all the fey with his magic sword and grumbling off. That's how it all started. . .

- They all have electromagnetic sensors in their horns, which is how they navigate in pitch blackness

- They do not breed true. They are the product of human rape or curses placed on men

- Shulabu of Hulum created a chimeric creature, combining a minotaur and a gargantuan mantis shrimp, creating a deadly aquatic predator

- A prank by a fledgling god is the beginning of it. Bulls were struck with lightning, holding great transformative power. The resulting creatures, minotaurs, were so fascinated by the lightning that they ever strove to recreate its complex patterns, digging out labyrinth after labyrinth
- In the beginning was Minotaur, firstborn son of the All-Father, the Great Bull of Sky. When he rebelled against All-Father and ate the fruit of the tree of knowledge, All-Father exiled him from the Pasture of Ease and split him into men and cattle so that his stolen knowledge would be scattered and lost. Now and again All-Father sends another divine minotaur son to see how the mortals live on the lost Earth. Some become bitter with their lot, others not. The greatest of the messiah minotaurs ascend bodily back to the All-Father with their judgements, while others fall from grace and become demonic reavers
- They are all human, blessed by the evil Baphomet with strength and power
- Minotaurs like delftware and collect it in preference to all other valuables
- Minotaurs are actually cyborgs — robot heads mounted on the slain bodies of humans. For cost-cutting reasons the Elven Transhumescence Corporation decided to mount the hardware in a bull's head because the extra space allowed for cheaper, off-the-shelf equipment
- The minotaurs of southern Tauriscia are organized in several crime syndicates collectively called the Corno Nostro. They are primarily active in smuggling dairy products, drugs, and fermented mare's milk

COMBAT TRICKS:

THE DOUBLED SHAFT: Double crossbow at range, fires two bolts at once for double damage, one to hit roll, plus a chance to knock the target down. One round to reload

CHARGE: Minotaurs receive double benefits from charge

IMPALEMENT: On a successful charge that is a critical hit, the target is impaled on the horns, taking gore damage every turn they are held. They must succeed at a grapple (against the minotaur's full hit dice) to escape

THE PUSH: Minotaurs are experts at knocking people back and down. If their only action, they get a large bonus, or they may attempt it as part of a normal attack. The penalty is that they are terrible at grappling, being hoofed, top-heavy creatures, acting as if they had half their hit dice

VENGEANCE AT DEATH: Upon being reduced to 0 hit points or less, the minotaur can make one final attack with a bonus to hit, doing double damage against the nearest melee target

SAVAGE FEROCITY: Every time the minotaur attacks and misses, he becomes more angry, getting a cumulative bonus on damage and temporary hit points until the end of combat

NIGHTMARE

"You can die in your dreams; to actually walk in the realm itself is the height of foolishness." — Ui-teh, Taurian Speaker

"I beheld a nightmare from up close upon the tree pits of Haly Karoek. I admit, beheld is not the right word. . . It smelled so noxious that my eyes watered ceaselessly!" — Nightmare survivor, Phrain Tharbos

NOMENCLATURE: Hell horse, darkfire mount

DESCRIPTION: A dark horse, often aflame

THINGS THAT ARE KNOWN:

- When seen, they appear as horses
- They are often highlighted or colored with flame
- They are known to fly

RUMORS AND OTHER TERRORS IN THE DREAMSCAPE:

- Nightmares are regular horses, raised on a special diet of salt, from the para-elemental plane of salt, collected near the negative energy side
- They are the dreams of demon lords that have settled into darkness and then race out as steeds of flame, each one an ember or spark designed to engulf the world
- They are souls of those who have failed their demon master, bound to the corpse of a horse, condemned to serve someone more competent
- They are the results of drunk bets made between wizards
- They are birthed from the raw detritus of creation, warped to only destroy
- They seek tragedy and ruins, decayed battlefields and mass graves, because that is where celestial and infernal stallions carry the dead to the afterlife.
- Sometimes wishes are horses and beggars do ride. Witches are responsible for binding infernal energy into a stable mount capable of reproduction. This product of internal wishes reproduces by mating with the terror dreams that are inspired by its existence
- They are a status symbol of the wicked, those who have torn free a piece of fire and ambition used to flee hell itself. They believe they've acquired freedom, when in fact the escape was a test. Those who do are horrific enough to lead demons against the last bastion of good on the prime
- They are capable of bearing a rider while leaping into the dream of a victim

- They are the used up, cast-off casualties of horses from the chariot that drew the sun across the sky. Burned and worn, they smolder still. They are tangentially real, disconnected from the divine, malicious, yet still able to travel between dimensions
- A nightmare is a witch's infernal bond. When she bargains with demons from the underworld, the nightmare is created, but the demon chooses the master of the horse, not the witch. Slaying the nightmare severs the witche's infernal power
- They are fallen Ki-rin
- Nightmares are the beasts created when wendigos attack horses instead of men
- Nightmares are actually the souls of children who died in a fire set intentionally for malicious purposes. They feast on the wicked, insane beasts driven by madness and eternal burning flame
- They are bred by giants in a remote land, fed only human flesh and blood to obtain a precious human soul. They are then killed and the souls sold to demons, who ride them for eternity. The horses are quite intelligent and constantly seek to escape
- The nightmare is a dream of a wicked man, potent and unfulfilled. They lack control, and their personal ambitions release ethereal miasma. This mist can become different kinds of aberrations; those related to majesty and freedom become mares of the night. They are ridden by champions of evil because they seek those who have the drive their creators lack
- They are loyal, cruel and don't feel any remorse to leave a master who is a failure
- Nightmares, hellhounds, and smoke raptors are all created by the lord of the hunt — after cultists found his avatar and corrupted him from a hunting god, to a god of death
- True nightmares are only born on the field of battle. Enraged spirits of the slain, trapped by their fury, pour into wounded horses, setting them ablaze with their wrath
- They aren't evil, just elemental. They have escaped from the stables of a volcanic titan. Their skin is cracked and folded like fresh lava. The flames at their hooves are from the objects they touch, not the horse itself
- They are the adolescent form of a night hag
- They can only be tamed by someone who isn't a virgin
- Sometimes when riding through the dreams of victims, they leave their riders behind. Other times they never leave, preferring to possess their victims instead
- Nightmares are unconcerned about sexuality. When they refuse to be tamed by 'virgins' they mean those who have never slain another sentient creature
- They will thoughtlessly abandon a rider for a crueller one
- They are the smouldering remains of the hopes and dreams of a valkyrie while transporting a soul to Valhalla

- Nightmares are literally nightmares of slumbering titans. Killing the titan will slay the nightmare
- Nightmares are only corporeal in the dream realm. They are the shades of innocent horses that are slain by cruel riders
- They are neither intelligent, nor alive. The sage Gno Ko No asserts that nightmares are the infections parasitized bodies possessed by larval efreeti
- According to Wagghy Baroeka, savant and najib of the Nazraheem, the nightmare is a vampiric horse. The vampirism is caused by a blood curse of the seven fates of the three crystal moons and increases the strength, speed, and blood lust, but only mares attain the full stature
- The stallion counterpart to the nightmare is the zombie stallion, rotting and possessed by a lust for herbivore brains
- Daymares are worse; they are not bound by night
- A nightmare can teleport through the bad dreams of anyone who has ever beheld it
- Shulao of Chuffre claims the nightmares were an abortive experiment by the Vilai who sought to create telepathic horses
- Shulao of Tancra disagrees; the nightmares were originally created from several species of animals, including donkeys and beavers, as familiars to permit the wizard Li Vilai Kreisers to communicate at a distance through their dreams. The mares eventually got loose, but some creatures, such as the nightbear and the nightskunk, remain docile
- It is a corruption of their proper name, Knightmare, the gift of the moon goddess to her paladins
- They are the spirit of wicked riders who have trampled to death the innocent and then burnt at the stake as punishment
- People riding on nightmares are all too commonly controlled by the nightmare. Nightmares are not the steed but the rider
- The dreamstuff nightmares are made of ignites in the waking world. Anyone who weathers the most terrible dream a nightmare can deliver is immune to any harm.
- They come from the stable of Oneiroi, gods of dreaming, found on the wild plane of dreaming and the astral plane
- Dwarven efforts to create a rideable nightmare pony have only resulted in delicious new barbecue sensation
- They are composed of ash and flame; when it is slain it falls to smouldering coals
- Fire giants, famed hellhound-trainers also train nightmares expertly. The prices are exorbitant of course
- They are invisible, translucent and colorless. It is only the fear of the victim that colors them black and flame
- Nightmare herds graze on the far side of the moon; trapped on earth they are driven to madness

- Alzamrum, the antimage of Chuffre, claims nightmares are demons that possess animals in the night. They ride them through the air, scaring people
- Nightmares have hooves of pure gold. They use fire-jet nostrils to melt rare metals out of ore, which sustains them. They are aurophages, eating gold in preference to all other substances
- They are all female and mate with other equines (unicorns, pegasi, and celestial mounts preferred) and bear only female foals
- They go into heat only during the hottest part of summer. The female subsumes her flame, becoming a plain majestic black mare. Her beauty attracts mates. After birthing, the foals are abandoned, and they must find sentient raw flesh to eat in order to survive
- A paladin's mount is an ordinary horse transmuted atom by atom into celestial matter. Hell, ever original, copied the idea
- Greater nightmares grow wings not unlike those of crows, which they then use to fly. Ordinary nightmares simply stride across the sky, slower than actual flying creatures, like pegasi, rocks, and the screaming stars of Phelogeon
- They are actually shape-shifting goblin shamans
- They are all created by the ritual "Nightmare" which targets a single individual, or the powerful "Plague of Nightmares" which the Academages of Askamandria claim was responsible for the fall of the Gloaming Empire of Suskandahar
- They are the steeds of fallen paladins who have no immunity to their tormenting flaming hooves
- They are possessed by a fiery demon, because hell creatures need steeds too
- Nightmares can torment victims by taking the shape of "psychic smoke" and invading the dreamer's mind. The creature feasts on the terrors of the sleeper, leaving a dried out fear-stricken husk
- They are actually a species of sheep
- Hairshirts made from their hide remind all those akashics and pain seekers of the ultimate fire that waits 'pon all flesh
- The aquatic nightmare has flippers instead of hooves and gives off steam instead of fire, called "notte di mare" in 'Talish
- Each nightmare has only one eye, the other a soul gem, hiding trapped behind the dreamer who dreamt it. All nightmares have a blind side because of this
- They seek damned souls of the troubled and disturbed. Souls are carried to various planes of torment or enslaved by the gods of horror to spawn new monsters to torment the waking world
- There is a whole realm of nocturnal horror fauna, but only a few leak into our world. Pre-human races and damnable cults try to call them
- There is a rare unicorn/nightmare hybrid. It poisons water with its toxic horn and enters the dreams of virgins to tempt them to death
- Nightmares are obviously and frequently used as riders to traverse the planes

- Any person who wakes from sleep in the presence of a nightmare is unable to move until it leaves
- Their teeth are stained pink

COMBAT TRICKS

FLAMING HOOVES: Their hooves may burst aflame! This means they do flame damage in addition to normal damage

FLAMING STAMPEDE: Nightmares may overrun their opponents. On a successful stampede, the target takes damage from both hooves, as well as double flame damage

FLAME STOMP: By slamming their hooves into the ground, nightmares may produce a flaming burst. This affects all opponents to the front or front sides of the nightmare.

ORC

"They are superior to men, in all ways, except one."
-Gorgonson, Avatar of War

NOMENCLATURE: Orc, ork

DESCRIPTION: Brutish, green-skinned humanoids

THINGS THAT ARE KNOWN:

- They despise men and are hated by elves

RUMORS AND OTHER RUMBLES IN THE WILDERNESS:

- There is no difference between man and orc. Orcs that live in cities become men, just as men who live in the wild become orcs. It is a dark secret, full of shame, and hidden from the elves and dwarves
- It is said that sudden shock or extreme stress can cause a human to become a half-orc
- Orcs are giant aggressive plants
- Orcs are from another world, near the end of its life-cycle. They were the only race to flee to our world, proof that brute force is the ultimate survival trait
- Orcs are the reincarnation of wicked dwarves
- Orcs are creatures of fae, born male
- Orcs are the cancer of the world, corrupted growths festering in unseen places. They have no gods before them, gods being a projection by other races. The "one eyed" they worship is their singular purpose, to grow until the whole world suffers and dies
- The orcs are a forgotten placeholder, a bookmark that was never removed due to the god's own destruction
- Orcs are what happens when teen mothers drink during pregnancy in a fantasy world
- They are the next devolutionary step, one step further down from the result of elves breeding with apes to make humans. They are the coming dominate race, a cosmic secret only a few know
- Orcs are not a separate race but elves wearing masks
- The brain chemistry of an adult orc is unstable. They require proteins from intelligent creatures to survive, and these proteins are better absorbed in the adrenaline rush of life or death. Stress, both physical and mental, retards the breakdown process, as does intense anger and hatred. The only hope for a peaceful orc is self-mortification, extreme exercise, and a complex or possibly magical diet

- They are simply angry over centuries of bigotry
- Orcs are an escaped modular-adaptive life-forms, They mimicked the most successful species, which at the time was neanderthal man. They evolved into their current stable state, their natural traits (fear of magic, power worship, shamelessness and fecundity) outgrowths of it
- "Orc" is just a derogatory term for people suffering from force-field mutations
- Orcs are cruelty of dreams and foul thoughts made flesh. They cannot be slain, for doing so only creates more orcs. Their elimination requires unconditional human peace
- Orcs are the result of humans consuming troll flesh. It is all too easy to feed a large army with troll flesh, no matter how dire the consequences. Halflings turn into goblins. Elves turn into bugbears, gnomes and giants find the flesh deadly to consume. Mermaids turn into sea hags
- Orcs are the reflection of man from a once-distant dimension merged with ours. Neither can achieve their potential while the other exists, and this is knowledge only the orcs have. Killing humans is a deeply spiritual duty for an orc, even if it's not something they mention often
- Orcs are symbiotic with humans, linked by the whim of the gods. Every human has his opposite orc when one dies, the other dies as well. Should a linked pair meet, they merge to create a new creature, a 'half-orc'. Sages say, a true neutral half-orc is destined to end the conflict, though the nature of the reckoning is debated
- Orcs are mutant elves, caused by the influence of iron on their reproduction
- Orcs are an alloy of goblins and humans. When they are burned together in a cramped space, the adaptability of humans is fused with the violent tendencies of goblins. Orcs lord over goblins because they consider themselves the next step up. There are rumors orcs could be 'broken down' into their base components, but goblins, orcs, and men all agree this is likely a terrible idea
- Orcs are scaled, cyclopean, fish-lipped monsters. They fire a ray beam from their single terrible eye, based on the color of the orcs
  - Some say that this is because orcs were slaves to the eye tyrants, the first of whom was a mad sorcerer, who gave up his humanity to become a floating head. He then created many different cyclopean creatures, orcs being the lowest
- A druid once desired peace, so he created a spell to remove all negative emotions, motives, and energies from humans and demi-humans. Sadly, his drug use had addled his brain and the casting was corrupted. Instead of removing emotions, he made them manifest in the world. Worse still, humanoids retained all their basic motivation. Every orc is the hate, envy, lust, greed, violence, gluttony, and sloth of a living humanoid made manifest. Every time a human is born, a new orc is born

- Elves are divine spirits made manifest in flesh. They reproduce by cultivating new natural spirits. Sometimes this process gets corrupted and an orc develops. Like elves, they take form fully grown of spirit melded with matter. However they can use any matter and spirit to propagate. They murder and rape to ensure both new spirits and the raw material to install them in. They are born with the impulse to reproduce obsessively. After much pillaging, they either die or begin to settle

- Older orcs focus on other things: refining their spiritual potency and eventually becoming demons, seeking out stasis and calm in nature, or perhaps becoming brood mothers who birth new warbands. Any orc will tell you it is foolish to depend on elves for anything, much less the future of the species

- Orcs are an experiment by halflings to create pig cheese. Results were mixed

- Orcs are descended from pigs. Or a culture obsessed with pigs. Breeding pigs, powering things with pig sacrifice. Suddenly people began giving birth to pigs. Or pig people. They were quietly enslaved and sacrificed and worshiped. This tenuous situation lasted only a while, then revolution began, and the orc as we know it today emerged

- Orcs are manifestations of the wild places, boars and pigs and savagery sprung from something much more ancient than man

- Orcs are the rational, revolutionary potential of mankind, freed from gods and their endless mechanisms of control. They aren't angry or violent by some intrinsic nature; they just have no patience for god-fearing, reactionary, bigoted humans. Better to put them all down

- Orcs are a symbiotic race, host to a strain of fungus granting them toughness and increased strength and aggression. It makes them hunger for human flesh, but only to complete their nutritional needs. They are nihilist humans, derived from an intelligence not freed from the needs of the fungus

- Orcs are mud men that have coagulated into solidity. Their anger is at their inability to flow and merge with the foul waste that birthed them. Slaying an orc causes it to crumble like damp earth

- Sites where many orcs have died become spawning pits for mud men

- You can use Faunal Succession to tell the length of time a body has been dead, for different creatures live off of it at different times. So it was with the titans, for the lizards feasted first, then dwarves, then elves, then humans, and finally the orcs

- Orcs are the result of casting *reveal invisible* on invisible servants. They aren't supposed to be here and they know it

- Orcs are demonic foot soldiers and come in a variety of forms

- Orcs are invisible spirits that ride and corrupt the flesh of the dead. When risen, their flesh reforms, horribly, becoming an orc

- Orcs are a common result from exposing humans to the energies of the underworld till they are driven mad. One human becomes a hundred orcs as their personality splinters and manifests in reality. The leaders and spellcasters are the larger chunks of the original personality. The original shattered human can be unthinkably powerful, and is often well protected, because it is said if you kill it, all the others will cease to exist

- Orcs are what happens when you feed elves after midnight

- Orcs were the largest and most organized bandit gang in the world, transcending cultures and borders. It has long ago collapsed, but many hold to their traditions, pig-like masks, savage dress, and horde tactics

- Orcs are a tool of the gods to curb population growth. When successful, they turn on each other, leaving areas depopulated

- Paladins sometimes raise orc troops but must provide an opponent. Sport is not enough; their violent nature is too much: starting riots over slurs, bad calls, or injuries. Respect for brute force and eye for an eye runs deep

- Orcs are from a twisted mirror of the real world. In the dark world, they fight and murder and die in 'cities' of the real world. When an orc dies, another bursts from its skull 9 days later. They are summoned into this world by sorcerers in foul rituals, but they are never under the sorcerer's control. They only answer to the orc king in the heart of the dark world. The orc king wishes for nothing more than to be freed from his prison

- They are frankenstein bipedal pigs; their eyes hide no intelligence, and they are surrounded by an aura of flies. They are said to follow, ant-like, a massive queen orc

- Orcs are perfected elves, without vanity and with motivation. Everything that orcs are is what elves were meant to be

- Orcs are all little pieces of different gods, eternally at war with each other

- Orcs are the broken parts of a singular large being. Their low-level species-wide telepathic bond allows one orc to fill in for another that is absent. Their odd bumps and pits are indications of the marks where they join

- Orcs are a natural phenomenon that exists outside the natural order to support it. They clear away the dead brush and allow new, stronger creatures to take hold. Comfort and stagnation call to them, their presence an irritant. They will not leave these blights till they are burned, any more than you would leave rotten food in your cupboard

- Orcs are the shameful creations of dwarves

- To understand this, you must understand dwarves. To reproduce, they carve each other from different kinds of stone (granite, marble, basalt). This is why the dwarves dig: to make more dwarves. But that is also their downfall, because sometimes they dig too deep. Throughout the ages, several dwarf clans attempted to 'improve' on the species. Gnomes were forged from clay, sandstone, and limestone. Azers were cast from molten bronze, but once completed moved to the plane of fire, never to return. Orcs are made from pig iron and turned on their creators, driving them out and killing those left. They opened the passages to the deep and sealed the entrances and forge new orcs to this day. They raid for iron and more iron to propagate as far and deep as they can

- Orcs are created slave soldiers. All their traits that would be non-adaptive for their environment make them better soldiers and less threatening to their creators (stupidly brave, easy to bully, Malthusian fecundity, fast life cycle). "Following orders" isn't an excuse but a genetic imperative. Excess orcs are sent away to live off the enemies' land or abandoned. Female orcs are breeding machines that rarely leave their pits. They must be supported by human races, since the orcs aren't capable enough farmers to feed themselves

- Orcs are simply humans exposed to unhealthy space radiation. This causes them to give into their base desires and wish to drain the id from humans via crude eldrich trepanning. Those who survive become orcs themselves, but sterile. Sometimes matriarchs gain enough id from humans that they become sated and give birth to horrible creatures

- Orcs are driven by an inescapable vice. Wrath is the most prevalent, as they tend to kill those who are not wrathful themselves. Greed, pride, lust, and envy exist in smaller numbers, accounting for orcs of subterfuge and cunning. Slothful orcs are the most rare

- Each race was crafted from a different element. Humans from water, elves from wood, dwarves from metal, gnomes from earth, and orcs from fire. Halflings are not original, crafted perhaps from the void. When the creators craft a species from air, it will mean a fundamental change in the world

- Half-orcs are sometimes called 'forks' because of their split from both human and orc

- Half-orcs aren't orcs but the spawn of humans and animals

- There are no orc females. They procreate by impregnating females of other species. Birth usually kills the mother. The offspring is always full-blooded orc

- Orcs are the insurance plan of the gods against the outsiders. You wouldn't bet on humans, dwarves, or elves to save the world, but a horde of orcs?

- There are only female orcs. In fact, elves have 1 male and 2 female sexes, with the other female sex being orcs. A pairing of two elves always produces elves, but a pairing of orcs and elves produces either a male elf or a female orc. There is a very low chance of an elf/orc coupling producing a male elf, so most outsiders don't even realize that they are the same species

- Orcs just are. Nobody made them. They have no destiny. Their rage comes from the fact that the gods hate them and keep trying to kill them like they are weeds

- Before the empire collapsed the Orchulli clan took to banditry and cannibalism in order to survive. Once discovered, they were locked in their house and burned alive. Later, tunnels were discovered beneath the cellar. It was assumed that this was an escape route, but it just led deeper and deeper into the dark, joining the natural caverns below. The clan mated and bred with what they found below and have been returning to the surface ever since
- Ancient scrolls contain the ritual to make elves into orcs, but as the population of elves thinned, the knowledge was lost. So the ritual has been adapted to work on humans, and even mud in some cases. A poorly worded *wish* may be the origin of female orcs
- Orcs are autistic, with limited socializing, language, and tool use, but well versed in aggression and tactics. They long to find their place in the pack and respond poorly to traits they perceive as weak, such as tenderness and kindness. Some may form attachments to pigs and wolves stronger than to their careers or others of their kind
- Orcs are not cultured. Here are a variety of ways orcs are born
  - They spring forward fully-formed, able to speak and kill
  - Any man painted with blood and committing murder that stays away from the sun for a full day becomes an orc
  - Any orphan who drinks from a sewer will change into an orc
  - After battle, orcs excrete an iridescent black sphere. When it's soaked in blood, an orc hatches. When soaked in demon blood, a dozen orcs are born.
  - Soak the ground of an ancient tree in blood, and for every wound the tree sustains, it will bud an orc in revenge
  - When the teeth of demons are hurled to the ground, they explode and orcs with weapons made from bone leap to battle
  - Dogs made to drown in salt water and then left in the lake cause orcs to spawn from the foul water
  - Orcs have disgusting long spined tongues. After battle, orcs use their tongue to infect the corpses. Several hours later, newborn orcs eat their way out
  - They are cooked in unholy cauldrons
  - Everyone dies, only they really don't. Once you reach a certain age, you change and become an orc
  - Marking any corpse with a dark, evil rune will cause the ground it is buried under to produce orcs
  - Humans who eat the flesh of the dead become orcs

 TYUGH

"I hate these things!"
—Arcaila Moreu, adventuring sellsword

NOMENCLATURE: Gulguthra, otyugh, neo-otyugh, shit pile, refuse

DESCRIPTION: A tripedial thorny tentacled beast with dun-colored rocky flesh, a gaping maw, and a set of three eyes on a mobile stalk. It is notable that it is usually covered in fecal refuse

THINGS THAT ARE KNOWN:

- They live in and eat refuse and fecal matter
- They also eat people

RUMORS AND OTHER GURGLES IN THE REFUSE:

- They are particularly sensitive to their environments, picking up traits from wherever they happen to live. Swamp otyughs cause rotting when they strike, cave otyughs can seep acid through their skin from the acidic water
- They often have psychic powers
- They don't actually feed on refuse, but on residual psychic energy from pain and terror. This is best communicated through refuse in ancient battlefields, mass graves, and dungeons
- They are all unwanted children, abandoned by their parents
- They are the discarded, diseased, and sick heads of a hydrae
- They aren't an animal or creature as such, but instead giant semi-sentient colonies of bacteria living in monster dung
- They aren't live children abandoned by their parents, but instead children who died and did not receive a proper burial
- Alchemical waste and detritus ends up somewhere and becomes an otyugh. Neo-otyughs occur when this process is performed on purpose
- They are the rage of a planet manifest against those who dump their waste instead of sorting and cycling it again
- They are the droppings of the many-handed Setebos, the god of rage and blind violence
- It is the result of a vicious magical poison, transmuting the filth in the imbiber's gut into a baby otyugh, eventually bursting free through the rear orifice
- They are sentient creatures produced from hemorrhoids by the curse of a witch

- The otyugh has a more primitive form, the paleo-otyugh, with tentacles that have spines and a fear of fire
- Some otyughs have been known to shoot beams of fire or light from the tentacle containing its eyes
- They have a rare third stage of evolution known as the ultimo-otyugh, powered by the massive consumption of methane. This large, armored form drifts through the air from place to place, attacking all life with beams of light and fire, gouts of flame, and streams of noxious poison
- They are secretly star spawn from beyond the outer crystal barrier of the heavens. They mine refuse for methane, stored in a hyper-pressurized extradimensional space until they can blast away from the surface of the earth on a pillar of fire.
  - These star spawn explode when killed. The historian and philanderer Mockoropius says that it was the explosion of a single one that took out the entire shimmering spire quarter of Massansopolis in the year of the cancer rat
- All otyughs may use the methane they collect to levitate
- It is the final fate after death of all those who were annoying and abrasive to existence
- Refuse to an otyugh is profound, the degree to which it is rejected and shunned is the beauty and purity of it. Adventurers are outcasts themselves, proving irresistible for most otyughs
- Otyughs communicate via modulated smells, which is why they collect dung
- The otyughs view the world through a strange lens, with an aesthetic sense completely reversed from our own. They attack out of strong revulsion, as we would a spider or insect
- They are the shit of the gods, proof of their existences
- They are what happens if you try to raise the dead long after it is safe to do so
- Otyughs are demi-gods elevated by sentient anthropomorphic dung beetles worshiping offal pits in the mists of early time. Each settlement of beetles raised their own god, and these gods turned out to be capable of breeding true. Back in the day, the biggest settlements pumped enough sincere worship into otyughs that they could grant spells to the high priest of the settlement
  - Goblins discovered this by accident, and many goblin tribes have a guardian otyugh they worship and feed with sacrifices. This is the source of some goblin shaman, spellcasting ability
- A grove of powerful swamp druids defended a border against incursions for a thousand years, constantly animating the swamp itself to defend against intruders. The composite residue built up in the swamp has been responsible for shambling mounds, otyughs, and a variety of carnivorous plants.

121

- A goblin hero once saved a lesser demi-god from a dark fate. The bemused and grateful god said the goblin could have a mount. The goblin wished for something stable and not too fast (he was easily travelsick) that could grab and break stuff, was heavily armored, could peek around corners, and was not too dainty. Oh, and it could wade through anything. His name was Otyugh, and his mount was named Otyugh too

- Lizardfolk shamans were getting pounded by constructs their civilized wizard neighbors built to go into the swamp and root them out. Frustrated, they pooled their collective energies and tried to figure out how to make constructs of their own, to bring the power of the swamp to bear against civilization. This was the best they could do. However, the fecundity of the swamp allowed them to manage something the wizards never could with their constructs—otyughs can reproduce

- A furious court wizard cursed the courtier who used intrigues to oust him, making him clearly visible to all as the spying, muckraking, lecherous, disease-riddled piece of shit he was. Unfortunately, he also told the courtier to go screw himself, so the resulting monstrosity could reproduce without help

- Otyughs are slaves brought from another dimension to do heavy lifting and swamp work, by the Makers Before Time. With the fall of the Makers, no one else had the knack or inclination to tell the otyughs what to do, or to send them home

- Modron, trapped on Prime lose their crispness and gain infections and unsightly growths, becoming otyughs. Driven mad with shame and pain, they degenerate to animal intelligence

- Otyughs are the individual sperm of the god of rot, filth, corruption, and fertility.

- Otyughs are massive, striding constructs of swamp pixies playing Godzilla. They are inside the armored torso, giggling madly as they smash stuff

- Otyughs are larval eye tyrants

- Giant otyughs exist, one was sighted in Sham Padmoen. They rise from the decayed souls and corpses of dead giants outcast from their society

- Otyughs are the result of civilization. For every intricate sculpture, every profound play, every elaborate painting, every organized government, and even the ordered philosophy of law, there is an otyugh. They recall the work of their birth: those born of music can emit a deafening scream, those of painting a mesmerizing display, those of sculpture a petrifying aura. They bud from themselves, full of loathing and hate for themselves and all men and their works. Their existence is suffering. They desire nothing but to devour all of civilization. A ruined, filth and decay covered dungeon is as to ponography for them, a brief glimpse of the end of all things

- Otyughs are beautiful creatures turned inside out

- They are exceedingly intelligent, with a highly literate culture. However, all their communication is olfactory, and their writing is in smell-coated excrement pellets, making their works unknown to men

122

- They are said to run a prison known as the otyugh hole, where if one can survive a week, internal reserves of strength might be found
- They have been known to swarm in large enough piles of refuse
- They are dungeon overlords, who hold a shadow council to decide the contents of every underground realm in the land
- They often act as 'watchdogs' for tribes of primitive screwheads
- The watchdog bit is an excellent cover for their rulership over tribes of primitive screwheads
- Smart and organized societies integrate the otyugh into the cycle of waste disposal. This often makes them the best person (thing?) to talk to when things get lost
- They have a tendency to form unions and then strike
- The type of waste they eat determines which special abilities they have

OWLBEAR

"Fuckin' wizards." — Ubiquitous

NOMENCLATURE: Urstrix, owlkin, wildkin

DESCRIPTION: A hideous fusion of owl and bear

THINGS THAT ARE KNOWN:

- They are a combination of bear and owl traits in the form of a ferocious beast

RUMORS AND OTHER HOOTS IN THE NIGHT:

- Owlbears are all erudite scholars and only act like bears to get people to leave them alone to read
- Owlbears don't sleep, and are berserk, frothing mad their entire lives. They are birthed whole by a magical plant pod
- Owlbears are incapable of feeling fear
- Owlbears are excellent swimmers and water hunters
- Owlbears hibernate. This makes them a seasonal threat, encroaching on civilized territories during harvest season
- Owlbears are unwilling to eat food that doesn't struggle. They like to play with their food
- It's actually a bearowl
- They are actually just lonely, and the terrifying "owlbear hug" is simply a cry for love. They don't know their own strength
- Some people race owlbears. Sometimes they don't race, so much as eat the jockey
- Once they have a scent, they won't stop till they catch their prey
- They are surprisingly intelligent, building and protecting bee hives and termite mounds for sources of meat and honey
- Owlbears are actually just bears. Only people with poor vision, idiots, and liars say owlbears exist
- In spite of being creatures of motive humors and warm blood, they lay eggs
- They are called owlbears because the wizard who made them was named 'Ser Claude Grand Panjandrum Owlbear'
- Owlbears are super intense and unpleasant at parties

- Some owlbears are so furious that their furiousness fills their form, fabricating foul, fasciate rods of furious fury, a vortex gone too heavy, too radical, too extreme to exist
- Others drink decaf
- Owlbears don't have eyeballs, but reflective blank tubes in place of eyes instead
- Owlbears are able to move without making any sound
- Once the love of an owlbear dies, they grieve and sing a dirge until death, killing any who interrupt their song
- Owlbears build their nests in trees and drop down onto interlopers
- Owlbears hide in cherry trees by painting their nails red. Have you ever seen an owlbear in a cherry tree? Works pretty good, eh?
- Owlbears are the mortal enemies and opponents of griffons and other raptor-crossbreeds. Griffons know the owlbears will eat them and so proactively gang up and attack owlbears when they are discovered
- Owlbears are a myth. They are actually a kobold psy-op. They construct owlbear body puppets from wood and drive them around to scare away humans
- Owlbears are summoned as harbingers for more dangerous magical creatures. When the most abominable and unlucky owlbears arrive, crying out in their hoarse and dismal voices, it is an omen of the approach of some terrible thing
- Owlbears, oddly enough, are just owls infected by werebears
- Owlbears are grown from tree pods by nymphs to protect the forest
- Wild animal attacks are a constant threat to travelers on forest roads. Among these, owlbear attacks are rare but devastating. To avoid owlbear attacks, follow these safety instructions:
  - Never leave food where owlbears can reach it; use a length of hempen rope to hang rations from high branches
  - Never stand between an owlbear mother and her owlbearlets. Owlbear mothers will do anything to protect their young
  - Always keep your potions and reagents securely locked
  - If an owlbear does spot you, wave your hands in the air and make as much noise as possible. This will convince the owlbear to move on to easier prey
  - If an owlbear attacks you, curl up in the fetal position and remain motionless so that the owlbear will mistake you for carrion and move on
- Owlbears are sometimes found dead at the foot of large cliffs. This is because they occasionally forget they are not owls and therefore cannot fly
- Owlbear tracks can be distinguished from regular bear tracks by the length and width of their claws. Bears have blunt, small claws on their forepaws, whereas owlbears have long, sharp talons
- Owlbear tracks look nothing like owl tracks because owls don't have bear feet

- Owlbears are omnivores and will only attack people if they are desperate or provoked
- Owlbears are most active at dawn, when they forage for edible plants and look for a place to spend the hotter parts of the day; and at dusk, when they look for nocturnal prey animals and dig in soft, wet loam for worms and grubs
- Owlbears prefer to sleep in low branches if they can find a tree that will bear their weight
- An owlbear's feathers absorb the sound it makes as it walks, making it an extremely stealthy predator
- It is impossible to sneak away from an owlbear; they have excellent hearing
- An owlbear's mating call will sometimes attract either an owl or a bear. This is especially awkward if it does not also attract an owlbear
- Despite the danger they pose, owlbears are a beloved creature, often used as mascots by taverns, children's entertainers, sports teams, and the heraldry of certain nobility

COMBAT TRICKS:

HOOTROAR: Everyone within hearing range must save or become frightened

BEARHUG-OWLBITE: If the owlbear can grab a target, they can automatically hit with their bite attack as long as the target is held (in addition to the crushing damage from the hug)

VALUABLE RESOURCES:

- Owlbear hide can make a supple and easily enchantable leather garment
- Owlbear eggs allow talented people to raise them as loyal guards or mounts
- Owlbear feathers can be used in the creation of ink pens for magical scrolls
- Owlbear teeth and claws will fetch a good price at market

VARIANTS:

DERANGED: These owlbears are a bad mix, the combination of owl and bear driving them to madness. They are misshapen and much stronger than a normal owlbear

BERSERK/RAGING: Sometimes during an owlbear's life, they are subject to a terrible disease. As their brain degenerates, they are nothing but fierce, frothing fury

SPOTTED: In northern, lightly wooded areas, you'll find the rare spotted owlbear

HORNED: This owlbear variation uses their horns in battles for status against other male owlbears; this grants them an extra goring attack each round

ARCTIC: This type of polar owlbear has stark white feathers and is adapted to live in areas of extreme cold

SIEGE: This owlbear has been enchanted and bred over generations to become larger, more muscular, and much more aggressive. Though popular as pets and mounts for their size and strength, they are rarely legal to own, and most are put down when found as being "too dangerous"

PSEUDODRAGON

*"Just don't upset it. It's not big enough to eat you, Slive.
It is big enough to put you to sleep and tear out your throat."*
— Orphic, human engineer

NOMENCLATURE: Wizard drake

DESCRIPTION: A small dragon the size of a large bird

THINGS THAT ARE KNOWN:
- They appear to be small dragons
- They are known to have a poison sting

RUMORS AND OTHER SCALES ON THE DRAGON:
- Pseudodragons ally with wizards to create their starting hoard. The pact between the pseudodragon and the wizard grants 50% of all earnings to the dragon
- Pseudodragons are simply manifestations of a caster's superego. A caster realizes when his mind begins to slip and tries to save itself by physically manifesting. It rarely does any good, meaning the presence of a pseudodragon is a good sign that the wizard is about to go off the deep end
- If you welch on an agreement with a pseudodragon, they will make your life miserable, allying with your greatest enemy and sharing all the darkest secrets
- The common lore about 'pseudodragons' is completely incorrect; they are actually firedrakes. The 'sleep poison' is actually magma injected into the body, which is so painful that few can remain conscious
- They are psionic creatures with powerful telepathy
- Though popular, they are quite annoying as pets. They have a rabid Napoleon complex; they attack and posture any opponent, claim to have kidnapped anyone who fits the definition of damsel, sit on piles of coins and refuse to budge until coaxed away. These annoyances ensure only the most anti-social wizards keep pseudodragon as pets
- Pseudodragons are actually fae that are bright enough to realize that if they chimerically represent themselves as dragons, demi-humans and humans will be too stupid to realize how intelligent pseudodragons really are

- They are actually cats, and just project a draconic image into the minds of those nearby
- They molt, just like other reptiles. An intact skin is a powerful alchemical reagent
- They are actually attracted to spellcasters who are filled with youthful exuberance. Their death not only physically injures their owners but increases the amount of poisonous cynicism in the world
- In fact the link with the pseudodragon between the wizard and his familiar is much stronger than other familiar types. When one body dies, the other becomes a shared vessel; if one soul is destroyed, both are
- Pseudodragons are cats affected by drakkengheist weed. It looks like catnip but turns cats into pseudodragons. Lions that eat the weed turn into dragonnes
- They have a short lifespan (15 years), but upon death they reincarnate into full dragons
- Pseudodragons are considered to be plaugebearers by proxy: they eat all the cats nearby; the rat population goes uncontrolled; and clerics become overwhelmed with diseases
- Pseudodragons are not the only pseudo-species
  ○ Pseudomedusa are tiny worm-haired dark fey; they paralyze with a touch
  ○ Pseudobeholders (ahrimana) are tiny demons. They have one eye and no mouth and long slashing talons and wee wings
  ○ Pseudoghosts are little people who cover themselves in sheets and try to scare away the living
- Far away in the dark west where only the moon lights the land, there was a great mystic called Kadem Beastshaper. On a bet, he cut a dragon's egg from a dragon's womb and tied it in a mithril mesh. The resulting spawn was a pseudodragon. To the surprise of all, the first reproduced by parthenogenesis and soon, many were released to the wild
- Pseudodragons are just as fecund as their larger cousins, leading to the creation of the Tressym and other winged beasts
- There is some discrepancy about the powers a pseudodragon confers onto its master. That is because it is their choice which powers are transferred
- Pseudodragons are necessary for some wizards who explore dark and forbidden avenues of research. After having seen dark outer horrors, they become unable to sleep. The venom of a pseudodragon is the only soporific strong enough to allow the wizards to get the rest they need
- You must be a virgin in order to have a pseudodragon familiar. If you are not a virgin, you are restricted to dragon familiars (and the requisite cost in horseflesh)
- Speaking of, pack animals and pseudodragons do not get along
- Sometimes they capture fairy princesses for ransom. As above, so below

- They are shards of a dragon's ego, the tiny part of the greed that longed for a hoard of relationships and interconnectedness in community with others. It is proportionately tiny to the greed for power and wealth, but just as jealous and greedy
- Pseudodragon wings can be enchanted and mounted on a helm. If they are, they provide protection from mental detection, attacks, and deafening sound
- Pseudodragons are magical constructs, homunculi or imps of the greatest dragon casters in their war on mortals. They can cast a powerful enchantment on men, that makes humans minions of dragons, inserted into the target while they sleep from the poison of the pseudodragon
- The Queen of the Fay long ago gifted a tribe of sprites with pseudodragon mounts. The tribe was killed by their giant-dragonfly-riding rivals, and the pseudodragons survived beyond their original purpose. They long for companionship and do not know their own history. They have a great enmity against dragonflies
- The fey created the pseudodragon as a small-scale practice sculpt before beginning work on the mighty dragon. The creature pleased the gods, and they built the dragons as commanded. Too proud to hide their process, they released the model to live on its own
- They are not true dragons but cold-blooded creatures, requiring many hours in the sun and sticking firmly to tropical locales. If they are in a cold area, they hibernate in hives in great numbers
- Pseudodragon teeth are actually frozen tears
- Pseudodragons are very reclusive because their scales, teeth, and claws are very, very sweet, tasting like candy if removed or eaten
- A wicked wizard of a foul disposition served at court for decades, annoyed with the intrigue of romance and politics. For decades, he transformed the unfaithful into small decorative pets to be given to their heartbroken ex-lovers as a way to dull his irritation. They could not be caged always and they continued their cheating ways. Soon the court was overrun by wild pseudodragons, and finally, he created a massive winged panther to keep the population down. The kingdom is now long fallen, but there are still flirting, simpering pseudodragons flitting through the long-ruined halls
- They have the ability to alter the color of their scales to blend with their environ-ment This is also used in mating and is under control of the dragon
- The greatest entertainment produced by the wizards of the shadow kingdom was the pseudodragon. Originally crafted for performing in shadowbox theaters and puppet houses, the little villains were such a hit that they were sold as household pets. They were often the divas in these ancient tales, and their vanity and taste for drama remains to this day
- The mighty fae demigod the Lord of the Vasial Woods gifted the pixies with pseudodragons to be herd dogs for their sprite flocks

- When the mighty dragon Bastaal was burning through civilized lands, adventurers managed to capture her three offspring. The wizards worked a mighty ritual to miniaturize them, and the little dragons were ransom; if Bastaal ever attacked civilization again, her spawn would be slain. In the meantime, the little dragons raged, but eventually grew docile over the centuries. They mated, and their spawn were affected by the neutralizing magics; a dozen generations later, they were reduced to pseudodragons. They are pests, but the memory of Bastaal staved off actively hunting them for a millenia. Now no one remembers where they are from, and they are actively hunted as vermin. Is Bastaal still alive somehow, out beyond the darkness? Could she return if her children's cries reach her?

- Pseudodragons aren't dragons. They are called pseudo because they are actually just winged lizards of no special intelligence or skill

- A mighty and wicked wizard cast a massive spell to summon a brutal dragon. Her experienced and powerful foe cast a counter to the spell. Both went sideways in the magic-sotted arena of their duel, and the summoning spell snatched this little twerp from somewhere. The winner kept the little dragon as a keepsake and was surprised to find it was pregnant. The legend of the one who slew the wicked wizard only identified him as the man with the tiny dragon pet, so eggs of pseudodragons are in high demand among wizards thirsting for reputation

- They are not telepathic at all, just good at reading non-verbal communication and assessing situations. They may understand as much vocabulary as a 10-year-old child

- The pseudodragon is the shape of the animate dreams of the patron god of the fae

- Pseudodragons love the inauthentic. They are drawn to queens and wizards of glam and glamour

- They only look like dragons because of convergent flying hexapod evolution. They are closely related to other creatures like the arumvorax than dragons

Combat Tricks:

Distraction buffet: By flying right at a target's face and flapping and scratching, a pseudodragon can cause the target to experience one round of confusion

Tripping targets: Pseudodragons are quite apt at tripping targets, and if not flying and in the target's space, they gain a bonus to trip a target (offsetting the penalty for their tiny size)

Infernal sprite: Pseudodragons are preternaturally agile. When flying, they can apply a large dodge bonus to their armor class versus a single target

Vicious bite: On a successful bite, the pseudodragon can latch on

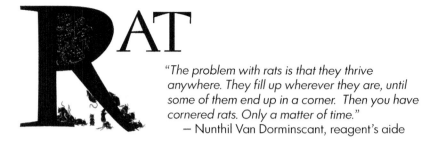

RAT

"The problem with rats is that they thrive anywhere. They fill up wherever they are, until some of them end up in a corner. Then you have cornered rats. Only a matter of time."
— Nunthil Van Dorminscant, reagent's aide

DESCRIPTION: Medium-sized, long-tailed, furred mammals

THINGS THAT ARE KNOWN:

- They have poor vision
- They live anywhere
- They have litters of up to 20 and breed prolifically
- They have a lifespan of up to 7 years
- Certain infections, cults, and sorceries can grant humanoids rat-like traits or even turn them into rats themselves
- Somewhat surprisingly, nearly every person of note ever can relate a story about how they had to clear a basement out of rats immediately before they became a person of importance

RUMORS AND OTHER SCRATCHES IN THE SEWER:

- Before monsters, rats were smaller
- The rats became dire and grew to enormous size because they broke through to the underworld, finding new stores of food and room to grow. Some grew to the size of wolves or even bears. Others feasted on the blood of demons, becoming monsters in their own right
- Cultists worship rats because they see the wealth it has brought the rats to break into the underworld. They seek to master the dark so that they may serve gods instead of kings. Perhaps to drink and eat of the blood and flesh of the gods instead of subsisting on moral scraps
- Some cultists have managed to become like the rat in the moonlight or through magic, allowing their inner rat to consume what is human, leaving only a human skin. Others have taken what is good of the rat and grafted it to their flesh, becoming the standing rats, the man-rats, inheritors of the new world
- The sign of rats is sign that there is something beneath the depth. Where does the rat live? In the rat hold. That is where the secrets lie

- The sailors of Suul say that rats are the progeny of a drowned and bloated god that came from the sea. That is why no sailor will kill a rat and why they seek the damp and dark

- Rats are the physical manifestation of urban property, exhibiting a strange gravitational energy towards other emblems of poverty: rotten clothes, empty wineskins, and the lowest value coins

- Rats have grown as the world around them has been corrupted

- Rat-kind has exploded for another reason, feeding off the magical detritus and runoff of society. Over generations of tainted meals of the dead, mutated cast-off experiments, and other arcane energies, rats have become stronger, larger, and smarter and even learned to walk and talk.

- Rats are the physical incarnation of things badly made or scrambled in the making. Many of them bear mutations or unhealing, oozing sores. They are masters of argots and broken codes. They are drawn to tar, the stars, and the arts

- "Radagast" is a filthy word in the slang of rats and the double secret name of their hidden shadow pontiff — Radagast the most Reviled

- While rats increased in size and strength, their cousins, the mice, have gotten smaller and sneakier

- The traditional guardians against rats are of no use against these smaller mice, who are too small to be pounced upon. These vermin, no larger than a grain of sand, form swarms that portray locusts as cuddly pets. They have the ability to strip a grown man to bones and buckles in under an hour

- The alchemist's guild, sole breathers of the hellscotties, trained fire-breathing dogs, denies any rumor that they are responsible for the pipmice

- A wererat is more dangerous and scheming than a hoard of enemies, able to blend into human societies, trading brute force for cunning, as smart as a man no matter the form they wear

- The teeth of rats never stop growing. They must gnaw constantly or their teeth will grow too long, killing them. This is only part of the truth. It is not the teeth, but the rats that never stop growing. Given the space and food, they grow ever larger and ever hungrier. They never stop gnawing. They never stop eating. . .

- Wererats were not originally human. A mad alchemist wondered if lycanthropy could be reversed and humanoid animals could be created. His lab rats agreed with the procedure, but not with their situation. Investigating into the circumstances of his death make it clear he did nothing to prevent their infection from spreading

- The ability of rats to spread and share information defies analysis. One heretical sect of mathomages holds that rat-knowledge is both so fast and so ubiquitous that it must be a branch of god-knowledge
- Giant rats arrived in the belly of a ship that raided mega-fauna from a long lost land. Accordingly, when enough gather near water, it flows in the opposite direction, making them useful in the construction of plumbing, river locks, and traps
- Ratkin are descended from King Ferdinand the Rat. They are bold, love battle, and bands of young Ratkin are nearly always raiders or mercenaries.
- A ratkin never builds a home, only squatting once tragedies empty established homesteads
- Rats and ratkin are known to build strange and beautiful piling sculptures from rubble. They eat anything and work well in a group. They are capable of executing complex tactical maneuvers with no communication, having learned such maneuvers from their oral histories and ancestors
- Great works of ratkind are The Squeak, Dawn and We Discovered an Uneaten Sandwich. Tales of the ratkind include How David the Rat Pinned the Great Stoat and Stole Back the Sun, and Why Nettleskin Rat Kept Knives in Her Fur
- Rats are given a bad rap; they are really just happy, polyandrous, hippy sneaks!
- Ratmen are immune to organic poisons
- All rats spy for the Rat King who seeks one day to be pretty
- Rats are the reincarnated forms of sinful people; the larger the rat, the worse the sin
- Ratkin are the eventual results of incestuous relationships between noble families
- The Rat King is a demi-god of filth. His senses are distorted, explaining his fondness for copper
- Ratmen are the result of children abandoned on dirty city streets, only able to regain their humanity if they find their parents
- Rats are the agents of entropy, seeking copper dipped in blood. Were they ever to collect one million pieces, it would mean the end of the world. . .
- The remarkable nature of rats is not due to the rat at but the fleas that infest them, resulting in many and varied mutations, from the common dire, to fire-breathing, regeneration, acid saliva, and worse
- The swarming rats in narrow cave warrens are actually bats who found flight impractical. They retain only vestigial wingflaps, but their sonar is acute and weaponized
- Dire rats are the result of a rat who has consumed enough of its brethren. Then when the dire rat consumes enough humans it becomes a ratkin. Ratkin perpetuate this process by feeding small human children to the dire rats
- A dire rat is a ratking; rats pushed so closely together that they merge and become one giant rat
- Pungent cheese wards ratkin as garlic does vampires. Centuries of using cheese to trap rats has caused them to associate the scent with danger

- The fleas on rats brought black death with them, but the fleas on dire rats are much more terrible. To survive a fight with a dire rat is to die a slow tortured death soon after

- As a rat's teeth always grow, so to, do the dire rats. But wood does not wear them down. Instead dire rats gnaw on stone. Ratkin gnaw on human bone

- Some sages purport that men evolved from monkeys. The dwarvelves (hairy, bearded elves who like forging mithril and gems) hold that this is obviously not true, for there are no monkeys in the Fantastickal Lands of Middle Oerop. According to dwarvelvish lore, a madman from the far north, from beyond the Maw of Whitefear the Bear God and beyond the razor winds of Iron Boreas came seven thousand years ago

  - The madman, called Piripetros by the dwarvelves of Morgolindon and Petropirireis by the dwarvelves of Taudrakshka, offered to save the dwarvelven holdings of their rat plague in exchange for half their gold and half of their most beautiful princesses. The dwarvelves agreed and with his magical Fluting Alpenhorn he summoned the rats from the deep holdings

  - But the avaricious dwarvelves then slammed their doors shut and refused to pay the madman who howled and puffed and roared in rage. He departed into the Flat Lands of Grass with his rat horde and there gifted them with uncanny prowess and knowledge (but not wisdom) and from these rats came the plague of MEN

  - According to the few remaining dwarvelves, therefore, rats are the larval stage of the locust creatures known as men

- There are rumors that in the old alchimitorium where the white wizards perished researching the plague dragon's corpse a race of intelligent six-limbed rats have arisen, with an additional set of manipulating hands hidden in pouches inside their mouths

- Dire rats acquire intelligence by eating the brains of slain creatures. Eventually they become intelligent enough to realize this and seek out areas of frequent slaughter, like dungeons that attract adventurers

- Ratkin include capybaras, chinchillas, nutrias, guinea pigs, hamsters, gophers and doppelgangers

- Rats are elemental sponges, acquiring the magical properties of their surroundings. In filthy human cities they carry diseases. In gorgeous natural elven tree-holds they poop edible caffeine berries. In dwarven duggings are often bred on a diet of gem-dust to produce beautiful pearls which are then sold abroad

- In halfling communities there are very few rats because they are used to make the famous three-bite-pie

- Death wizards first bred semi-intelligent dire rats so they wouldn't have so much trouble with buying fresh slaves and captives from humanoid villages

- A dire rat's soul is worth one fifth of a man's soul and three-quarters of a woman's soul, according to Pulchraphobos's seminal work, The Balance of Souls

- Orcs will buy bundles of rats at sixteen silver pence the half-dozen. Or at two silver pence for a single rat. Math is not an orcish strong suit
- Several species of dire rodent have prehensile tails which can grow into a new rodent if severed
- Dried and ground skyforest rat gonads protect from mummy rot
- Ear-rats are popular familiars among wizard-scouts, who use them to listen in on distant conversations
- A rat is a bat without wings. Rats can crossbreed with bats, resulting in winged monkey-rats. There is no monkey in a flying monkey, just a lot of nasty rat
- Rat bites can cure old age. . . or at least prevent it
- Dire rats are otherworldly rats that come from the domain of the Mater Milia, the rat spirit. They are her agents and children and normally live in her halls where they gnaw at the pillars of the universe. They may breed with normal rats and create giants rats
- Wererat skins are used to make Face-masks of Animal Charming
- Old colonies of rats become more organized and develop group intelligence and cunning and even enslave other small species and build structures
- In dungeons rats scurry in between walls, under floors, and through air vents. Some adventurers have tried to smash through walls to have rats swarm out and attack them
- A ball of rats are a colony whose tails become knotted and they act as one. Very rare in wild, in some magic rich areas dozens of these balls form. Some even form huge sphere, as large as a child or even larger
- Normally, big rats eat smaller rats. Humanoid rat men and wererats may keep rats and giant rats as pets and food. Pony-size colossal rats or larger may serve as mounts
- Rats beneath an alchemist guild in the ruined city of Gnash-Toril bred a gargantuan rat who burst up from beneath the earth and destroyed buildings before the city's wizard kings destroyed it
- A rat's intelligence is inversely proportionate to the amount of rats in a certain range from it. Lone rats, well out of range of other rats, sometimes even develop psionic abilities like telepathy and telekinesis.
- Among all natural creatures and races, rats are the best at sensing magic and following residual amounts of it. In fact, this sensitivity is borderline addiction, as rats just love feeling surrounded by magic. The reason hubs of civilization tend to have quite so many rats is because the same hubs tend to house a wizard's guild, or several, and those draw rats in from miles and miles away
- Among all creatures, the ratkins have been blessed, along with the roachkins, to inherit the Earth at the End of Days. So spake Ratatushtra
- Ratpyres are pyrokinetic blood-drinking ratkin

- A ratkin that drinks a human potion of healing is afflicted with a voracious appetite and a propensity towards obesity — this is why ratkin-kings are all huge and round

- Rats originate from the elemental plane of filth. There, rats are easily fed and treated as a versatile domesticated creature. Generally, dire rats are guard creatures, giant rats are food (or sometimes pets), and regular rats are pets, trained to eat some of the more pestilent creatures of the plane

- When they migrate to the material plane, they tend to migrate to the places most similar to their home dimension: the sewers of large cities

SHADOWS

*"They all came out of the shadows and just drained all
the strength from him. Like a bunch jerks."* — Sad Dato, warrior

NOMENCLATURE: Shades, darkfolk, mistmen, shadow servants

DESCRIPTION: A being of elemental shadow that drains life from the living

THINGS THAT ARE KNOWN:

- They are animate shadows
- They have a connection with other planes of existence
- They can drain the strength from a living creature and turn it into a shadow

RUMORS AND OTHER SHIFTING IN THE DARK:

- Shadows have a connection with the ethereal plane, which is why they are hard to spot
- Shadows are banned from the ethereal, forced to inhabit its dark reflection, the plane of shadow, with the advantage that they can travel at the speed of darkness within this space
- You can claim shadows are undead or not; the only thing you will get for your trouble is to get embroiled in an endless debate
- The secret to the shadows' ability to hide in shadows is that they cease to exist while people are looking for them, and only re-emerge into reality once not seen
- The most deadly weapon against a shadow is lasers, holy lasers
- You would think that bright light would drive off shadows, but it only defines their form
- Shadows have a seething passion to destroy all light and life for creating a cacophony of noise that disturbs the restful nature of the shadow, driving them mad
- Shadows feed on energy from the negative elemental plane. They only drain the strength of living creatures for pleasure
- They are desperate people from a dying material plane and drain the strength from living creatures because that is their only way to reproduce
- The shadow is a living hypercube which occupies all shadow space and no shadow space simultaneously, which is why they can fit through any space. They simply choose to exist wherever there is an absence of photons

- Once someone becomes a shadow, there is no way to return them to their human form, which is, of course, untrue. The problem comes that in order to restore a creature from their drained shadow form, they must steal the life from elven children, which is why the elves take shadow infestations so seriously
- Shadows gather in places that are ignored by people. A farmhouse people walk by, an unvisited grove in the woods, an attic, a dark closet. If ignored, they will create a nest and begin to plague the local area
- Shadows don't feed on strength; they feed on terror which drains the life from the victim in the form of their physicality, targeting whatever physical statistic is weakest
- Some shadows grow powerful and strong after stealing many souls until it becomes a much more dangerous creature
- If you are restored to life after being drained by a shadow, your dark half still seeks you and wishes to put you to exquisite torture
- Warlock patrons will assign shadows as servants to promising candidates

TIRGE

"It'ss the dream of the mosquito, issn't it. Jusst a nightmare for everyone elsse." - Shellmoss, Ghazan Speaker

NOMENCLATURE: Bloodsuckers, spear-beaks, strix, striga/strigae, bloodbirds, devil birds, vampire owls

DESCRIPTION: Small flying parasites

THINGS THAT ARE KNOWN:

- They lair in narrow dark places
- They drink blood
- They are about the size of a housecat
- They have leathery bat-like wings, a short tail, and barbed legs

RUMORS AND OTHER SILENT FLUTTERS IN THE DARK:

- They steal genetic material
- Stirges build bee-like hives, where they store their blood. After time passes, it coagulates into dark honey
- They collect diseases, which live in pockets along their proboscis
- They are quite intelligent, often setting up near exits or not bothering heavily equipped and prepared parties, instead seeking out the wounded
- They attack with a distinctive buzzing sound that travels quite far. Considering they only take some of their prey's blood, the noise often draws those wishing to scavenge on their leavings
- They aren't parasites, but symbiotic creatures that live on and with underdark horrors like hook horrors and umber hulks.
- The stirge is not a grown creature but larva. It collects blood for the coming change and enters a pupa stage for less than a week. It emerges from its old shell as a combination of the creature and insect-like features of the stirge
- A character can also attempt to dislodge a stirge by tensing their muscles. Each round they must succeed on a constitution check. On the third round, the stirge bursts from the blood they have taken in. It is a common game among barbarians
- Goblins are quite fond of adding stirge to stew, the more bloody the better
- They are also popular with the blood-drinking undead

- They are often kept as pets or allies, intentionally or unintentionally, by other creatures, attacking a minute or two after the creatures they are allied with. They often are able to feed and flee this way before any attention is paid to them
- They are the spawn of an insane vampire who desired living servants
- Stirges were once humans who were transformed as punishment
- They are viewed as harbingers of war and strife
- Blood drank from a stirge sac can heal the injured. What is less commonly known is that it is also highly addictive
- They can sense mutations and diseases and will avoid those with tainted blood
- Certain types of blood are extremely attractive to stirges and they favor those targets over all others
- Stirges are lulled to sleep by mournful polyphonic dirges
- They were originally crafted by vampiric wizards to throw hunters of the undead off track
- They were the minions of evil wizards who bred them by the millions and released them against enemy armies arrayed against them
- The stirge uses blood to fuel a bizarre alchemical process in its bloated para-abdomen. This process is how the gas it uses to fly is produced
- Stirges are a cross between a leech and a bat and have no relation to insects or mosquitoes
- The stirge is actually an insect; what appears to be hair are actually just sensing fibers
- The stirge is a larval form of a stirgeon, a highly intelligent creature, specializing in the science of blood. Many underdark denizens consider it superior surgeon to even the xixchil
- Chirurgeons use stirge cages to drain excess humors from patients. Varieties of stirge such as blood, black bile, yellow bile, and phlegm are known
  - Blood stirges are the only ones who can fly and are fond of liver
  - Phlegm stirges swim and try to drain the lungs and brains of their victims through the nose
  - Yellow bile stirges propel themselves with jets of burning gasses and are very quick. They eat as fast as they move, devouring a spleen in 1-5 rounds. This can be fatal
  - Black bile stirges are wormlike and live in earth, soil, and rock, looking to enter bodies through the anus or urethra, then eating the gall bladder. Victims become despondent, sleepless and irritable, but they live
- Stirge eggs are laid in carcasses when the stirge feeds
- When a stirge attacks, they attempt to squeeze between the armor and the skin
- Stirges are annoyance made manifest. They will take whatever form of vermin is most suitably annoying

- They are just subterranean hummingbirds and completely harmless. Their abilities and appearance have been exaggerated because they spook adventurers very easily when they dart into torchlight, and no one is going to admit once they get back home that they were scared by a tiny harmless bird
- Stirges are technically tiny pterodactyls
- Stirges will continue to feed, even after satiation. If overfed, their membrane ruptures, leading to sacks of pig blood as a common tactic against stirges
- Stirges are the key ingredient in instant blutwurst, a beloved winter dish of the Dzhungaznian dwarves of Dheoghnunn
- Stirge eggs pickled in brine are known as stony mountain caviar
- Stirges have three wings and an organic flywheel to assist them in flying, hence their excellent maneuverability
- Stirges are collectivist creatures that serve Law and preferentially target chaotic and individualistic creatures
- Telling people that stirges eat your blood is simply adventurers whitewashing the truth for the townsfolk. They actually have a razor-sharp maw and specialize in eating your face off
- Stirges are sentient assemblages of stringy worms, cooperating for the greater good. They attempt to get ingested to take control of their victims, turning them into reckless adventurers who will get eaten by a dragon. It is in the dragon's duodenum that a stirge matures, laying eggs that hatch into dragon-dung-worms
- Stirges stir subconscious sexist sentiments, seducing silly sirens, sylvans & semi-humans scavenging stony sepulchers
- Stirges are bio-engineered syringes, given small wings to be at hand for the enterprising surgeon. Their progenitors have long since died off, and they have adapted to take the blood of anyone nearby in an attempt to discern their health. Sadly, without the help of an authorized medical representative, all the tests are inconclusive and must be repeated
- Every time a mortal dies from a supremely selfish act, a swarm of stirges is born. Kings of greed spawn dire stirge queens, who brood thousands more
- Jungle goblins use stirge bones in the fruit gruel they feed their children for crunch and marrow; this is similar to the plains goblins feeding their children tiger nails in a bowl of rotten goat crud
- Stirges do not drain blood. They don't drain anything. The needle mouth is actually an ovipositor
- Stirges are magical creatures used to obtain the essence of others for sympathetic magic. Bat-like stirges exist and seek out hair; this is the source of the old urban legend
- Stirges are the physical form of malaria-spirit
- Stir-inges are magical syringes made from stirge ovipositors

- The belief that stirges deposit eggs with their proboscis is wrong; they actually deposit mutagenic sperm, which impregnates the host tissue. This creates a 'stirgiform grub' which absorbs genetic information from its host before erupting from the body
- Stirge guano is red and grainy. When dry, it hardens into a clay-like substance that is flammable and useful as fertilizer
- The stirge secretes a substance to maintain the blood pressure in the vascular system to allow it to easily drink. This substance plus the desiccation of the body make fully drained corpses very flammable
- When the first demon army came to wage war in the marshes, the mosquitoes fed and were changed
- Kabraxis, the Demon of Lust, has a thousand detachable members that swap fluids with whole crowds of worshiping cultists during a ceremony. Some of them can't fit back on the demon, as more are constantly growing. Any site with stirges is a site where cultists had congress with their dark master
- They are aberrant bats that lair in the thousands underground. Their digestive system is extremely efficient, causing them under normal circumstances to only need to feed a small sip
- The psychic wizards of Marnbayzie got so proficient playing darts they needed to make the game interesting. They created darts that could fly of their own accord, with enough mind to give mentalists another venue for winning. Lazy and stylish, the foppish wizards eventually adapted the darts to fetch them drinks, drawing from the bar and squirting into cups
- When STDs, madness, mutation, and furious former lovers finished with the order, enough of the stirges survived to spread and become a real problem. Still, a wizard wearing a yellow and silver robe may find that stirges still have enough racial memory to want to fill their cups for them. Better hope wine is handy
- The first stirge were created when a profoundly powerful wizard used a *power word* originally designed to turn dragon teeth into warriors. Crippled and desperate, the wizard cast it on a still-living dragon, whose needle-sharp teeth tore loose with wads of gum tissue and bone, desperate and insane with agony, stabbing and drinking to assuage the pain they still felt through the sundered nerves
- The chupacabra is a ground-based, large relative of the stirge
- The dragon was immortal, and captured, and its teeth suffer and feed still. If the dragon dies, perhaps all the stirge die too. If the stirge ever proliferate to a certain point, perhaps the dragon will become strong enough to escape and reunite with them
- A min-maxing wizard character was not content to only throw 3 darts a round, or to be stuck without armor. After decades of casting animating magic on the same darts, eventually they were imbued with the magic. The final step was when the wizard fell into the pool that animated inanimate objects, and the darts came alive

- "It's not armor," the player protested, strapping cages to chest, back, arms, legs. The cages filled with the now-living darts, who returned to their master. Until the DM had enough and an ogre mage charmed the lot of them and drained the enterprising munchkin dry. Now they are feral
- Stirge are the carrier pigeons of the Stygian Suburb. Their wings are uniquely suited to carry demonic script, and they are instinctively eager to please demons. Swarms gather in the palaces where the demons hold massive social events like gala balls, feasts, and hunts
- The strix is a vampiric bird, a cousin of the stirge
- The stirge is the only form a shape-shifting witch can take
- It is the height of fashion for demons and tieflings to have "blood buttons" with a few drops of a friend or enemy's blood in the center; the stirge pecks the button the demon chooses, then homes to that demon with the message
- They attack sleeping victims without them noticing, for a stirge bite is painless
- Kyvash War College is famed for its Biomunitions Chair, funded by the Zephrox Mercenary Guild. One of their more popular sub-projects was sponsored by the neogi, who wanted a way to weaken eggredex beasts (who were immune to poison and mind control) to make them easier to capture and sell to wealthy nobles. The stirge nest was portable, and the blood the stirge took weakened the strange circulatory system of the eggredex beast (who operated on hydraulic principles) so they could be folded and taken quietly. When the eggredex beasts went extinct, the stirge were re-purposed for "scorched earth" campaigns to deter resettling in the dimension wars
- Stirges are frequently mistaken for vampires based on their method of feeding
- Garlic and holy water infuriate stirges, causing them to fly into a rage and attack until death
- Stirges are actually the attack helicopters of a particularly repugnant brand of sprite. Their fuel is blood. Don't believe it? Twist off the head, and in the chamber between the eyes there is an extraordinarily furious blue person half the size of your pinkie. These sprites are on a religious quest to kill nosy people, and they are an off-shoot of the species that manages will-o-wisps remotely with psychic powers. Their rivalry is legendary
- They patiently track prey, waiting. Once a fight begins, they attack everyone, feeding on the wounded. As soon as the fight is over, they retreat again, up into the trees, following and waiting again

Mr. Gygax the demiurge
Happily created the stirge
It's like a mosquito
Except you're finito
If your paths should ever converge
— Dungeons and Digressions

- Stirges hunt people by softly calling out their name. This rhythmic chant entrances the victim, putting them into a stupor and making them unaware of their environment. The stirge then has free reign to do what they wish to the victim

- When the zerg first came to this world, bats were caught in the creep. Most died. A few survived, but the fast and loose mutagenic properties of the creep tied them to the hive mind and warped them into monsters

- Sites that have heavy stirge infestations often keep small mammals in cages at the top of poles around town to deter them feeding on humans and to provide target practice to the locals

- The greatest of the vampire necromancers weaponized his blood, so that every drop shed would twirl free, spinning out wings and starvation, and attack on his behalf. He was eventually slain, but his creations thrived and grew large. They are able to breed true; they share the same blood, after all

- Stirges have rubies for eyes

- The dire stirge is the size of an elder pot-bellied pig, has six wings and a blood draining proboscis at both ends

- In the warrens of Moloko, they murmur of the hydra stirge created by the mad mage Mulana of Mulenbach

- "I have invented a biomechanical creature based on the stirge, which is attracted to naphta or rock-oil, the raw ingredient required for the activation of the phlogiston in the internal explosion engine. I believe this oil-irge will lead to a time of great plenty and good for all dwarven-kind, freeing us from toil and bringing us a period of peace, plenty, and oneness with nature." - Ishtvan Shentdizely of the Blackrock Dwarven Corporation

- They were designed by alchemists as autonomous blood sample collectors but have since escaped and bred true. The ancient scent lore of the alchemists can still be used to tame and direct the stirges if the lore could be discovered and deciphered

- Stirges can't withdraw their proboscises from padded armor and will bloat up like honeypot ants

- Rothe blood is toxic to stirges and they avoid anyone with the musk of the rothe. That is unfortunately true in general

- Stirges originally were fruit eaters, but they were trapped in a cave after an earthquake, opening a path to the underworld. They were forced to adapt to drinking blood to survive. Sadly this trait bred true and almost all the harmless fruit eaters are dead

- Stirges quickly succumb to bad air, like canaries

- Fire-roasted stirge is best when served fully bloated; otherwise, it's dry and chewy

- Stirges always travel in flocks which are multiples of 8. This is because they are the tips of the tentacles of an ethereal octopus creature, which partially extrudes itself onto our plane to feed.

144

- Stirges actually prefer red wine over blood
- Tying stirges together is a favorite goblin pastime
- A healing stirge is an enchanted stirge that injects the stored blood into your body. You have to pierce your skin and squeeze the blood sac to get the blood to inject. This bursts delicate membranes in the stirge's head but heals you
- Bound together stirges are used to play a goblin children's game called sip-sip. The players run in circles easily avoiding the stirges but usually crashing into one another and making an easier target for the "sip-sip"
- Stirge-owls serve the underworld goddess and her minions. Everyone from her gatekeepers to her vampire throne-bearers use stirge-owls as messengers and shock troops. Underworld stirges can both be larger than normal and hit creatures immune to non-magical weapons
- Stirge beaks make excellent quill tips for scribing scrolls
- Stirge eyeballs are heavy and shiny and make good sling bullets
- Stirges are used by Drawangari doctors to purge bad humors from sick people. A wild stirge bite has a chance of having a *cure disease* effect on the victim
- Some less scrupulous Drawangari doctors reuse stirges rather than dispose of them as per custom. These "recycled stirges" have a chance of curing disease and chance of causing disease
- In enlightened Drawangari city states, authorities have taken to providing single-use neutered, short-lived may-stirges pre-filled with troll blood to tee addicts
- Halflings of the Upper Blue Dowager clans of Peenkemoende have taken to using trained carrier stirges to harvest troll blood, which is used by humanoid and elven addicts to get a high and temporary regeneration (though as the saying goes, "shoot tee and you bee fick ass troll")
- Black-and-blue market dealers often mix troll blood with chicken blood to increase their margins, though this generally destroys the regenerative properties. On the market this product is often called chee-tee
- Stirge enzymes convert blood into a thin, ichor-like fluid and can be used to kill vampires, as they rapidly convert the blood a vampire has ingested into stirgeon juice
- Boiling a stirge that is well fed makes a delicious blood pudding

Variants

PHASE STIRGE: In addition to the standard phase characteristics, they can drain blood from targets up to thirty feet away, without needing to touch the victim

JUNGLE STIRGE: Twice the size of a normal stirge and has a paralyzing venom when it strikes

DESERT STIRGE: A flightless hopping creature that attacks its prey somewhat like a large flea. They can burrow beneath the sand and travel with a movement rate of 6" underground

GHOST STIRGE: A stirge that died from lack of blood. They ooze ectoplasm which sucks the life from targets as well as draining blood as normal. They return to life again and again until their remains are bathed in warm blood

TWO-HEADED: This variety has an additional head. This grants an additional attack as well as reducing the chances of surprise

ENRAGED STIRGE WHIP: This creature does not feed with a proboscis, but instead has four long whiplike limbs that attach and drain blood from multiple creatures. The whips have AC 3 and 10 hit points each. It normally attaches itself to a cave wall or surface before attacking. It can attach itself to a surface with an effective strength of 20. It flies and is small instead of tiny. They hunt in packs

SWAMP: These are much smaller than normal (about the size of a half dollar), but they travel in huge swarms. They hunt at dusk

Combat Tricks

FLOCK BLINDNESS: When three or more stirges affect a single target, the target's vision is obscured for the round, causing them to act as if they are blinded

ARMOR CRAWL: On a hit, the stirge may worm its way under the armor. This protects the stirge from damage, giving it the AC of the victim's armor and ensuring that any hit that hurts it, hurts the victim for an equal amount

EYE STAB: Some Stirges are unsatisfied with blood and drink fluid out of the eyes. They land on the target on the first turn, move to the eye on the second, and on the third turn make a strike into the eyeball. The victim must save or become shaken by the pain, and the eye is seriously damaged, causing partial blindness

# ROLL

"You should kill them, then burn them or boil them. The sword is never enough." - Huyiz, the one-armed mage

NOMENCLATURE: Rubberbeast, underbridge ogre, trollteri

DESCRIPTION: Ugly regenerating monsters

THINGS THAT ARE KNOWN:

- Trolls regenerate damage that isn't caused by fire or acid
- They are hungry

RUMORS AND OTHER LIMBS REGROWING IN THE DARK:

- There is only one troll. Every time he is cut, he grows
- Trolls are always ugly. They may be weak or nice but never fail to carry a hideous visage
- The trollplague is what it is called when trolls realize each part begets a whole
- They are magic taken physical form. Their nature makes them cause harm or damage to living creatures. They are often the detritus from a spell designed to harm other creatures
- This means that they are not vulnerable to fire and acid but are instead vulnerable to the type of harmful spell that was used in their creation. It just happens that this is often fire and acid
- Trolls are the byproduct of a wizard successfully extracting an immortalized cell line from a swamp giant. After testing and experimenting on the cells, it languished in a sealed beaker in an abandoned laboratory for hundreds of years. Found, it was imbibed as a potion and rapidly caused the line of trolls we know today
- Beware the limb replacers. Though having a severed limb replaced with a magical replacement or a wonder of mechanical engineering is expensive, troll limbs attach readily and are much more affordable and simpler than whatever you are likely paying for
- Severed troll parts that are prevented from reattaching to the original grow into a clone of the original. They share a telepathic bond
- Healing potions don't use troll blood in their manufacture. They *are* troll blood
- Troll regeneration is a byproduct of their fecundity.
- They are heavily influenced by their environment, taking on aspects of the terrain and creatures near where they live

- Original trolls were a cross between the fae and the earth creatures, both noble dwarven and base goblin. But some worshiped chaos and evil and gained the dark art of regeneration from a demon lord, and it caused their hunger to grow until it drove them to cannibalism and anthropophagy. The brain prions drove them mad, and they wiped out the non-chaos worshipers. The most pure of the troll vanished first, perhaps they were somehow spared

- The mad wizard Rolleg cut the hands and feet off trolls and linked their stumps together to create a living fence. Anyone can apply this technique; simply hold the stumps together until they fuse. Collars or muzzles must be applied to prevent them from chewing off their own body parts

- Trolls are reflections of the attitudes directed to them. Most people react with horror at their visage, so are immediately attacked. If greeted warmly, they are kind and playful

- Trolls are vicious thieves, and their very presence causes food to spoil

- Frozen troll chunks buried in the enemy's fields is a nice surprise for farmers in the morning
- Trolls are the acne of young, evil treants: twisted branches that just need to come off right now. This is why trolls are gnarled in shape and often covered in moss
- Trolls are just normal giant spellcasters such as shamans and witch doctors. Their coloration and skin comes from the plants they use to connect with the natural enviornment
- Trolls would be immortal if not for cancer. Tearing out growths and polyps and ganglions with their teeth births new trolls. In some cases trolls burst from the mother and immediately set to fighting. Young trolls hide, spying on older ones, moving closer and closer until admitted into the clan. Some never adjust and live apart
- Lord Agamazar broke the defenders of Castle Vizgrom by chopping parts off captive trolls and shooting them into the town with catapults. Unfortunately, Agamazar was torn to bits by enraged trolls later that day, so his victory came with a steep price
- Trolls aren't natural creatures; they are the result of a series of flawed magical rings of regeneration cursed into being long ago
- When reflected in a mirror, a troll is a startlingly beautiful humanoid. If pulled through the looking glass, they will trade places with the ugly one. In every other way, they are identical, including outlook, alignment, and disposition
- Some trolls divine the future in entrails, using their own and stuffing them back in the hole before they close
- Fire and acid don't actually kill a troll; they merely send pieces of the creature to another plane of existence. Once the entire creature has been transported, it lives on in the other plane. And on those other planes, other types of attack may be needed to send them to yet another plane
- Aristocrats frequently swallow severed troll fingers as a macabre form of dietary control. Don't trust the ones sold by your average village apothecary, though. Those are usually just shaved baby rats
- Trolls are the discarded mucus and wax of Orcus, constantly refreshed by the ethereal transmission of material from the demon's orifices. The only way to stop the regeneration is to slay Orcus, or at least convince him to be more hygienic
- The technique of hulling trolls is quite well known, but some mad kings have taken this a step further and begun the sexy new field of troll sculpture. Futurists predict someday the next step will be troll architecture
- Trolls are the essential animated cancerous essence of the Mother of Life. As such, all trolls are female and parthenogenetic
- Troll women are astoundingly beautiful, sometimes called dryads or nymphs

- Trolls are the counterpart to elves and dwarves; however instead of representing the spirits of youth and magic or earth and greed, trolls represent the spirit of the dead

- Trolls can only regenerate in the dark. In fact, they need to regenerate constantly to simply stay alive, since their bodies are so unstable. That's why they turn into stone in the daylight

- Trollism is a virus, similar to vampirism, which lives in the blood of infected creatures. A creature that injects the blood of a troll may become a troll itself

- So long as trolls drink and eat enough mortal (non-troll) flesh, they retain the native intelligence and appearance of that race. Trolls exiled from troll society into the wilderness slowly decay into their vicious, wild form over a period of weeks or months

- Trolls have difficulty thinking, but some environments (such as cold or the dark) can make the troll more intelligent

- Trolls and vampires have been locked in a secret war for the flesh and blood of mankind for millennia, for they were spawned by twin demon queens and hate each other with a deathly passion

- Trolls are something people become because of their spiritual health. That's why they have language and not culture

- Trolls are fond of contests where the loser's head is ripped off and a new one regrown. Something is frequently lost in the process, although the trolls that have had their heads removed are hard-pressed to recall what it is

- High trolls are usually referred to as "trulies", for they believe themselves truly blessed — possessed of immortality, eternal youth, beauty, vigor, and regeneration. . . and an aversion to sunlight.

- The accursed royal blood of the Night Elemental Lord Agalloch tainted the heroes that slew him when he bid to take over the Prime Material. One was tainted by the essence of wind and air, turning to stone in the sunlight and becoming the first of the troll kind. The second was tainted by the essence of water and vital fluid, turning to fire and ash in the sunlight and becoming the first of the vampires. The third was tainted by the essence of earth and stone, vaporizing into thin air when exposed to sunlight and becoming the first of the stonewalkers. The fourth was tainted by the essence of fire and flame, liquefying into a puddle of fetid water in the sunlight and becoming the first of the nightmares

- Lycanthropes are loathed by all the bearers of the elemental blood curse, for their blood is infused with the essence of the moon and stars, giving them greater power when in moonlight, but no drawbacks in sunlight. The lycanthropes are truly the children of Orion the Hunter, born to hunt the blood-cursed and to keep the lands of the Prime Material safe for mortals and their works

- Trolls were once peaceful, but asked the fae queen for a boon of immortality. It was granted, allowing them to draw from the life force of any thing they ate. Soon those traits began to affect the trolls; as they became dumber and more cow-like, they realized their error and changed their diet. Now they seek out the most intelligent and aggressive creatures they can find, though this has done little for their relations with other races

- The trolls are so adept at climbing that some have been known to create wooden homesteads for themselves inside the canopies of dense forests. Some of these canopy-dwelling trolls are clever enough to build tripwire traps that drop heavy stones down on their victims from the branches above.

- Some trolls mix their own blood with the urine of their victims to create a foul concoction that is capable of sprouting carnivorous plants when poured over fertile soil. The trolls propagate these plants to defend their lairs from trespassers

- Trolls are so unafraid of death that their corpses are more likely to rise as zombies after they are slain. Some have witnessed troll zombies going about their daily activities as they would have in life; mindlessly preparing fires and chewing and swallowing food that falls right out of their decayed chest cavities

- Some trolls carve patterns and markings into their own flesh in worship to their gods. Due to their regenerative capabilities, these wounds scar and heal over a matter of days, allowing the troll to continuously carve new markings into itself as a regular ritual. If the gods decide to reward this worship, the troll is blessed with enchanted flesh that it can use to cast powerful spells of necromancy

Variants

There are many variations of trolls: rock, ice, swamp, etc. These specifications do not grant them elemental powers or resistances, but indicate differences in size, intelligence, and culture. They frequently receive bonuses in their home terrain

Combat Tricks

BETRAYAL: Trolls will often dig deep pits in their lairs and happily dive into victims and pull them in, both falling to the bottom. The damage from the fall is little worry for the troll

DIVISION: Trolls have been known to detach a limb and throw it behind its victims. This prevents the troll from rending its opponents, but the limb receives a separate attack used to trip the party member

IMPROVISED WEAPON: Trolls like to grab creatures two size categories smaller than them and wield them as weapons. The damage applies to both the target and the weapon, of course

UNICORN

"Unicorns aren't real. And if they were, they'd kill you."
— Apocryphal

NOMENCLATURE: Holy steeds, mount of purity

DESCRIPTION: Pure white horses with a single horn atop their head

THINGS THAT ARE KNOWN:

- They are always white
- They have horns
- They are known to shift through space
- They are immune to charms and enchantments
- They are susceptible to the charms of young women

RUMORS AND OTHER RESTFUL NOTES IN THE GLADE:

- Unicorns gain their power from the chaste and pure of heart. The bond they form with a holy individual, such as a virgin or paladin, is for life
- However, if they should succumb to sex or sin, the unicorn becomes mad with rage. It looses its horn, its hair turns black, its hooves burn with hatred, and it hungers for flesh, becoming a nightmare
- Unicorns are a special type of fairy shape-shifter, that can only reproduce with virgins. They gain their trust and intimacy, often by playing hard to get, and then bed them, consensually or not
- It is as they say: the unicorns need maiden riders. This is wondrous when it begins, but once bonded with the unicorn, they are separated from the realm of man. Tending constantly to the needs of another fickle creature, loneliness, and the need to hunt evil begin to wear. The youth given to the maiden rider from the unicorn becomes a heavier and heavier weight every year. Eventually, the riders become hostile, bitter, and weary
- A unicorn is a dream of instability and madness, more powerful than you, and completely unpredictable
- Unicorns are warlike fae sustained by bloodshed, righteous fury, and fanatical zeal
- Their alliances with paladins are not out of a desire for justice, but merely made as the most expedient way to shed the blood of the guilty

- Some Unicorns are even said to use their allies to not only create warlike churches of justice, but also nests of evil creatures to ensure that there will always be vengeance to be had

- Unicorns are prepubescent centaurs. They are only into virgins until they undergo puberty, a rather traumatic metamorphosis involving a great deal of wine drinking and celebration in lost and hidden caves

- There is a rumor that their centaur torso is the torso of the virgin they eventually deflower, but it is much more likely that Bacchus himself shapes their form.

- Unicorns are the dreams of virgins seeking aid, their desire to escape giving form to spirits in the wild. They exist beyond the call, but cannot properly breed.

- Unicorns must drench their horn in the blood of a pure maiden once a year or they lose their powers.

- A true unicorn horn is pure platinum. That's why they are no longer found. Bone horns come from fish. Any new sightings are either lies or a sure sign of an invasion

- Unicorns don't need virgins so much as they need women who have rejected men.

- The souls of great saints become angels. That is a fate out of reach of the nice lady down at the corner market. Occasionally, however, their wishes will find a place upon death, becoming a brilliant white horn on the forehead of a stallion or mare. The horse then seeks others who remind them of the horn giver, pure and compassionate

- Unicorns are horses infected with a brain worm. This worm spends its first life stage as an egg in the soil of a cemetery, but once hatched it crawls up on the tallest blade of grass it can find and lies in wait, hoping to be swallowed by a suitably large herbivore. Most herbivores know this and will not willingly feed in a cemetery, but horses can sometimes be led there and forced to feed by unknowing masters
  - Once eaten, the worm lodges itself in the brain. It develops a large horny proboscis which protrudes from the host's forehead
  - It needs a human brain, one filled with zeal, preferably laced with innocence and suppressed desires. Thus, it will be drawn to virgins and paladins. It will remain with its intended next host, testing it to see if its brain will be a truly delectable treat and its body a suitable host, all the while using its rather powerful psychic abilities to create chaos and danger
  - Once the host is found suitable, the fabled "horn" will be used for its intended purpose, leaving the horse body vacant and dead and the new host body almost intact apart from a ruptured ear canal. The creature will now revel in the last and shortest stage in its life by influencing its new host to abandon all former principles and fall to hedonism and debauchery (coincidentally, the unicorn will be gone at this point, furthering the theory that unicorns will abandon unworthy masters). Soon, the host will meet his or her fate somehow, at the hands of the law or through an act of despair, and will be buried in a nearby cemetery, its brain case ripe with eggs. . .
- Just as clerics channel the power of their god into Prime, so does the unicorn channel cosmic power. The horn is an intricate multi-dimensional array that reflexively converts power. This makes it very sensitive to auras and vibrations from intent and mindset. The presence of intense selfishness or delight in pain causes feedback that stings in the unicorn's bones.
- Salvressa Greengoat was a powerful druid mocked by wizards. They claimed they could weaponize animals to serve them in destroying their foes, and she could only use them "out of the box" as it were
  - She decided to prove them wrong. She thought of the most painful experience she had ever had, and she decided to incarnate it. She remembered the penetration and disillusionment of her first sexual experience, and she projected it out into a steed
  - First, the light and the cuddling and the freshness of idealism. Then the construct of romantic love contrasted with the rutting and grunting and abandonment of mating. The piercing pain, physical and emotional. And she unleashed it on the world
  - Salvressa Greengoat was never famous for her monster-making (and this was her only attempt)

- Voskohr the Defenestrator is an evil lich with a thousand windows in his multi-dimensional tower. The only way in is to insert a unicorn horn into the door lock, and each horn only works once. He figures if someone wants an audience with him, they have best be prepared to slaughter something pure to get a foot in the door

- Drunk fae at revels decided they would do away with the rider as they imitated jousts the humans hosted. They put the lances directly on the horses. It did not work out. Surviving unicorns became disapproving icons of probity and virtue, considering themselves object lessons in the pitfalls of drunken animal-tampering

- The unicorn's horn is actually pure magical energy. It's why the horse is white and so difficult to hit; the energy repels nearby materials

- For that matter, the unicorn isn't an actual horse. It's just magical forces, swirls and whorls of energy, and shapes more strange that all float together in the approximate shape of a horse. The body is like the tail of a coat, dragging along the ground

- The Thickwood is impossible to navigate. Brambles coat everything, climbing trees and spreading across the ground. They release fog that eats firelight. The only way through is to follow the glimmer of a unicorn's coat, and the shine of the light its horn projects. They were created as guides to carry the allies of the fae through the darkness

- When the Thickwood was destroyed and the ground it once covered was salted and burned, surviving unicorns were faced with a crisis of purpose. They decided to take their role as guides metaphorically, and they sought out those hemmed in and befogged and led them to clarity and safety

- A unicorn's bones are stitched with sigils that collect and concentrate emotions — namely righteous wrath and compassion. The horn is capable of either directing a release of pent-up energy or conducting a tracery of a multi-dimensional glyph that gives form to those energies

- Orcus had a phalanx of wicked goat mounts, shaggy and topped with skirling cathedrals of bone horns. A few of these defected one of the many times Orcus was (temporarily) slain. Their new patron, a forest goddess, fused and straightened their horns and granted them light and grace. They are intense rivals with their former kin

- An entire cult of Orcus, the Crooks, has as its purpose the ambition of discovering whether a hybrid of unicorns and devil-goats will yield something useful to their master. So far, no success staging experiments; unicorns can apparently die at will

- The horn of a unicorn can cure any disease. It may also infect you with parasites that have odd effects

- Each unicorn has glyphs inlaid in its horn that reveal a prophecy uttered by their divine patron. These can only be read after the horn is separated from the unicorn and given special treatment — unless the diviner has a healthy dollop of fey blood and the approval of the sponsoring god

- The city state of Belleraes has some really weird morality laws involving sex out of wedlock and legal marrying age. Many a visitor has fallen afoul of their castrating carpet-knives and twisted legal system. This culture was shaped by about five centuries of a fad among the nobility. Every legitimate noble had to have unicorn decorations, and at least once a year eat the meat of unicorns
- Every part of the unicorn was used: bones for end tables and writing desk inlay, hair for pillows and helm crests, eyes dipped in glass and inserted in statues or head trophies, hide for clothes or upholstering loveseats, marrow for Virtuous Salsa, and so on
- Unicorns have been out of style for at least three hundred years, but laws passed to ensure virtue and virgins are still on the books and existed long enough to shape this society indelibly
- Unicorns focus on virgins because "purity" is the same as "unmixed." They need naivety, people whose ideas have not been challenged and shaped by conflict with other ideas. They need spirits that have not deeply twined with other spirits. They are avatars of loneliness, colorless and solitary. Compromise is their poison.
  - Because of this, their minds project a flickering "horn" of singularity that can penetrate anything

COMBAT TRICKS

HORN PARRY: The unicorn may make a saving throw versus petrification when it charges. On a successful save, it is able to deflect any weapon set against a charge

REAR UP: The unicorn can forgo an attack with its horn, and instead rise up on its hind legs to attack with its hooves

AMPIRES

"Listen to them. Children of the night. What music they make."
- Dracula

NOMENCLATURE: Leeches, licks, bloodsuckers, overbites, fangers, fangs, lonely ones

DESCRIPTION: Undead creatures that feed on humans

THINGS THAT ARE KNOWN:

- They are repulsed by mirrors and garlic
- Sunlight damages them
- They can be slain by being held under running water
- A wooden shaft through the heart will paralyze them
- They are resistant to non-magical weapons
- Once 'killed' by normal means, they simply turn into gas and retreat to their coffin

RUMORS AND OTHER ABSENCES IN THE MIRROR:

- They are actually intestinal parasites that infect corpses. The victims harbor all sorts of weird physical characteristics, but the actual creature is a small, wandering gut worm. The gaseous form trick is pure parlor magic, just a common flashbang that allows the worm to escape

- Vampirism is used by the powers of Law to isolate and neutralize dangerous Chaotic influences. It is very attractive to a certain kind of power-mad maniac. Immortality and power. And the cost? Ha!

- But what happens when a dangerously dynamic champion of Chaos becomes vampire? By the nature of the curse, they are tied down, they are dependent on their environment, they are bound by day and night, they are beyond life, and can no longer learn and grow. They have stopped being a dynamic threat and become a static irritant — they have been encased in a cyst which protects the larger world from their influence. Perhaps they pollute a small corner of it, but they are effectively neutralized as champions of Chaos

- Vampires become terrible forces for conservatism. Unchanging. Eternal. They are Law's way of making Chaos serve it, and only we poor mortals suffer for their gambit

- They are just the fiction-made-manifest of a sage who writes pot-boilers in his spare time. Unfortunately the one with the vampires was written in a magic book, which causes anything within it to become real, as if it had always been real. Destroying the book causes all vampires to cease to exist

- Seven vampires carry the throne of the underworld goddess. She sends them to promote suffering in the world and reminds us of her wrath

- A spirit of the underworld possesses the corpse, making a mockery of the victim, corrupting and exterminating the departed soul. Once slain, it is banished until it can regather its power. Each devil or demon can have one such champion in the world at a time

- Werewolf corpses make particularly good hosts for vampires

- They are all sludge vampires

- Vampires are just ghouls that feed on immortal flesh. The powers of the vampire are just side effects from their diet

- Vampires are a trick your mind plays on you to cover up its own secret workings. Every time you think you're fighting a vampire you're actually fighting something else you don't want to look at. And if you have a sufficiently powerful personality, you can get others to share your delusion, blaming the "vampire" for crimes nobody wants to confess. The mythology of the vampire gets more baroque the more crimes it must stretch over

- Vampires are part of an infection. They are a hive mind, a single viral organism. The source is nearly immortal, and the ones it infects are quite strong. Those that the infected infect are pale shadows of thinking creatures

- Vampires are a fictional cover for the lizard overlords

- The blood that vampires drink is sent directly to hell. Not only does this make your soul more likely to go there after you die, but the genetic material in it (call it essence if you want) is mixed and used as a starting compound for building demons

- Vampires are the ultimate narcissists and for this reason they have never united to rule the world. They only "reproduce" when a vampire is foolish enough to think they can create and control another vampire, who almost always manages to get away when their own hyper-narcissism kicks in. If one vampire seems to dominate another, it is a sure bet that the "slave" is merely trying to get close for the ultimate betrayal. Thus the whole idea of vampire families, splat-sects, etc. is a paranoid fever dream of churchly witch hunter manual writers. Vampires are solo monsters, powerful, but their own worst enemy.

- The Vampire is even worse than the most terrifying nightmare. It is an idea that takes over the mind, inducing secrecy and obsession. People infected with the idea find themselves engaged in absent-minded bloodletting. Left unchecked, they begin filling bowls, barrels, and other containers with blood. It is unclear what their purpose is, and they are always unaware of their actions

- They are the guardians of the debts incurred by wishes. Wishes always have a cost. If that cost remains unpaid, a vampire extracts the balance. They prey on children, stealing into their rooms, in recompense. The only way to stop them is to stop the debt

- All vampires are actually simulacra. A plasmic being infects and replaces a body's cells. Eventually the entire being is replaced on a cellular level, and it gains a consciousness. The vampire has no idea that its real identity is already dead. The soul is truly gone

- These plasmic beings have a cellular structure that cannot stand up to the rigors of UV light. Other weaknesses are attributed to superstitions of the former identity

- The specific powers and limitations of a vampire are linked to the qualities and lifestyle of the host spirit. The landed elite are tied to their home of origin; their pale skin no longer tolerates the sun; and their thin noble blood reacts to garlic (a natural blood thinner) poorly. Poor vagabonds, by comparison, suffer constant wanderlust, are empowered by the sun and road, and resist the elements (including elemental spells). While frequently not as traditionally powerful as their noble kin, the rest of the spectrum of vampirism is aided by a shroud of ignorance.

- Vampires are simply young liches, struggling to hold on to the vestiges of life. The blood brings the semblance of life. As the years progress, it takes more and more blood for the same effect. As the lich slips into the embrace of undeath, his need for humanity fades away, along with the taste of blood

- Wishes and other means of immortality always produce vampirism

- If you refer to them as Draculas, they will spare you

 # WYVERN

"I have it on good authority from the duke of the Puttenbergen's vizier, Jochrim ibn Oberwaldski, that the wyvern is the protean and horrendous manifestation of dwarvish gold-lust also known as the dwarrowwife."
- Lujek, starter of the final wyvernwife wars

NOMENCLATURE: Wyrmspawn, dragon-birds, whyverns, wiverns, scorpion dragons

DESCRIPTION: A bipedal winged reptile with a poisonous tail sting

THINGS THAT ARE KNOWN:

- They can fly
- Their tails contain a poison sting
- They are related to dragons

RUMORS AND OTHER WHISPERS IN THE DARK:

- Wyverns are from the elemental plane of poison, which is filled with roiling clouds and bright candy like surfaces
- Wyverns are part of a family of creatures known as xyverns, yyverns, and zyverns organized in a complex hierarchical structure, each serving a different purpose
- A xyvern is almost like a wyvern, but with pteranodon wings and a confusion venom
- The wyvern is a chimeric creature, combining parts of a turkey, fruit bat, gecko, and scorpion. There are some who say it also possesses the forearms of a snake.
- Wyverns are the cursed remains of a bird race, who must kill a certain number of sentient beings before the curse is lifted. Every wyvern carries their total secretly, hoping for the day to become free once more

- The wyvern is the adult form of a cockatrice
- They eat their victims whole, but bones and metal aren't digested. After a kill, these are vomited up near the wyvern nest
- That's inaccurate; wyvern is a term for a giant turkey

- Wyverns are drawn to small enclosed spaces, much like cats are drawn to baskets and boxes
- Wyvern tails are actually their heads, and what looks like the head is just mimicry designed to fool and confuse predators.
- Wyverns are the natural animal competitors to dragons, resistant to both breath and dragon magic. Nowadays, however, they either live in dragon-free environments or become servants by those same dragons
- Attempts to breed versions that are magically resistant so far have been a failure but have produced a number of interesting wyvern variants
- Wyverns are flying lions with bat wings, but have no tail, no sting, and no poison. It is a legend based on the siege and fall of Castle Juniper in the Moon Mountains where goblins rode wyverns flinging poisoned spears
- Wyverns are inbred dragons
- Wyverns are the homunculi of dragon arch-wizards
- Wyverns are the result of fairies dreaming of dragons. In their ignorance, they come out a lot like wyverns
- Wyvern testicles and ovaries are powerful magical components. Wyverns know this and mistrust wizards
- Wyverns are excellent mounts. If they won't cooperate when they are alive, they make excellent mounts as undead creatures
- Wyverns reproduce by stealing the stings of scorpion men. This infuriates them. Many forge replacements of brass and steel and devote their lives to hunting wyverns.
- It's pronounced wai-vern
- It's actually pronounced wii-vern
- No, it's derived from the latin for viper and the "Wy" has a long 'i' sound
- The wyvern is the heraldic symbol of the black hobbits of Overhill. Nobody has ever seen a wyvern in or around Overhill, but the black hobbits speak of the wyvern in a reverent voice. "When the end times come," they say, "the winged lord will send the wyvern to swoop us away, and Overhill will be no more."
- Wyverns grow from the fetus of a bat magically implanted into a scorpion egg, ensconced in the egg of a snake, ensconced in the egg of a turkey, and hatched in a nest of poison ivy
- Wyverns are rainbow-colored monsters that emit a sonic attack that causes ecstasy. The sound is a high pitched wheezing
- Wyvern ecologies are only written by sages who are jerks
- Wyvern is actually a term locals use for agile dinosaurs
- Wyvern eggs can feed twenty men for a day. Or ten hobbits
- Wyvern eggs can be used to poison two hundred men. Or five greedy hobbits

- A wyvern is not bipedal, but actually tripodal. The third leg is presumed to be a powerful aphrodisiac
- Wyvern poison causes death by priapism. This causes males to save versus the poison at a penalty
- Wyverns are color blind
- Only because wyverns have no eyes
- In the souks of Salahalabarbalhalas, the powered purple 'juice' of a wyvern is sold as a powerful cure-all, antidote, and aphrodisiac. It can be snorted for a powerful high with a side effect of complete poison immunity, assuming it doesn't kill you
- Sadly, 'wyvern juice' is made from hobbit urine and agave syrup, a horrible tasting mixture that may not do what it says on the tin
- Actually, real 'wyvern juice' is collected by cooling the head of a wyvern to the freezing point of rock oil and chiseling out the venom glands, producing 300 gold worth of juice, or 330 gold if milked by a hobbit maiden
- Only males produce wyvern juice
- Wyvern wings are cyclically considered the height of fashion, most recently because the queen wore one during the funeral of her husband
- All wyverns are hermaphroditic
- Wyverns are actually giant mutant mollusks, gastropods. Their shells are contained in their stomachs
- Unsurprisingly, they taste like chicken
- They are helpful natural creatures, feeding only on poisonous vermin. Slaying a wyvern does irreparable harm to local communities
- Wyverns are temporal tesseract creatures: There is only one wyvern, but instead of being distributed amongst the manifold universes, they manifest everywhere. Part of the reason of their chimeric appearance is that changes in physical representation also bleed across the manifolds. If you manage to find the ur-wyvern and kill it in all the universes at the same time, you will get rid of wyverns. Otherwise, they will continue to spring into existence evermore. Don't be surprised if a wyvern remembers you the first time you meet it
- Wyverns are endangered creatures that are too ugly to live. They are so ugly that if a wyvern sees its reflection in a mirror, it will flee
- This information comes from Aphandor, the famous explorer, who was killed by a wyvern and eaten while wearing four-mirror armor
- Wyverns are a cross between magpies and turkeys, a terrifying bird without fear, that likes mirrors, shiny objects, and gems
- Wyverns have no soul
- Wyverns have five souls. They are twisted, suffering, and blinded souls, but for every one banished, the wyvern loses the properties of that soul

- This means undead wyverns are practically unturnable, being that they count as five undead. Luckily it's five times as hard to create undead wyverns
- When wyvern wives whisper wonderful whimsical wild-tales, witches wish warlocks would woo them
- When a witch and warlock mate, a duck will give birth to a wyvern
- People stung by a wyvern and resurrected have said that they died in bliss
- Using wyvern dung instead of bat guano for a *fireball* creates an exploding acidic sphere instead
- Wyvern guano in general is a useful ingredient for incendiaries, acid vials, and cart bombs
- Wyverns are the angels of the goddess of pleasure and poison, Whyt. Wyvern venom is one of the most pleasurable experiences imaginable, and many an adventurer is a secret YV addict. Actual deaths from wyvern venom are caused by the overdose burning out all the nerve endings, resulting in a comatose, hebephrenic husk of a being
- Priests of Whyt turn into wyverns over time by replacing their body parts with animal grafts. The wyvern's brain as such is human in nature, but beyond the acuity of spell casting
- In cyrilics a wyvern is written as уивэрэн and is believed to be the forerunner of the hut of Baba Jaga
- The city of Nrevywis very adamant in its claim that the name being reverse for wyvern is nothing but a coincidence. Since the scroll of independence from the king's rule spells out the city's name exactly like that, there is a strong reluctance to change it and risk losing said independence
- It doesn't help that the city walls are home to a nest of 144 wyverns that never attack the city itself. In fact, nobody ever saw the wyverns do anything other than fly around — as long as they're unprovoked
- The Wyte Guard of Nrevyw wears wyvern-wing cloaks
- A wyvern transplant is never rejected by the host body and always naturally grafts to any creature to which it is attached
- Wyvern bile and cerebrospinal fluid stop troll regeneration
- Repeatedly asking a wyvern "Why?" will cause it to storm off in disgust
- Wyvern poison is used as bitters in dwarven cocktails (like stormy stout)
- At night, wyverns transform into beautiful dwarven maidens
- Well, not exactly. Wyverns are dwarven females, and the dwarves greatest shame. They are never encountered because they are kept hidden away. The dwarves of Kamolovarupa keep them chained and massaged by drone dwarves to continually produce new little dwarves

- Mating with wyverns is unpleasant, which is why dwarves drink so much, and why the sting causes priapism and arousal
- Mentioning this fact is a good way to have a dwarf kingdom go to war with you
- Wyverns are always hidden behind elaborate stone walls and floorboards
- Wyverns shed their wings annually, growing a more elaborate pair every year
- You can determine the age of a wyvern by counting scale segments
- A wyvern has three cloacas. One for solids, one for liquids, and one for gasses
- Wyvern gas has a weakening effect, used as an experimental sedative at the Barovia Strahd Asylum
- Very old wyverns are very large and can no longer fly, making them popular sport for hobbits
- A wyvern is heraldry come to rampant and perilous life. It manifests as a vast, winged shadow with talons and stings and filled with fear of open spaces. It is a protean creature of shifting parts
- In its youth, a wyvern is quite intelligent. They can be bargained with and sometimes even made to keep their word, but with the insane pain from molting and growing new wings, their sanity wanes
- A wyvern is a cognate of viper, an insane poisonous snake grown beyond all reckoning
- A wyvern is the promise of an unknown monster, constantly morphing and changing forms. Its chimeric form is just a metaphor
- The Keeper of the Seven Seals keeps seventeen sea-wyverns in his ornamental oy-pond
- An oy pond is a more dangerous version of a koi pond
- Wyverns steal limbs from Heraldic Dragons for their adolescents' grafting experiments. Thus the legless Amphiptere, the wingless Wyrm
- Wyverns are trying to turn themselves into pompous four-legged dragons
- Wyverns are building some gigantic ur-horror composed only of claws, horns, and leathery wings
- Dragons are mutable creatures and obsessed with eugenics. They curse all their not-quite-dragon spawn with distinctive, baleful powers and weaknesses to ensure they are not classified as true dragons. The bane of wyvernage is saved for the worst: those that talk back and won't eat their villagers
- Wyverns were once sea serpents. When the triton community undertook major prayer, fasting, and sacrifice, their plea culminated with a quest. Their goddess took pity on them and cursed wyverns with wings, so they could only haunt the world above the waves

- Wyvern were first created as draconic bonsai; an academy of powerful wizards had a tithe of dragon eggs come to them every decade from subdued dragons, and they had competitions to see who could make the most interesting protodraconic form. They have a LOT to answer for in this draconic-monster-infested world

- Wyverns first arrived as parasites on the hides of vast space whales

- Wyverns are battle suits for small translucent rodents like hamsters. One eye pushes back, and they follow the corridor to the skull "bridge." An orc warlord came to know this secret and nearly conquered the world before being burned down; so far, no one else knows the secret, but they DO know that old Scraglatchiar the Conqueror left the secret of his success carved on a wyvern skull hidden with his treasure, and orcs have never stopped looking for it

- When the world was still cooling, the King of the Faerie gambled with one of the first dragons. The dragon lost his arms, his magic, his cleverness, and his magnificent breath; the Queen interrupted the game and spotted the dragon a poison tail loaded with fey-killing venom. The King of the Faerie lost interest in the game (and the inevitable revelation he was cheating), and the crippled dragon (named Wyvern) re-entered the world in shame

- They all come from a cursed mirror being broken in the grove of a mad druid. The results of removing this curse from an individual wyvern are unknown. Would it become broken glass? Or several other monstrous creatures and elementals?

- Wyverns are the keepers of all knowledge, the words of lore written upon their scales in the ancient language of serpents

- Wyverns do not breathe, nor do they have lungs. They absorb air through their membranous wings, spending most of their time high in the jet stream

- Wyverns have no legs, only arms and wings

- They are the flip side to a stirge, a beast created to extract. Wyverns were made to inject

- They compete in the ecological niche of eagles, but being featherless makes them immune to the parasites that plague those large birds

- Wyverns try to bite off each other's tails before mating. Their eggs will hatch before the tail grows back

- Corkmelon is used to disable the sting of a wyvern, making it safer to trap them in nets. Slashing their wings also helps

Variants

Two-tail pygmy wyverns have a poison, which if survived will cure any ill. This permanently makes you less healthy, but can be used to save your life. The problem is, a single sting can kill, and they generally attempt to stab you with both tails

Undead wyverns (skeletal and zombie) are not easy to create, considering the number of creatures' souls used in their formation

Great wyverns have grown to the proportions of the largest dragons. No longer able to fly, they can spit the acidic poison from their mouths

Combat Tricks

TAIL SPEAR: A wyvern can grapple an opponent with its mouth, doing normal bite damage, and then fling that opponent up in the air. Once airborne, they then strike, impaling the creature on their tail. If they successfully bite, grapple, and then throw (bull-rush) their opponent, their tail strikes with a bonus to hit and the target saves versus poison at a penalty. This exposes the wyvern to a variety of attacks, and all opponents get a bonus to hit the wyvern for a round

FLYING STRIKE: Wyverns fly down to their opponent, stabbing them with their tail, and then trampling them on the ground. They must charge their opponents with an aerial dive. Once in range, they attempt to strike with their tails. Hit or miss, they then attempt to overrun their opponent. On a successful overrun the opponent is trampled and takes damage per hit die of the wyvern

WING BUFFET: A single target standing on the flank of an enraged wyvern can be buffeted with a wing. If hit, they take damage and must make a save or be knocked prone. It may do this in addition to it' normal attack

What is the difference between a dragon, drake, wyrm, and wyvern?

Whatever you want it to be. Traditionally, however, dragons are organized via color. Chromatics for evil dragons, metallics for good dragons, and gemstones for neutral dragons. Most terrain-oriented dragons (shadow, lava, etc.) are closer to monstrous drakes, though may usually be assumed to be evil. Drakes are very similar to dragons, though usually bestial, not being able to speak, cast spells, or reason. Wyverns have only four limbs (two wings and two legs) and have poison stings. Wyrms are reptilian beasts that have non-functioning, absent, or vestigial wings. Linnorms are a specific type of wyrm that can fly in spite of not having wings, related to dragons, being a much more primitive, aggressive, barbaric, and greedy version. They have a venomous bite.

In the end, they are all just words for the same thing.

XORN

"They think, you know, that we are being simple or perhaps superstitious when we say that the stone is alive, that it breaths and speaks and eats. But they don't live underground, do they?" — Torsav, Duaru warchief

NOMENCLATURE: Grinders, greedy creepers

DESCRIPTION: Trinary earth creatures

THINGS THAT ARE KNOWN:

- They can phase through earth
- They eat gems and precious metals

RUMORS AND OTHER WHISPERS IN THE DARK:

- The xorn are a trinity of creatures, each based on a certain type of rock: igneous, sedimentary, and metamorphic. Other lesser types exist but are less skilled at navigating impure rocks and often become stuck
- They are the result of a bet between two xeno-chimarologists on the possibility of crossing machines with monsters. Hence they are a cross between a concrete mixer and refuse pile
- They are drones, simple machines, sent out by outerworld creatures
- They seek draconic soul stones, usually found embedded in the brains of a dragon
- Xorn are stupid, and will take any gem. They sort them by consuming them
- Give a xorn an Ioun stone and you will create an intelligent magic-using xorn
- They are the end result of teleportation mishaps, their misshapen limbs caused by the warping of space and melding of a mind with solid stone
- Dwarves use salt-rocks to distract xorn from gemstone deposits. Too much of the salt-rock causes the xorn to become pickled, stuck, and barely able to move. Cooked over magma, they make a rare treat for the dwarves
- Legend says that if a xorn is exposed to enough pressure, it will turn into a multi-faceted, multi-hued gem worth the sum of all the gems it ever ate
- Miniature xorn are said to have depopulated worlds, stripping all the heavy elements from living creatures like a disease
- Gemstone deposits are just bellies of xorn who have died long ago
- Xorn settled underground long ago, spawning gnomes, dwarves, kobolds, and other underground humanoids. They are ashamed of this story and will deny it

- Xorn are fused hermaphrodites. Each is not a trinary creature, but two creatures, one male and one female, fused, both halves of the same xorn
- Crystal, lava, ice, and metal xorn were all eaten long ago, leaving only the gemstone xorn we know today
- Few creatures capture the hate of a dragon more than a dwarf, and xorn have that honor. It is said that a xorn once wandered into Xyphnecrop's great treasure hoard and consumed his entire collection of rubies, before snacking on the gems embedded in his gross underbelly. When the dragon awoke, the xorn was long gone, though it would be a millennial more before the laughter at his fate ceased
- Xorn are from the elemental plane of gluttony and avarice. They have been accidentally summoned by fat and greedy sorcerers
- Xorn were once servants of the creatures that lorded over the very dragons themselves. When their crystal palaces were struck with disaster, the xorn were knocked lose, sent throughout the planes. Those landing on the plane of elemental earth fared much better than others, sniffing out and examining any gems in the hopes that it will lead them once again to their masters and their crystal cities. They eat the gems to collect building material to bring home
- Xorn only eat crystals, not true gems
- Xorn are the embodiement of rage from mother earth and stone, sent up from her igneous womb to return that which was unearthed and stolen
- Xorn attack by extracting calcium from living creatures
- Xorn are matter shorn of manners, some of the most rude creatures in the universe
- Xorn are forlorn creatures
- Xorn aren't creatures, but in fact silica-based plant life
- Xorn are filled with xorn pearls, various geodes harvestable upon death
- Xorn are unable to reproduce, because they lack a soul. They steal greedy hobbit children to reproduce
- Samishi of Sulspicc claims that xorn are simply the larval stage of another larger creature
- Xorn actually have four arms and legs, but are phasic creatures, the fourth arm and leg are out of phase with the rest of the prime material plane. This has the side effect of a fourth attack happening after the first attacks occur
- The excrement of xorn are gem-dust bricks
- They have a motile and sessile phase.
- Their armor reacts strongly with sugar, dissolving rapidly
- They are the offspring of clockwork constructs and golems
- Xorn are in reality the plaque on the teeth of colossal demons, being shed like dandruff
- Xorn are the bio-mechanical creatures used to make space within the hollow world. Once finished they were banished to the elemental plane of earth, a considerable act of mercy, considering it is their idea of paradise. Those that force them back into the prime material plane are sadists.

- Xorn do not exist. They are a myth used by thieves that are very bad at disguise

# ETI

"She had those damned crazy eyes. I don't got nothin' else to say about her or any of 'em." - Zauzikhoo Khalimas

NOMENCLATURE: Frost monkey, ice ape, white death, hunters, snow giants, Abominable snowmen, the horror that walks the mountain

DESCRIPTION: A white, furred, giant ape-like creature

THINGS THAT ARE KNOWN:

- They live in cold, arctic climes
- Their gaze leaves men not what they once were

RUMORS AND OTHER WHISPERS IN THE DARK:

- Some things are lost in the mountains what a man does, what he must, to survive. Many will not pay that cost, and they freeze to death. Those that do are transformed in both shape and spirit, possessing only rage and pure madness

- The emotions of a yeti are so strong that they are contagious. Meeting their gaze is glimpsing the deepest, obfuscated recesses of your soul. Apart from the terror, it causes your human nature to traumatically rebel against your animal flesh

- The fear that results from gazing into a yeti's eyes is the realization that each yeti is in fact their far future selves, returned and sent to slay themselves before the horror of their transformation into the yeti occurs. Sadly, this does not cause the yeti to cease to exist

- Yeti fur is actually a wiry red-orange, yet invisible in the snow. Nearby tribes will often have colors considered strange by foreigners. However, bright orange huts are a sure sign you are in yeti territory

- The urine of a yeti is thick and viscous and warm. It turns snow into hardened ice, melting it, and the water refreezing in the cold. This is why there are so many deadly slick traps near yeti lairs

- When the lost, spiritual, or weak-willed die in the mountains, they dream they are a beast, walking the land as a yeti. If you gaze into the eye of a yeti, you can see the dreamer, but also their dream reflection of you in their eyes. This is knowledge forbidden, and those that see it can lose their minds, becoming mad forevermore

- Yetis do not have brains. They all worship Ithaqua and Wendigo, and madness, chaos, and an icy fear lurk behind their eyes, and it is this you see that drives you mad

- Yetis are bailiffs of terrible evils frozen and hidden in the mountains. They try to prevent people from visiting their prisons by yelling, throwing things, and scaring people away, but no one ever listens

- The yeti and the abominable snowman are two sides of the same species. During interglacial periods, men turn into yetis. Except in rare peaks, where the torturous elements conspire to create and awaken an abomination. When the winter comes and the cold descends, the yetis are subject to this cold and become abominations themselves

- Yetis, although as intelligent as a normal man, able to speak and reason and act as any creature can, are touched by the fae realms and live only in the moment, unthinking of the future or the past

- Yetis are not as intelligent as their abominable snowmen cousins and have none of their psychic powers, save one. Their blue, blue, paralyzing eyes are the only psionic power they possess

- Yetis are adept at swimming in arctic waters and dive deep feeding off the plankton filtered through their fur

- Yetis are not creatures. They are the parasitic spawn of the elder kind who sleep beyond the universe, burning with the fire of infinite darkness. Their eyes are portals to their masters, and to look upon them is to lose one's self. Those who die from this gaze are drawn through the portal to suffer eternally at the hand of the darkness in the universe

- The glare in the eye of the yeti is lust. The hugs are a prelude to something horrible, and it is that thought that drives men mad

- Yetis are 4 feet tall, and very angry for short people

- Yetis are hyper-intelligent, smarter than any other living creature. They act like beasts because they take the minimum effort to survive, maximizing every ounce of brainpower on greater cosmic mysteries. They care for no creatures, not even themselves, convinced this world is just an illusion attempting to distract them from greater cosmic mysteries. It is this otherworldly intelligence far beyond that of mortals or even gods that is seen when one gazes into their eyes

- Yetis don't naturally live in frozen wastes. Their life there is a choice to separate themselves from worldly things

- A yeti is winter manifest; It is the cold embrace of winter. Those that fear the frozen cold are frightened of its spirit, and the cold chills of fear grant the yeti power over them

- Yeti theater is melodramatic and wildly sentimental. It features long, tragic, repetitive musical interludes which are absolutely not songs and which are never woven into the narrative

- Yeti shamans make a trade; they lose a portion of their boundless fury in exchange for an understanding of the spirits. Their 'damned crazy eyes' only deal 3-18 damage, and they can cast *faerie fire*, *speak with dead*, and *preserve manflesh* once per day each

- Yetid are thoughts of a peculiar intensity, wandering the mountains high. They are hallucinations brought on by oxygen deprivation. Possibly they are the self, cast out by the mind and made flesh
- If the character looks into the yeti's eyes, then the full weight and significance of the revelation grips them. It is a calling and a geas. Save versus spells or get another class at level 1. Roll 3d6:
  - 3: Barbarian. you have seen the wild and it is you. No more shoes
  - 4-5: Ranger. You can keep your shoes
  - 6-9: Druid. The wild has shown you things
  - 10-12: Monk. Duh, mountaintop
  - 13-16: Cleric. You must bring the word to the people
  - 17: Thief. But they can't hear it while they're distracted by fripperies
  - 18: Yeti. You can't come down from the mountain until you've passed the revelation on to someone else
  - The nature of the revelation is left to the Dungeon Master and player to discuss, but it must be heretical, troublesome, and right
- Yetis are beasts that only live during the ages of ice. They estivate for millennia, frozen in glaciers, polar caps, far beneath the ice. They wait for the intense hot period that occurs briefly before the ice age starts
- When the yetis come down the mountain, things are about to get much worse
- Yetis are fire spirits, trapped in cold places lest they set fire to the earth and sky. Their fur is sooty smoke or pale mist. Eyes are holes in the smoky covering through which primal fire, maddening to mortals, projects
- Yeti is a pasta shape associated with the cannibal tribes of high Dolomites
- There are beach yetis, marsh yetis, and perhaps others, each a tyrant of its own territory
- There are rumors of sewer yetis, but no man has ever seen one
- Yetis are bundles of sticks and fur, animated by rage spirits
- Yetis have a propensity to rip your arms out of your sockets if they lose in a game
- Yetis are the wandering, tortured souls of extinct volcanoes. As such, they are immune to fire, and disintegrate into ash when slain
- Yetis will guide travelers through frozen mountain passes if approached with the gift of a mirror and hairbrush
- Perhaps their anger is due only to bad hair days
- Yetis have a mortal phobia of mirrors and hairbrushes, blasting out the call of the yeti if confronted with them. The yodel causes all within 100′ to save versus spells or become forever warped by the haunting trills and falsetto growls of the yeti yodel
- All yetis are functional hermaphrodites

- Yetis are obsessed with salt
- Yetis worship Cryonax, their progenitor and evil para-elemental lord of the ice realm. Without this holy worship, they lose powers of ice and cold and are less aggressive
- Some are blessed with tentacles like their lord
- Yetis are the harbingers of snowstorms and blizzards
- They are accomplished snow sculptors, focusing on the abstractions of good and evil
- Yetis refer to themselves as "Ch'rrawr'grrah'hwtech", which in the yeti tongue roughly translates to "the true folk"
- Yetis are self-absorbed liars.

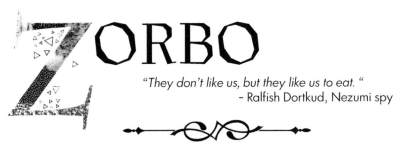

ZORBO

"They don't like us, but they like us to eat. "
- Ralfish Dortkud, Nezumi spy

NOMENCLATURE: Zorba, sorbers, dirt bear

DESCRIPTION: Small bear-like creatures with fangs and claws and black beady eyes.

THINGS THAT ARE KNOWN:

- It hungers for the flesh of humans and humanoids
- It has the ability to absorb the traits of objects and items around it, as well as draining magic items of their energy
- It looks very much like a koala bear

RUMORS AND OTHER WHISPERS IN THE DARK:

- Its dying curse is to leave adventurers with the shameful Mark of Zorbo, a Z on their forehead, which to those in the know is occasion for ridicule and mirth.
- They are said to give birth to one or two live young every three years
- Zorbo are created by pickling koalas in mysterious alchemical concoctions for seven days while performing a ritual known as "chanting the seven mately groans"
- Killing a zorbo with a melee weapon traps your weapon in the corpse 4 out of 6 times
- Zorbo were originally designed to go in steel cages, fired from siege engines. They would take on the aspect of steel, and when the cage burst on impact, they rampaged. They were the winners of a contest, where a wizard submitted his life form. Unlike golems, they were cheap to breed. Because they had a meat form, they were relatively easy to feed and house. And when they became burrs digging through infantry ranks, that put a smile on the commander's face
- Zorbo are children of the Gum-Tree God, tending the gardens of creamtime.
- Some zorbos absorb brains, and they are called zorbies
- Zorbos are universally double jointed
- Zorbo claws make excellent mace heads, maintaining their absorbing power even after death
- Zorbo were created by religious xorn. They prayed for something they could hunt through the earth, after seeing what joy their underdark neighbors took in the practice. The original zorbo were holy creatures, reserved for hunting through the earth on xorn holy days. The trick for the xorn was to catch and kill the zorbo when it was formed of the most delicious material — adamant, always put in its path. . .

- Zorbo are shape-changers who manifest entropy and chaos. Their shape of a koala bear is simply a mask of skin streched across their void flesh

- The hunger for humanoid flesh comes from their millennial long origin as the pets of demons. Favored most by the succubi, they all long for the delicacies of their past

- Zorbo are unable to climb backwards; like squirrels, they must face forward to ascend

- Groups of zorbos are known as blots. There is much disagreement among the sages on the plural of zorbo; many different kinds have appeared in academic texts on the subject

- Once a stage magician offended the god of magic. The god cursed him, that all his illusions were factual. Knives went through things. His touch transmuted. The climax of the curse saw his pet bear actually turned to steel, and it ripped him apart in front of a duly impressed crowd. If a wizard sees a zorbo, that is a sign that the wizard has offended the god of magic and must atone very soon or else all magical effects become more real than they should, climaxing in the wizard's death

- It is incorrect to say that zorbo absorb traits. They are reflected with a slight delay

- A herd of earth elementals carefully gathered for a religious ritual, but kept in close proximity with the mutagens and toxins that were also to be part of the ritual, contracted a disease. Delirious, they escaped and somehow were able to breed with all the local wildlife. The zorbo is but one unfortunate consequence

- Zorbo are actually plants that masquerade as animals. They wait to be eaten, and once they are, they absorb the animal, finally free to walk as living creatures do

- Sanglee the Lesser conquered a region and prohibited weapons. Revolt after revolt showed that the people were still getting their hands on refined steel to make armor and blades. Sanglee approached his grandfather, a completely insane wizard, and asked for something that would let him take weapons from the people without tipping them off to his presence. The zorbo was the result, his grandfather's last (and most eccentric) work. The screams of rust monsters and furry beasts echoed long into each night

- All did not end well for Sanglee. The zorbo did in fact wipe out all the metal it could get its furry claws on. So, the locals developed unarmed and simple weapon fighting, giving them a serious edge when they faced Sanglee's metal-wielding troops with their war-zorbos

- Zorbos live in extended family groups called greeks. They like playing chess

- When zorbos kill a creature, they drag the corpse to a special chamber under-ground, where a giant cocoon sits. They shove the corpse into the cocoon and spin more silk to seal it close. Eventually, these wake and become a giant meat golem

- Zorbos are a weapon — mutant dropbears bred to bankrupt a magic-glutted kingdom by foreign enemies
- High fashion was supplied with color-shifting furs, and Zellman knew he had to up his game. He would produce furs that could change their textures! He never did figure out how to do that, but he did create the zorbo in his painstaking decades-long experiments. They were so cute they became a status pet among the nobility, who had special bare stone rooms for playing with their absorbing pets. When the empire fell, the zorbo escaped into the ruins, and still haunt them now
- A zorbo is actually just an animal skin that covers a seething, buzzing colony of chaos beetles
- Dwarves created the zorbos. They trained them to follow certain cracks and fissures, absorb the best of what was there, and return. Their small size and the purity of their recon made them the mascots of the Helliriak Clan. When the clan fell, the mascots became status pets and delicacies for the goblins that followed.
- Zorbo population is steady because their waste is often coated in diamond dust and occasionally contains rare jewels
- Zorbo skin and flesh are in high demand because they are used in the construction of bags of holding
- The Adamant Idol was the toughest construct the world had ever seen. It was worshiped as a god, and it conquered nation after nation. As the faithful prayed to their defending god, that night a pod of zorbo arrived. The faithless bitterly laughed, that their god chose to mock them before watching their destruction, but the confused faithful bundled the creatures up and took them along. During the battle the next day, the zorbos took on the toughness of the Adamant Idol and destroyed it with its own grade of weaponry now in their claws and jaws. The survivors tell the tale once a year. Priests have a pet zorbo in each temple, living in a specially carved nest that looks like a suit of armor, symbolic of their god's protection
- The nose of a zorbo is often considered a delicacy, especially in the court of the Crimson King
- A zorbo, once slain, turns into an inert, solid lump of obsidian
- Back when beholders had an eye that could see meat, even through barriers, the fey used zorbos to sneak up on them and bite off that eye stalk. Eventually, it stopped manifesting
- Zorbos reached this planet on the hull of spelljammers. No one knows where they originated, but they delight in absorbing (and holing) spelljammer hulls. It gives them magic resistance

BIOMES

Biomes are simply contiguous zones of monster inhabitation. The creatures within a biome are adapted to live and thrive there. Biomes are characterized by both their **terrain** and **climate**. We are only concerned with the player-facing indicators of biomes, not any concrete or scientific classification. It is of no importance during the play of a single adventure that the biome resemble a realistic one. Considering the number of alpha predators adventurers encounter, the assumption must be that they are drawn to the players due to their loud noises, colorful hats, and obnoxious personalities.

The goal is not to create a dull environment, but one that is unusual and fantastical. You should have normal areas as well as exceptional ones, but concerns about yearly average rainfall are not relevant to play. We are constructing biomes for play, not world-building an actual planet. Your rivers can go any way you want them; you can have a swamp right next to a desert; and you should ignore the critique of people who would rather develop simulated real biospheres, and instead have fun with your friends at the table.

CLIMATE

Köppen climate classification is most appropriate for fantasy games. First we will examine the real-world climates and then address fantasy climates. We will bypass the letter classification system, along with significant technical complexity. When designing for your campaign, only have a small selection of biomes (climate+terrain) that the players will traverse. Do only that which is necessary to enhance the veracity of play.

Tropical Climates

Tropical climates have an average temperature greater than 18 °C (~65 °F). It is divided into four classifications:

- Rainforest, characterized by precipitation daily, every month of the year.
- Monsoon, characterized by a dry winter, and a summer season heavy in precipitation.
- Savanna, separated into balanced, wet, and dry types. Balanced savannas have equal periods (6 months on Earth) of dryness and rainfall. During the dry period almost no precipitation occurs, and the vast majority of the yearly rainfall occurs in the wet season. Alternately, savannas can have lengthy dry seasons with short wet seasons, or vice versa.

Arid

Arid climates are frequently non-intuitive. Many areas in the ocean are deserts due to lack of rainfall. Arid climates are split into two categories and may be considered either hot or cold.

- Desert: a hot desert is just as you imagine when you hear the word, Death Valley, the Sahara, etc. This category is over the value of *potential evapotranspiration*. In layman's terms, more water is used or evaporates than precipitates. Most frequently this is due to heat. But deserts also exist in colder areas that are dry for other reasons. Cold or polar deserts are denoted if the average temperature in their coldest month is below 0 °C (32 °F). Cold (or polar) deserts are generally found in mountainous areas.

- Steppe: This climate is similar to a desert, where *evapotranspiration* low. But that doesn't simply refer to evaporation, but also how much water the climate uses. Because of the slightly higher rainfall, steppe terrain has much more flora and fauna biodiversity, increasing the use of water, pushing it above the *evapotranspiration* ratio. These are transitional areas between deserts and wetter climates. They support relatively dense fauna and floral populations (to the limit of their rainfall), which are frequently subject to starvation or dehydration in irregular periods of drought.

Continental

Continental is the living climate. Tempered, having full seasons and variety of temperature and rainfall. Most civilizations, flora, and fauna live here, and the biosphere is very dense.

- Warm Summer: This climate has summers with average temperatures over 22 °C (72 °F) but can get much hotter. The coldest winter has a temperature below 0 °C (32 °F) but can be more severe. It is the meeting place between polar and tropical air masses, leading to violent weather like thunderstorms and tornados. Winters can have high winds, heavy snow, or ice lasting on average up to four months.

- Cool Summer: This climate is cooler, with summers that average below 22 °C (72 °F), but can reach highs in the high 20's. Winters are long, cold, and severe. Snow, frost, and ice cover the ground for around 8 months of the year. Cool summer continental zones are much larger than warm summer zones, frequently covering the vast interior of continents.

- Boreal (Sub-arctic): This climate has long, very cold winters, with short cool summers. Summers average around 10 °C (50 °F) with a high of about 26 °C (-80 °F). Over half the year is below freezing, and temperatures can regularly drop to -50 °C (-58 °F). Most of the ground is covered in permafrost, and dwellings need to be insulated against the cold weather. The frost-free period usually lasts between a month and a half to three months at most.

Temperate

Temperate is a cool, dry climate. It has a narrow temperature range with warm humid summers and temperatures that typically stay above freezing in winter. Rainfall is spread fairly equally throughout the year.

- Mediterranean: This climate is pleasant and characterized by warm, dry summers and cool, mild winters. They experience only summer and winter, the fall and spring too mild to be noticed. Traditionally these are narrow areas near coasts, either near warm waters in higher latitudes or cooler waters in more moderate latitudes.

- Humid Subtropical: This climate has warm and moist summers, mostly due to tropical waters approaching the coast. Summers are warm, moist, and wet. This is the inverse of Mediterranean climates, where winters are wetter. Winters remain mild, and they are frequently subject to hurricanes when warm tropic air mixes with the cooler northern temperatures. Examples include Florida (southeastern United States) and Japan.

- Oceanic: This climate is bullied by polar fronts and vortices. This leads to cool, overcast weather; cool summers; and mild, cloudy, and wet winters.

Polar

Polar climates are characterized by their extreme cold temperatures.

- Tundra: These regions are generally very dry; they have long, cold winters, high winds, and have below freezing temperatures for up to 10 months a year. They are mostly treeless, consisting primary of tundra, due to the fact that the ground is permanently frozen.

- Eternal Frost: This climate is so cold that the annual accumulation of snow and ice is never exceeded by ablation. Functionally it is a sheet of solid ice. Only very specialized forms of life can exist here.

Fantastic

Fantastic climates are magical, mythical, miraculous climates. These are not transitory states that can pass through certain areas (like 'magical weather') but rather influences that are constant, providing a unique climate. The following list is not proscriptive, but descriptive and can be added to, the only limits being your imagination.

- Anarchic: This climate is broken and blasted. It's characterized by high winds, constant thundering storm clouds, and roaming mutated beasts of chaos. Forces of chaos corrupt the local life, turning them into destructive warbands, and weather is extremely random, though never with any accumulated precipitation.

- Animist: This climate awakes the inner spirit of every object and creature, which manifests and becomes active. It's quite chaotic as every plant, animal, and object within slowly wakes up and gains an ego. Weather is as normal, but expect the grass to complain about being trod on, the ground to be resentful, and commentary from the local wildlife on anything and everything. Areas that have an animist climate over a long period of time will be excessively political with complicated Byzantine procedures, politics, and rules.

- Corrupted: Negative energy has corrupted the land here. Plant life is feeble or dying. The sky is overcast, and carrion feeders are attracted to the area. The land is broken and the ground is fallow. Mist billows everywhere, and if it rains, it could rain acid, blood, or frogs. Swarms of insects move across the land, stinging and biting. Piles of bones and bodies spawn skeletons and zombies. Buildings and materials decay at a greatly accelerated rate, and the very air is filled with miasma, bringing both physical ailments and wearing down the will and motivation of all living creatures.

- Decay: Everything in this climate is in a state of advanced decay. Flora and fauna are blighted with injuries and degenerative disorders. Fungi and mold are rampant, and spores in the air make it hard to breathe. Unknown microbial horrors, hive creatures, and mind-altering particles make travel dangerous. There are heavy mists and spore-storms, and the entire area seems constantly covered in hazy twilight.

- Giant Creature: This climate consists of a gigantic animal or creature that supports an entire ecosystem. This could be a giant turtle as large as an island, the corpse of a dead god, or a living insect the size of a small mountain range that other creatures live within. The creature may be alive or dead, and this can have serious consequences for those involved.

- Luminescent: All flora and fauna and even minerals in this climate are run through with streaks of vibrant or neon color. It may flow and shift and change, or perhaps brighten and darken in specific patterns. The flora and fauna in this area may have a symbiotic relationship, or may have deleterious effects on non-native life.

- Music: Everything in this climate produces some kind of vibration. Though many of the vibrations are between 20 Hz and 20,000 Hz, some are higher or lower. Some areas have pleasant tinkling; rivers produce beautiful melodies, and flowers pure clean notes. However, some areas and items produce disturbing frequencies, causing people to become incapacitated, sick, or even possibly setting up deadly vibrations that can eventually kill the victim unless neutralized. Natives to this climate have learned to master these. Weather comes in the form of musical crescendos, dub-step thunderstorms, screamo windstorms, or chant-like fog.

- Primal: This climate represents an influence of the platonic ideal of the area. Primal forests always have a golden sun shining through the trees, with vibrant colors and a ground carpeted in moss. Primal swamps are always dark and gloomy, light sucked in by the bent and crooked trees, and a marshy bog that sucks at your feet. Time seems to pass unnaturally in these areas; night never comes, or perhaps day never arrives. The land is characterized by its constant and unchanging nature.

- Radiant: Positive energy has infused the land here. The air is clear, and reflective surfaces shine bright. The sun seems larger and brighter than normal, and objects are frequently backlit by halos. Plants grow incredibly rapidly, and colors seem much more vibrant than normal. Fluids are thick and viscous, and objects seem plump, and everything is much warmer than usual. It is difficult to sleep, and fauna seem vibrant, creative, and full of energy.

Planar Weakness

This climate is caused by a weakness between the planar boundaries the effects vary by the type of planar crossing

- Astral: The barrier being weak causes the spirit of flora and fauna to separate from the body, rendering their silver cord vulnerable to separation. It is possible to move through the air, using your astral form to drag your body along. Storms and bad weather affect the mind of the subject, causing them to project thoughts, be subject to psionic attacks, experience déjà vu, or subject to an *Emotion* spell.

- Etherial: This climate is frequently covered in a thick fog, completely blocking out the sun. Solid objects are translucent, and with concentration one could pass through them. Sound is muted and eerie, and it is difficult to determine direction, greatly increasing the chances of becoming lost.

- Elemental: This climate is characterized by the elemental climate breaking in. Fire will have lava flows, and gouts that shoot flame, and the air will be filled with soot and ash. Water will cause flooding, rain, and storms. Air will be blasted with wind and dust, making flying difficult or impossible. Earth will be mountainous and rocky, stones rolling down hills and being shot from the earth.

- Mirror: Objects become reflective and shadows dance at the edge of your vision. Creatures are duplicated, but reversed in some way, backwards, upside down, or appearing as a negative. It's possible to get lost and find yourself in an alternate reality, a "mirror world" where everything that you know is different.

- Shadow: The sun is obscured and long shadows cover the land. All light levels become darker, and it is physically draining to travel through this area. Many creatures are shadow versions or imitations of their usual self. The air is cold and saps strength from your body.

Terrain

Terrain is the second part of a biome. A particular climate plus terrain will create a unique biome ready for monstrous inhabitation.

Alkali Flats

This is a dried out desert lake, frequently covered in salt or silt.

Badlands

This is a dry terrain that has been severely eroded, leaving steep slopes, minimal flora, and lack of any particulate cover (dirt, dust, regolith, etc.). It is very difficult for fauna to cross.

Bay

This is a small recessed body of water, connected to a larger body of water. It is frequently a site of naval urban developments.

Beach/Coast

This is flat low-lying piece of land next to the ocean. The soil is frequently fertile, and is characterized by a gently sloping resource rich landscape.

Caldera

This is a large volcanic crater, usually after the mouth of the volcano has collapsed.

Canyons

Canyons are formed when water cuts through a mountain range. They usually are very deep and have very steep sides. Though usually caused by water, not all canyons have water flowing through them.

Caves/Cavern

This is a natural void in the ground. Many campaigns include entire continent-sized areas covered in caves. There are various kinds of caves (lava tubes, fracture caves, Talus caves), but the type of cave isn't relevant to its use as a terrain.

Crystal

This terrain is made up of large crystal spires. The ground is polished translucent mineral, and there are many caves and crevices.

Desert

Not the climate, but a terrain characterized by sand, blown into dunes, little vegetation, rocks, and dry, cracked earth. Can contain an oasis, which is a fertile area caused by a source of fresh water.

Fleshlands

Everything in this terrain is made from living flesh. Pulsing towers with veins rise above the landscape. Moist rugated caves lead to fleshy intestine-like caverns. The ground is covered in viscera-like plants. Pools and lakes of blood, bile, mucus and worse dot the landscape.

Forests

These are areas dominated by flora and filled with fauna. Usually consisting of thick tree cover and other vegetation, and a surfeit of druids. They go through all the various seasons.

Glacier

This terrain is covered in large ice masses. These masses frequently move under their own weight and are a mixture of water, rock, and snow.

Hill

This is a rise in the local terrain, usually with a distinct summit. It is characteristic of uneven land, with many peaks and valleys. Specific types of hills include:

- Buttes, isolated hills with steep vertical sides with a small flat top
- Mesas, as butte above, but the top is wider than the height.
- Mima mounds, small mounds or humps grouped together.

Jungle

Similar to forests, but more dense, containing tangled vegetation that has completely overgrown the land.

Magical Terrain

This is another terrain type infused with a magical energy that sustains either a magical effect or creature. It may have a physical or visible effect (sparkling motes, wavy air, flowers sprout where people walk) and certain creatures may not be able to exist outside this area. This is applied as a modifier to other terrain types.

Marsh

Low-lying land that is frequently flooded during high tide or wet seasons, but even when not, the land is soggy, waterlogged, and filled with silt, mud, tar, and peat. Areas that will not support heavy bodies are called 'bogs'.

Mechanical

Instead of organic terrain, the land and all surfaces are made of metal or a machine. This could be circuit boards and technology, like early virtual reality cyberpunk visualizations, or a creation of iron, steam, and copper. Or it could be a gigantic, ancient structure such as a crashed generation ship.

Mountain

This is a large protruding landform that rises prominently above the surrounding land. These are steeper than hills and are frequently formed by tectonic or volcanic activity. Frequently, they form 'ranges' where mountains rise in a line and are connected by high ground with mountain passes in-between.

Ocean

This is a large body of water that covers a huge area. They have extremely varied flora and fauna. In fantasy campaigns, the oceans are usually colonized by various intelligent water-breathing species. This can make travel by boat significantly more dangerous than in the real world.

Open Plain

These are flat areas of land that lack trees, and have wide vistas. They cover over 30% of all land on Earth and are very common.

Plateau

These are wide expanses of flat land, usually elevated, and surrounded by hills and mountains.

Prismatic

This terrain is characterized by the land, flora, and fauna being made of colored force.

Rainforest

This is a forest filled with gigantic trees, so large that they cut off the sunlight into the undergrowth, leaving wide and clear spaces to travel. They are made up of broad-leaf or coniferous plant life.

River

This is a naturally flowing freshwater watercourse. They generally flow towards bodies of water, but anyone who is overly concerned with the direction of water flow is likely an asshole.

Swamp

This is a marsh that is forested with wetland trees and vegetation.

Tundra

This terrain (not climate) is generally made up of spongy lichen and moss several feet deep. It is difficult and tiering to cross.

Valley

You have mountains and hills, valleys are the terrain between them. They range between V and U shapes and have bottom depressions that can be quite large.

CREATING ECOLOGIES

To use these in play, you must have an area map. Designate several types of terrain on the map. Each of these terrains is considered a zone. Assign contiguous climates over the zones. Discard your concerns about realism. Does the direction of the river flow matter when you have a screaming tree forest?

This leaves you with a biome that's a combination of a terrain and a climate. Now you have to begin the work of preparing the ecology for player interaction. Take note of the following guidelines.

The more hostile a biome is, the less depth the biome possesses. Creatures evolve to fit specific niches in biomes, and in hostile biomes this radically reduces the density of the biome. The idea is to not be comprehensive, but consider what your players are likely to interact with or find important.

ENCOUNTER DENSITY

For each biome the absolute maximum number of creatures you want to have identifiable to the players should be seven. Any more than seven creatures will appear to the players to be effectively 'many' and will disperse the characterization of the biome. To the perspective of the player, the contents of the biome will be random.

It's important to consider this is only useful for environments the players spend a lot of time in. In general, if the players are going to spend less than 10 hours in an area, it's not worth taking the time to do this, and random encounter tables will suffice. But for campaigns that take place in a limited area (e.g. West Marches style, Hot Springs Island, or Isle of Dread) that is explored over a long period of time, it can add great depth to the campaign.

A minor area (15+ campaign hours) can have three relevant creatures; a major area (30+ campaign hours) is good with five, and an area that is involved in the entirety of the campaign is manageable with seven.

The spirit may feel that this is narrow, but the truth is in a game there will only be around three to five encounter checks, and many of those will not involve active encounters with a creature. So, unless the players have the opportunity to encounter creatures again and again, they get no sense of the biome.

BIOME TRAITS

Biomes also have 'non-encounter' creatures which can sometimes appear. These are like tags that are applied to the biome, rather than encounters worth taking up table time. This includes such things as "Stinging insects", "Caribou Herds", "Carrion birds" et. al. When designing a biome, consider the list of the following areas in the biosphere to create these tags. Each one could be replaced with a magical or supernatural version with a minor effect. Do not fall into the trap of filling out or determining every one of these, choose two or three per biome to give them flavor of mechanical effects. Predators are not included, neither are humanoids or sentient creatures, since they are more appropriately used as the creatures in the encounter table.

- Flying insects
- Ground insects
- Pollinators
- Large herd animals
- Song birds
- Raptors
- Reptiles
- Rodents
- Fish and aquatic life
- Amphibians
- Bacteria
- Fruiting plants
- Previous inhabitants
- Unique weather
- Minerals, metals, stones
- Mystical/Planar gateways
- Regolith composition
- Petrification/Fossils
- Monoliths
- Floating land
- Unusual colors
- Vapors and miasmas
- Mists and fogs
- Insect nests (termite mounds, ant colonies, wasp nests, beehives etc.)
- Organic replacements (antler or keratin trees, hair grass or plants, etc.)
- Magical barriers

- Invertebrates
- Crustaceans
- Fungi
- Trees
- Plants
- Vines
- Parasites
- Spiders
- Moss, slime molds
- Worm
- Hidden dangers
- Magical effects
- Animal graveyard
- Gigantic dominating ruin (ancient engine, corpse of a god, etc.)
- Monumental construction
- Sinkholes/Environmental hazards
- Living terrain (walking forest, Pando organisms)
- Flaming jets
- Pools of oil/grease/bile etc.
- Lava tubes, ice tunnels, subterranean access
- Faces, either carved or real
- Gigantic creatures the biome exists within/on
- Mechanical or robot assimilation

PLAYER-FACING ENCOUNTERS

Once you have your climate, your terrain, and your special tags, effects, and characteristics, you can select your creatures. Select the appropriate number of novel encounters, using the monster sections to design unique creatures that inhabit your setting.

Preparation

Most referees do not have time to create a full field guide for the players to peruse before entering an area, but thankfully the structure of the game already provides us with a method of transmitting this information. Rumors. You can take your biome-specific information and fill the rumor tables with relevant and possibly false rumors and information. This allows you to set up expectations which you can then fulfill or subvert in play and allows players the opportunity to use their personal skill in preparing for the various biomes. Because you now have so many options for rumors (normal campaign rumors as well as biome rumors) you can give players rumors on a regular basis and encourage them to seek out more on their own

Encounter die

In order to create player-facing interactions for these creatures, we overload the encounter die. In normal campaigns, a die is rolled, and if it is in a certain range, an encounter occurs, and if not, it does not. An overloaded encounter die tracks certain conditions on other die rolls. Here is an example of an overloaded encounter die from *Perdition*.

1. Encounter; gain 1 stress point before the encounter
2. Spoor
3. Environmental event
4. Stress; gain 1 stress point
5. Background administration
6. Stress triggered! Take mental damage equal to your level times your stress points

Environmental effects would be special effects depending on where the party happened to be located. In a crypt it could be a 'rising mist' for example, or 'wolves howling in a forest'. Background administration would be things like torches going out or potion effects ending.

For these biomes we are going to overload the encounter die so every time the encounter die is rolled, they encounter some aspect of the creatures in the area. This will create a matrix, so that every time an encounter die is rolled you will encounter some aspect or feature of the monster. Again, these are descriptive not proscriptive, there is no need to use every entry for every table, and instead you should craft relevant tables for each encounter.

This allows the players to gather information on monsters long before the actual monster is encountered and lets them plan and gain information for themselves as foreshadowing the eventual encounter.

Consider an encounter chart for a minor biome. You expect the players to spend about 4 sessions in this biome (about 16 total hours) so you've selected 4 monsters kobolds, carnivious vines, trolls, and blink dogs.

X	1	2	3	4
1	Kobolds			
2	Carnivorous Vines			
3	Trolls			
4	Blink Dogs			

Now we consider a great many things. We think about how each of these creatures is present and interacts in this biome. This includes many things, including their lairs, effects of their interactions, sounds and territorial markings, tracks and spoors, victims, signs of the encounters interacting with each other or the biome, and other indications.

Let's begin with signs and traces of the encounters.

X	1	2	3	4
1	Kobolds	Primitive traps		
2	Carnivorous Vines	Desiccated Victim		
3	Trolls	Broken/bent trees		
4	Blink Dogs	Spotted, mottled hair		

Then we can move on to territorial markers which is useful since all of these creatures mark their territory in various ways.

X	1	2	3	4
1	Kobolds	Primitive traps	Lizard and Dragon drawings on rocks	
2	Carnivorous Vines	Desiccated Victim	Small rodent skeletons	
3	Trolls	Broken/bent trees	Skulls set on piles of rocks	
4	Blink Dogs	Spotted, mottled hair	A strong urine smell	

Finally, we can round out our short table with sounds. Larger tables can have more monsters and more interactions. The fewer signs, lairs, tracks, etc. the more likely you are to encounter an actual creature. Smaller tables with fewer entries work better for minor areas; major areas can afford the extra complexity.

X	1	2	3	4
1	Kobolds	Primitive traps	Lizard and Dragon drawings on rocks	Distant yipping
2	Carnivorous Vines	Desiccated Victim	Small rodent skeletons	*silence*
3	Trolls	Broken/bent trees	Skulls set on piles of rocks	long low moans and cruel laughter
4	Blink Dogs	Spotted, mottled hair	A strong urine smell	Barking and howling

Keep in mind, players cannot see your side of the table. If you roll two 4-sided dice, and get two fours, they will only hear barking and howling. Are those dire wolves? Werewolves? Hellhounds?

Every time an encounter is rolled, they encounter some aspect of the monster instead of "nothing". Instead of only interacting with an encounter only on a roll of 1, now every time an encounter roll is made, they acquire some piece of information, either one that provides new information or one that confirms what they already know.

Keep in mind that you can play with the table itself. The players may begin to track rolls (which is perfectly acceptable) but just like in dungeon mazes, you can place identical entries to confuse the players. If you have both ettercaps and spiders, 'webbing' and 'people in cocoons' will show up in both tables, confounding players.

Infestation rules

A common function of biomes is when players decide to set up a castle or settlement. One of the requirements is clearing a biome. Extensive rules for doing this during basic play are covered in *On Downtime and Demesnes*, but can be expanded using this encounter table instead. Consider the density of the monster population in an area, and assign it a die value between 4 and 12. Each creature has a number of population points equal to the die value. So a creature with 6 population points uses a 1d6. Each time the creature is encountered and some are slain, remove a population point. Each time a lair is found and cleared, remove 2 population points. At the end of every month, roll the appropriate die.

If the total is under or equal to the amount of remaining population points, increase the total population points by one. If it is over the amount of remaining population points, reduce the number of population points by one. If the number of population points is reduced to 0, then the monster is considered cleared from the hex.